# KNIGHT'S FEE

ROSEMARY SUTCLIFF

# KNIGHT'S
# FEE

*Illustrated by*
*Charles Keeping*

NEW YORK HENRY Z. WALCK INC.

# Contents

# THE NEW LORD OF ARUNDEL

His name was Randal, Randal the Bastard, Randal the Thief. His father was a Breton Man-at-Arms, and his mother a Saxon lady, one of several who had waited on the old Countess. She, having nothing to live for, had died when he was born; his father had been killed when he was four years old, in the constant warfare along the Welsh Marches, and neither among his father's people nor his mother's was there any place for Randal. The only person who had ever shown him any kindness, and that was of a somewhat rough and ready sort, was Lovel the Huntsman, who had taken him over from the time when the woman who sold cheap wine to the men-at-arms had thrown him out like an unwanted nestling because with his father dead there would be no more money for keeping him. Lovel had brought him up, or rather, allowed him to bring himself up in the kennels along with the hound puppies, and treated him as he treated all the rest of his charges, thrashing him mercilessly with the same long oxhide whip when he was wicked, purging him with buckthorn in the spring, and sitting up with him when he had the colic.

He was nine years old now, going on ten, and officially a dog-boy, but in actual fact just something of no account, to be kicked by anyone who felt like kicking, and plenty of people did. Sometimes, when he had been kicked particularly hard, or Lovel had used the whip more savagely than usual, or when he was especially hungry, he would crawl away into a dark corner and indulge in a welter of self-pity, wondering if his mother knew what they were doing to him, until the tears made white stripes down his dirty face to echo the red stripes that the oxhide lash had made on his scrawny brown back. But for the most part he contrived, somehow, to enjoy life.

He was enjoying it now, in this hot, blue August noon, lying on the gatehouse roof to watch for the new Lord of Arundel. He should not, of course, have been on the gatehouse roof, and at any ordinary time, since the only way of reaching it was up the guardroom stair, there would have been no chance of his getting here. But the workmen who had been doing something to the roof had left their ropes and tackle for pulling timber up in position, and where there was a rope, Randal could climb, especially with a projecting buttress to shield him from interruption. They had left some of their timber up here too, ready for use, and between the stacked beams and the parapet was a small secluded strip, well out of sight of the sentinels who paced to and fro on the roof of the great Keep.

Randal lay on his back, lapping up the sunshine until he felt that it was pouring right through him so that if he got up he would have no shadow. Nothing to see but the coping stones of the high, crenellated parapet on one side, the stacked timber on the other, and overhead the burning blue laced with the flight of swallows. He heard the bustle of preparations going on in the bailey far below him, the Master-at-Arms bellowing orders, the high voices of the women, the pad of hurrying feet on the beaten earth, all small and distinct with distance. Somewhere below the gatehouse two men were talking. Their voices carried up to him along the face of the wall.

'They should be here soon,' one of the men said. 'It must be full two hours agone that Gilbert Goaty-Beard rode out in state to meet them.'

'A fine thing 'twill be to have a Lord of Arundel here in his stronghold again,' said a deeper voice with a note of recklessness in it. 'Three years of Steward Gilbert and our saintly Lady Adeliza is more than enough for any man's belly, while the Old Lion sits in his own abbey of Shrewsbury, making his peace with God.'

The first gave a snort of laughter. ''Tis to be hoped he managed it by the end. It must have taken quite a bit of doing . . . Aye well, at least we shall have better living than we've had in these past years, with the Lady so busy feeding the Poor and the

2

Church that there was naught but outworn plough-ox beef and watered beer for her own men-at-arms.'

'Aye, young Montgomery won't make *that* mistake.' There was a deep chuckle.

Silence followed, and then the first man spoke again, reflectively. 'Young Montgomery . . . You'd think, seeing what's come of the Conqueror leaving England to a younger son and only Normandy to the eldest, that the Old Lion would have more wisdom than to do the same thing.'

'Meaning that the two cubs will be at each other's throats? Na, na, I've known those two since they were children. They were devils then and they're devils now, but they don't turn their devilry against each other. If 'tis true as they say, that de Bellême rides in with his brother today, then I'd say more like they're planning to turn it against—someone else. 'Twouldn't be the first time. They have no more love for Red William than have most of his Barons, I reckon, and they're as fire-headed as he is himself.'

'Careful with that sort of talk,' the other man growled in sudden caution, and Randal, listening in his sunbaked corner, heard their feet scuffle, and the lowered grumble of their voices as they moved away.

He reached for one of the three dried figs that he had stolen from the kitchen—he always stole anything he got the chance to, because nothing ever came to him otherwise—flicked away a couple of flies, and bit into it. It was soft and very sweet, sticky with the heat, and added to his sense of holiday. He sat up, then scrambled to his feet and peered out through the nearest crenelle.

It was like being a kestrel, up here; a kestrel hanging in the sky, looking down on the thatched roofs of the little town beneath their faint haze of woodsmoke, on the Hault Rey looping out through the downs, brown and swift under its alders, winding away through the tawny marshes to the sea; and nothing as high as you were yourself until the oakwoods on the far side of the river valley started climbing the downs again. A little breath of wind came siffling over the shoulder of the woods, and blew a long wisp of hair that would have been barley pale if it was not grey with dirt, into the boy's eyes, and he thought that it brought with it the faint sound of a horn.

He thrust the hair out of his eyes with the back of his dusty olive brown hand in which he held the rest of the fig, and pulled himself up with a foot in the crenelle, staring out along the track that followed the flank of the downs. Far off where it ran out from the deep-layered shade of the oak woods, a faint cloud of dust was rising.

A few moments later the trumpets of the Castle sang from high on the crest of the Keep. The new Lord of Shrewsbury and Arundel was in sight.

Truly in sight now for the dust cloud was rolling nearer, and under it Randal could see a dark skein of men and horses. Nearer and nearer. They were pouring up the track through the town, between the staring townsfolk and scratching dogs who had crowded to their doorways to see them go by. Colour and detail began to spark out from the general mass, and the blink of light on sword hilt or harness buckle. Some of the Arundel knights who had ridden out with Sir Gilbert that morning wore the new fashionable long sleeves and trailing skirts to their tunics that all but tangled in their stirrups; but the newcomers, straight from warfare and the Welsh Marches were shabbier and more grimly workmanlike. Several of them wore their padded gambesons, and here and there was even a glint of ringmail from men who had worn harness so long that they had forgotten how to wear the gayer garments of peace time.

Randal leaned farther and farther out, his half-eaten fig forgotten in his hand, his gaze fixed on the man who rode at their head. It was the first time, at least to remember, that he had seen this new Earl of Arundel, Hugh Montgomery, whom the Welsh called Hugh Goch—Hugh the Red—from the colour of his hair and maybe for other reasons also. He was a tall man in an old gambeson, who rode bareheaded, flame-haired in the dusty sunlight, managing his black Percheron stallion as though he and the beast were one. Sir Gilbert the Steward rode beside him, leaning confidentially toward his ear; and on his other side rode another man, red also, but a darker red, the colour of a polished chestnut. Randal knew him well enough, for he had

4

seen the Old Lion's eldest son before; Robert, not Montgomery but de Bellême, for he had taken the name of his mother's lands in Normandy. His gaze flickered from one brother to the other and back again. The man-at-arms had called them the cubs, because the old Earl their father had been called the Old Lion, from the strange golden beast on a red ground that he had on his war banner; but Randal thought suddenly that what they really were, were birds of prey—like the great, beautiful, half-mad hawks and falcons in the Castle mews.

Half a length behind de Bellême rode another man who stood out from the rest almost as much as the red-headed brothers, a long, loose-limbed man clad from throat to heel in monkish black—save that no monk ever wore garments of that outland-ish cut, and the long, fantastically wide sleeves falling back from his arms were lined with the shrill, clear yellow of broom flowers. He carried no sword, this man, but a light harp on his saddle bow, and played and sang as he rode, his voice coming up on the little wind, light, but strong and true above the swelling smother of hoof-beats; and him also Randal knew, for anyone who had seen de Bellême before must also have seen Herluin, de Bellême's minstrel. But it was on Hugh Goch that all the boy's attention was fixed, as he leaned farther and farther out from his perch while the head of the cavalcade swept nearer, the baggage train of its tail lost behind it in the white, August dust-cloud.

The trumpeters on the Keep were sounding again as the fore-most riders swept up to the bridge. The horses' hooves were trampling hollow on the bridge timbers. Hugh Goch was directly below him now, in another instant the dark tunnel of the gate arch would have swallowed him and it would be time to dart across the roof and hang over the other side to see him come riding into the bailey; and in that instant, as the new Lord reined back a little, looking up at his inheritance, the thing happened. A very small thing, but it was to change Randal's whole life. He dropped the half-eaten fig.

Before his horrified gaze the dark speck went spinning down-ward for what seemed an eternity of time. It struck the black stallion full on the nose, and instant chaos broke loose. The

5

great brute tossed up his head with a snort of rage and fear,
plunged sideways into de Bellême's bay, and flinging round in a
panic that was as much temper as anything else, went up in
a rearing half-turn. There was a flurry of shouts above the
savage drumming of hooves: 'Look out, for God's sake! . . . Ah,
would you now?—Fiends of Hell . . .' The stallion had become
a mere plunging and squealing tempest of black legs and rolling
mane and flaming eyes and nostrils. He would have had a
lesser rider in the ditch before a heart might pound twice, but
in Hugh Goch he might have been trying to shake off part of his
own body. The red-haired man clung viciously to his back, and
Randal, staring down with wide, horrified eyes, saw him whip
out his dagger and hammer with the pummel between the laid-
back ears. In a few moments it was over, the black Percheron
trembling on all four legs again, and the chaos that had spread
behind him sorting itself out. Hugh Goch swung him round
once more to the gate arch, and reining him back with a merci-
less hand that dragged his bleeding, bit-torn mouth open
against his throat, sat looking up, straight up along the face of
the gatehouse wall, until his eyes met those of the boy, still leaning out from the crenelle and no more able to move than if he
had suddenly become one of the Castle stones.

Hugh Goch's face was white and thin under the flame of his
hair, long-boned and almost delicate, but his eyes were the cold,
inhuman, gold-rimmed eyes of a bird of prey, and looking into
them, Randal was more afraid than he had ever been in his life
before. For a long moment the two looked at each other, the
dog-boy and the new Lord of Arundel, and then the power of
movement returned to Randal, and he darted back from the
crenelle, and turned and ran.

Half-sobbing in terror, he made for the ropes and scaffolding
that he had come up by, and almost flung himself over the
edge. The ropes tore the skin from the palms of his hands as he
dropped, but he scarcely felt it, and a moment later he was
crouching in a bruised heap on the narrow rampart walk behind the curtain wall. He heard the hollow clatter of hooves
pouring through under the gate arch, and a reckless burst of
laughter caught up by a score of voices, and knew that Hugh

Goch was turning the thing into a jest. But it would be an evil jest for him, if the Lord of Arundel knew him again. With one hunted glance at the scene in the bailey, where the Lady Adeliza and her women stood waiting and all the Castle had turned out to see the new Lord ride in, he gathered himself up and bolted. He ducked under the hand of a grinning man-at-arms stretched out to catch him, hurtled down the rampart steps and dived panting into the dark alleyway behind the armourer's shop.

Over the years a veritable town had grown up round the inner side of the curtain wall, like the fungus that grows up round a tree stump; barracks and mews, stables and kennels, granaries, armouries, storehouses, baking and brewing sheds, all jumbled and crowded together in higgledy-piggledy confusion, and Randal knew the ways round and through and under the confusion better than almost anyone else in the Castle. So now he took to it as a small hunted animal taking to furze cover, making for the only sanctuary he knew, the kennels, right round on the far side of the bailey behind the vast mound of the Keep.

He reached it at last, stumbled in through the walled court where they turned the hounds out while they cleaned the kennels every day, and dived, still sobbing and shivering, into the darkness of the open doorway. Inside it was surprisingly cool under the thick thatch, and sweeter smelling than the Great Hall, for they changed the hounds' straw every few days, the Hall rushes only two or three times a year. There were no humans there, for Lovel had been sick with some kind of fever in his own quarters these three days past, and Gildon who was supposed to be in his place would be round on the far side of the Keep with everybody else. But the hunting dogs greeted him with thumping tails, great tawny shapes rousing from their noonday sleep; Beauty stood on her hind legs to lick his face, but Garm sniffed at him whimpering, as though he smelled the boy's fear. Randal stumbled straight through them, up the long, barnlike place towards the little shut-off lair at the far end, where Lovel kept his whips and leashes and medicines, and had a fire-place for warming sick puppies. Next to this lair was a corner partly screened off with hurdles, and into this he turned, and flung

7

himself down in the straw between the two huge, brindled shapes that already lay there.

Bran and Gerland accepted his coming, though woe betide any other hound that came trespassing round their side of the hurdles. The two great Irish wolfhounds had been the old Earl's constant companions until he left the world for his abbey three years ago, and since then, refusing their allegiance to anyone else in the Castle, they had chosen to take up their quarters here with Lovel, who had the right smell. The only person, save for the huntsman himself, who could do anything with them was Randal, who stood little higher on his two legs than they did on their four, for they were about the size of ponies.

Now they made room for him as an equal, and he crawled between them and lay shivering with his face buried in Gerland's neck, telling them over and over again in a terrified whisper, 'I didn't mean to do it—I didn't mean any harm—I didn't . . .'

For a long while he lay there, his heart hammering against his ribs as though it must fly out of his body, his breath coming and going in little jerks, his ears on the stretch for any sound that might mean the hunt on his trail. But he heard only the usual sounds of the Castle, and bit by bit his heart quietened and his panic died down a little. 'He'll forget,' he told himself. 'If I can keep out of his way for a few days, he'll forget all about it. And he *did* laugh—afterwards. Maybe he wasn't so very angry after all, maybe it was just the sun that made his eyes look like that.'

So he lay, telling himself over and over again in the same frightened whisper inside his head, that the Lord of Arundel would forget, while the long, hot summer's day crawled its length towards evening.

About sunset, Gildon came with the great baskets of raw meat, and the baying and snarling that always broke out at feeding time sounded from end to end of the long kennels. Bran and Gerland got up and shook themselves and went out, proudly pacing, to demand their share, the royal share, and Randal was left quite alone. He was hungry too, as hungry as the hounds. Usually at this time of day he went up to the Keep and hung about the kitchen below the guardroom, waiting for the food that the Great Folk had not eaten to come down from the Hall. He had eaten with the hounds before now, but he did not really like raw meat. But this evening he was too afraid, too afraid even to creep out of his corner and fight one of the hound puppies for a lump of worn-out horse meat.

He heard Gildon grumbling and roaring away as he always did, between cracks of the lash, until at last the feeding time uproar dwindled down into contented snufflings and the sound of bones being gnawed and Gildon hung up the lash and went tramping off.

In a while Bran and Gerland came back and lay down again with contented grunts, stretching themselves out for sleep. Randal was hungrier than ever, but at least, now that they had come back, he did not feel quite so alone. Presently it was dusk in the kennels, and the sky turned water green beyond the little high window just above him, and there was one star in it, not bright as yet, because the sky had still so much left of light, but like an infinitely small white flower hovering there. Randal lay and looked at it, curled into Bran's warm, brindled flank, and the soft, sleepy sounds of the hounds stirring and settling all about him. And little by little, despite his fear and hunger, the familiar sights and sounds that he had gone to sleep with almost ever since he could remember, wrapped themselves around him.

It seemed that he had scarcely fallen into an uneasy sleep before he was awake again, to the golden gleam of a torch through the screening hurdle, casting a ring-streaked freckling of light across the piled straw and himself and the brindled hide of the hounds. The light wheeled across him, footsteps were coming along the central aisle, and Gildon's voice called, 'Randal— Randal! Rouse up now!'

The next instant the full, fierce light of the torch was flaring raggedly into the narrow corner, making him blink with the dazzle of it, as he crouched back against the wall. Gildon stood in the opening, holding the torch high. 'Come on now, up with you—you and the hounds.'

He made a sudden movement as though to catch the boy and

9

jerk him to his feet; Randal ducked, as he always did when anyone looked as though they were going to hit him, and Gerland
whined deep in his throat, troubled by the torch, for even a dog
that has been free to sit by the hearth all his life does not like
fire that comes at him on the end of a stick.

'Wha—what do you want? What is it then? Leave me to
sleep,' Randal began, and slid down again into the straw, playing desperately for time.

''Tisn't me that wants you,' said the man. 'It's Earl Hugh
that's finished his supper and taken a fancy to see his father's
wolfhounds again.'

Randal gave a little choking gasp, and pressed back against
the wall, his eyes darting from side to side as though in search
of some way of escape.

'Lovel,' he protested stupidly, 'it's for Lovel to take them.'

'Lovel is sick, as you know full well, *and* you know that you're
the only other living thing in Arundel Castle that those brutes
will pay any heed to!' The man stirred him roughly with a foot.
'What's amiss with you? Come on now, do you want to keep
Hugh Goch waiting all night?'

Randal stared up at him, wondering desperately if he could
tell Gildon the truth and throw himself on his mercy, but he
saw that it would be no good. Gildon was angry because he, a
grown huntsman, was having to rout out a boy of nine to do
what he could not do himself. It showed all over his broad,
piggy face in the torchlight. He would have no mercy. Well
then, if he set Bran and Gerland on to him, while he, Randal,
ran away? But that would mean noise enough to rouse the whole
Castle, and he could not escape while the gates were shut for
the night, and so he would be hunted down and most likely
dragged before Hugh Goch, which would make it all the more
sure that Hugh Goch would know him again. The thoughts in
his head ran round and round in circles like frightened mice, refusing to stay long enough for him to think them; and he found
himself obeying, because he could not think of anything else
to do, scrambling to his feet, catching up the hound leashes
that the man tossed to him. One leash with the special knot on
to Bran's wide, bronze-studded collar, the other on to Gerland's.

Somehow, fumbling because he was blind and half-crying with fright and his sense of utter helplessness, while Gildon swore at him for being all thumbs, the thing got done.

'Come then, Bran—Gerland boy—good hounds!'

A few moments later he was scurrying across the still crowded bailey in the warm summer darkness, with the huge, feather-heeled wolfhounds loping on either side of him, and Gildon with the torch following hard behind. They climbed the Keep mound by the covered way, and were passed through the inner gatehouse into the courtyard in the midst of the huge shell Keep, and, with the hounds leaping ahead on the ends of their leashes, climbed the outside stair to the Great Hall.

The skin curtains over the Hall entrance were drawn back because of the warmth of the night, and the archway was full of smoky, amber light. The flaring brightness of the torches, the colour and noise and press of life within, stopped Randal on the threshold like a blow between the eyes, but Gildon thrust him forward, and all chance of escape was cut off.

# A GAME OF CHESS

THE rich smell of food lingered in the air from the meal that was just over, mingling with the sour smell of the rushes on the floor, and the smoke of the torches held by a score of squires stationed round the walls hung in a drifting haze under the rafters, so that the light was thick, and the whole scene swam in it as in murky, golden water.

The new Lord of Arundel sat in his great chair, leaning an elbow on one carved front-post and his chin in his hand, to watch a man who was dancing on his hands before him while another played a bagpipe; but as Randal stood just within the arched doorway, his mouth dry and his heart hammering, Hugh Goch looked up and saw him with the hounds in leash, and impatiently gesturing the strolling tumblers out of the way, crooked a finger to him in summons.

Somehow Randal found himself walking forward up the crowded Hall, the two great wolfhounds stalking on either side of him. He kept his shoulders hunched and his chin tucked down, staring at the rushes as he walked, with a crazy hope that if he did not look at Hugh Goch, Hugh Goch might not recognize him. He had reached the step of the dais now, and halted, still staring at the rushes.

'Ohé—a sight from old times, eh, Robert?' He heard the Lord of Arundel's voice above him. 'I scarce ever remember our father in Hall that he had not these brutes or others of their kind lying at his feet.' And then, 'Bring them here to me, boy.'

Randal had just enough sense to know that the order was for him and that he must obey. He climbed the step, and stood again staring down—at a pair of feet shod in rose-scarlet cloth with fantastically long toes. Ever after he remembered the chevron pattern of gold that ran down the instep, and the withered yellow head of ragwort among the rushes beside the left one, that made him think of the salt-smelling marshes where they took the hounds for exercise when they were not hunting. Hugh Goch was snapping his fingers to the two great hounds, laughing as he failed to get any response from them. 'Hai! My Bran—my Gerland, don't you know the bad black smell of the Montgomery blood?'

'Since you so clearly remember our father with his hounds, Little Brother, have you forgotten 'twas his pride that they answered to no one else—even of the Montgomery blood?' De Bellême's voice was like Hugh Goch's, but with a note of mockery, darker in tone as the flame of his hair was darker in colour.

'It seems that they answer to the boy,' Hugh Goch said. 'Look up, boy. You should be proud that you can handle my father's hounds, not hanging your head. Look—up—I say.'

It was smoothly spoken, with almost a sheen of laughter, but the smoothness was terrible. Slowly, Randal raised his head, feeling as though his eyes were being dragged upward, over the great iron-hilted sword lying across the man's knees and the beautiful, ruthless hand that held it there, over the violet-coloured breast-folds of a cloak, until they came to Hugh Goch's face, white under the flaming hair, with the red, rough marks that his mail coif had worn at cheek and chin and forehead giving it somehow the look of a mask. He was leaning forward, his gaze waiting for Randal's face as it turned slowly up to his, waiting, as it were, to swoop. And the boy knew as he met the golden eyes that Hugh Goch had known him from the first moment he entered the Hall.

'Do they always do what you tell them, my father's hounds?'

Randal, his eyes caught and held so that he could not look away, whispered through dry lips, 'Mostly, my Lord.'

'Show me.'

'What—would my Lord have them do?'

'Bid them go back to their kennels,' said Hugh Goch, softly.

Randal, terrified as he was, suddenly found himself able to think again and think quickly. But all his thinking told him was that if he did not send the hounds away, they would fly to his aid when he needed it—as he would need it—and that then no matter whose throat they tore out first they would be cut down, here in this dreadful place full of men with swords; and Hugh Goch knew all that, and was enjoying the situation.

'Bran,' he whispered, 'Gerland,' and as they looked round questioningly into his face, he slipped the leashes from first one collar and then the other. 'Go back! Off to kennels. Off now!'

He stood watching them as they bounded away down the Hall and disappeared through the archway into the darkness; and the panic whimpered higher into his throat as he saw them go.

'You are indeed a hound boy,' said the soft, amused, terrible voice behind him. 'They say that the Saxon blood always makes the best hound boys and hunstmen. Now turn again to me, you Saxon brat.'

Randal turned.

'So,' Hugh Goch said conversationally, 'we meet again, boy who throws rotten figs at his Lord.'

'I didn't——' Randal protested wildly, staring like a trapped hare into the white face with the gold-rimmed eyes of a bird of prey. 'I did not—it was not me—it——'

'No? In this Castle of Arundel, there are no doubt many boys with skin as dark and hair as pale as yours?'

'I didn't—I didn't——' Randal babbled. 'Oh my Lord, I meant no harm.'

'Oh no, you meant no harm.' Hugh Goch's laughter became suddenly a snarl. 'The gadfly that stings my wrist means no harm, I break it under my thumb-nail, none the less.' His hand flashed out and gripped Randal's shoulder, the long fingers biting as though they were tipped with iron, and began to drag him to and fro, shaking him with short, snapping movements like a dog with a rat, until he was sick and crowing for breath, his neck all but broken and his eyes set in his head.

When at last the Lord of Arundel flung him down, he fell all asprawl, gasping and crowing and clutching at his shoulder that felt as though it had been torn out by the roots, then somehow struggled to his knees.

'Take this *thing* away and thrash it,' Hugh Goch was saying,

15

'but stop short of killing it. It is too good a hound boy to waste, and we can always thrash it again another day.'

Randal heard the words, and with the certainty of a ruthless hand already swooping to catch the scruff of his neck, gazed wildly and imploringly among the faces on the dais. He saw de Bellême looking on as at a jest, the Lady Adeliza with her mouth buttoned and her eyes cast down; faces that laughed, or were uneasy, or simply did not care; and out of them all, one face that was not shut to his agonized appeal, looked back at him. At the last instant, with the hand of one of Hugh Goch's squires in the act of closing on the neck-band of his ragged tunic, he rolled clear, scrambled across the dais on all fours and flung himself at the long black legs of de Bellême's minstrel, clinging to them with small, desperate hands.

He felt a quick movement above him, and an arm was laid across his shoulder—but so casually that it seemed as though it had happened by chance—and a light and lazy voice said, but not to him, 'Hands off, my friend.'

Out of the startled hush in the Great Hall sounded Hugh Goch's voice.

'You have something there—an ill behaved puppy—that belongs to me. Pray you hand it over to my squire, for training.'

And the lazy voice replied, faintly drawling, 'Let the Lord of Arundel forgive me, I fear I am something too busy.'

A gasp riffled round the Hall, a laugh bitten off before it was begun; and then complete silence save for a dog scratching under one of the benches. Randal, whose face had been hidden against the minstrel's knees, looked up, and saw the two men watching each other above him. Hugh Goch's eyes were all golden, the pupils contracted to mere pin-points of black. 'Too busy? And what then is this busyness that has no outward showing?'

'I make a song,' Herluin the Minstrel said blandly, his own eyes wide and very bright under the lock of mouse-coloured hair that fell across his high, sallow forehead. 'I make songs as well as sing them, did you know? And the songs I make, folk sing and whistle afterwards—and laugh at when they are meant for laughter. This song that I make now is meant for laughter;

16

it is a song of how a great Lord spent as much rage as would set all Wales in flames on one small boy who dropped a half-eaten fig on his horse's nose. It will be a good song—very funny.'

By now the whole Hall, breath in cheek, was watching the two men who faced each other on the dais. Years after, when he was a man and had some knowledge of courage, Randal knew that for sheer, cold courage he had seldom seen the equal of Herluin the Minstrel, that night in the Great Hall of Arundel.

It seemed that Hugh Goch thought so too, for he said after a few moments with his lips smiling over the teeth, 'You are a very brave man, Herluin, my brother's minstrel.'

Herluin shrugged thin, expressive shoulders, his brows drifting upward under the hanging lock of hair. 'I leave the martial virtues to my Lord and his kind. My toy is the harp, not the sword.'

'A toy that you use for a weapon, and to good account for your own ends, however,' said Hugh Goch, dryly.

'Nay, I am a peaceable man, and a lazy one. But—I am such a creature of whim—I have a mind to this boy.'

'So-o?' Hugh Goch said softly. 'And do you then suggest that I give him to you?'

Herluin smiled. 'Ah, la no. There must be so many who come craving boons of my Lord, and I was never one to run with the pack; while my Lord, generous though he is, must grow weary of so much giving. No, since—I think—my Lord finds poor entertainment in the juggling turns that we have endured through supper, I would suggest that we change the order of the evening to something that may prove more amusing, and play a game of chess for the boy.'

For a long, silent moment Hugh Goch looked at his brother's minstrel, red brows knit above the fierce golden stare, while Herluin, his arm still lying across Randal's shoulders, smiled sweetly back, and the whole Hall waited. Everyone knew—even Randal, still clinging desperately to the minstrel's long black legs, knew, for in his kind of life one learned many things—that the new Lord of Arundel was a gambler to the bone. He saw little flecks of light begin to hover far back in the golden eyes.

'Truly there was never a minstrel like you, Herluin,' said

Hugh Goch, 'but how if we say that tonight we are all of us suddenly in the mood for minstrelsy, and cannot spare you from your harp?'

'As to that, Little Brother'—de Bellême spoke in that dark, mocking voice, with a flash of pointed teeth in the fashionable red, forked beard—'I never yet found any means to persuade this Herluin of mine to wake his harp when he was not minded to.'

Herluin cocked one eyebrow at him. 'Na, I do not think you ever have,' he said in a tone of cordial agreement; and a moment later, detaching Randal from his legs with a 'Hy my! What is all this clinging for, Small One?' lounged to his feet with the slow, somewhat fantastic grace that was very much a part of him, and made a deep bow to the Lord of Arundel that expressed without words how completely he was at my Lord's service and ready to play chess.

Hugh Goch stared at him a moment longer, then flung up his head with a snarl of laughter. 'I have done many things in my time, but never played chess for a human stake before. So be it; I am in the mood for something new.' Then, with a long, contemptuous stare at the thronging faces all turned in his direction, stamped to his feet. 'But not here, to be a raree-show in my own Hall . . . Ohé, Reynald my Squire, set out the chess board in the Great Chamber, and bring wine there, and a torch that we may have light to play by. No, since the outcome of the game concerns the brat somewhat nearly, let him come and hold the torch for us himself.'

And so, a short while later, everything seeming unreal about him, Randal was standing with a long resin torch flaring in his hands, in the Great Chamber above the Hall. The Great Chamber was by right the private quarters of the Lord and his Lady, and since the Old Lion had been away making his peace with God in Shrewsbury Abbey, it had of course been used by the Lady Adeliza and her women. But now there was a new Lord of Arundel. Sir Gilbert the Steward had ventured one trembling protest, earlier that day, when he found that Hugh Goch intended instantly to dispossess the Lady. 'It is but a short while before your Lady Mother goes to the nunnery where she has chosen to spend her widowhood; might it not be kind to leave her the Great Chamber until she goes?' But Hugh Goch had made the situation quite clear. 'If she were indeed my Lady Mother, who knows, I might scrape up enough of filial piety to leave her in possession. She is my father's second wife and her long sheep's face raises the devil in me by the mere sight of it. Splendour of God! Cannot you find her another corner of this place to patter her prayers in? You had best try, for I warn you that I lie in the Great Chamber tonight if she lies in the brew house!' So now he sprawled in the carved chair beside the empty hearth, his sword still across his knees, while Herluin the Minstrel had settled himself, long legs outstretched, on the cushioned bench opposite; and on the table between them, at which the dispossessed Lady of Arundel had taken her supper, for she seldom supped in Hall, lay the chess board with its white and crimson morse-ivory pieces marshalled like opposing armies.

Hugh Goch had drawn red, when they tossed a silver penny for sides, and said laughing, 'It is fitting that I should command the Red Queen and her train. I warn you, I always play better with my own colour.'

And so it was for Herluin, sitting with the white ranks before him, to make the first move. He took his time, considering, then put out a long musician's hand and moved one of the pawns forward.

Randal heard the faint click, very sharp and clear, as he set it down.

Hugh Goch, leaning his elbow among the thick, harsh hairiness of the great brown bearskin flung across his chair, took up a piece that glowed in the torchlight deep ruby red, and set it down in its new position with the same clear, decisive click.

All his life, Randal was able to remember that scene in its every least detail, the torch making a ragged core of light in the heart of the crowding gloom, and in it, the intent faces of the two men, and their intent hands, and between them, on the magpie-chequer of the board, the two armies of fantastic shapes that marched and pranced and wavered to and fro, each with its finger of crowned or helmeted or horse's-headed shadow

19

moving beside it; the half-seen, half-lost glint of a bird with a
serpent's tail gold-embroidered on the bed hangings; the king-
fisher fire in the heart of the jewel that held Hugh Goch's cloak
at the shoulder; the click and silence and click again of pieces
picked up and set down, against the distant surf-sound of
voices and bagpipe music from the Great Hall beneath their
feet; the very smell of rosemary and hot resin from the torch in
his sore and smarting hands. And yet, at the time, none of it
seemed quite real. It was all like one of those dreams so vivid
that when you wake the taste of them remains with you all day.

His shoulder ached where Hugh Goch had all but torn it
from the socket, his legs ached with weariness as the time went
by, and his head swam a little with hunger and the strangeness
of everything. Somehow he went on standing and standing, as
the time crawled along, shifting his weight from one leg to the
other and back again, trying to hold the torch steady so that it
did not dribble or flare; and all the while, with an aching intensity, watching the board. He had never seen chess played
before; until this evening he had never even heard of it. He had
no knowledge of opening gambits, of a pawn sacrificed to better
a knight's position, of cunning combinations played out, and the
skilled marshalling of pieces in the face of a devilish red attack
and a menaced white king. He did not know what they were
doing, these men with their intent faces and hovering, deliberate
hands, only that they were moving about carved figures of
kings and queens and little squat knights on horseback and
high-mitred churchmen; and that in some way that he could
not at all grasp, his whole life from that time forward as long as
he lived, depended on the pattern that they made.

At first they played easily, as it were lightly, leaning sideways
to the board, pausing sometimes to drink, when a squire came
in to pour more wine for them into the cups that stood at their
elbows; sometimes talking with the people who wandered up
from the Great Hall to see how the game was going. Presently
de Bellême came up, his sword chape ringing on the circular
stair, to lean on his brother's shoulder and watch the play,
pointing with a finger. 'Watch out for your bishop.' And a little
later, 'Ye-es, I've seen almost this game played out before—

between Red William and Duke Robert.' He laughed 'Maybe our Red King should challenge his brother to play for the lordship of Normandy and England. He might get the thing settled in that way; it seems he's not likely to by tramping round the Duchy with his hired mercenaries as he's been doing all this summer.'

Hugh Goch looked up quickly, echoing the other's laugh with that soft laughter of his that was like a snarl. 'Have a care with that kind of talk, Great Brother . . . Maybe Red William feels something safer with a hired army behind him than with a dumb-sullen English rabble that trusts him as little as his Barons do, or as he trusts his Barons—and maybe with as good reason.' A long, meaning look, lit with reckless amusement passed between them, while Herluin pondered over his next move.

Randal had some idea what they were talking about, at any rate in part, for he knew (had not the whole South Country been grumbling with it for a month past?) that Red William had called out the fyrd, twenty thousand English foot to serve with him against Duke Robert, and then sent his own chaplain, Ranulf Flambard, to meet them at Hastings and take from each man the ten silver shillings coat-and-conduct money provided by his district, and send him home again, while the money went to the King to hire mercenaries.

'A trick such as last month's at Hastings does not earn trust,' de Bellême said. 'And so, with bad blood between the King and his English, comes maybe, sooner or later, the chance that *other folk* may turn to good account. Watch out for your bishop, I tell you, or my minstrel will have you checked in three moves.'

The game went on again, and gradually, as it laid a stronger hold on the players, their faces grew more absorbed, they straightened little by little from their lounging positions and sat square to the table; the wine was left untouched at their elbows, and they ceased to be aware of onlookers. Presently de Bellême shrugged and strolled off down to the Hall again, where the strolling jugglers were still amusing the company. And then at last, a long time later—but Randal had lost all count of time by then—Herluin took up one of his knights and made a move

with it that seemed no different from the many moves that had gone before, and set it down with a small decisive click, and said, 'Check, Montgomery.'

'Ah? What?' Hugh Goch snapped, dropping back his own hand which had been poised for a move. His gaze went quickly, questioningly, over one after another of the pieces, while Herluin suddenly relaxed in his place, watching him with a little smile hovering behind his cool, light eyes.

Hugh Goch's white face seemed for the moment to darken and narrow. Then, abruptly, he laughed, and crashed up from his great chair, oversetting several of the pieces as he did so.

'Checkmate is it? Checkmate to the Lord of Arundel? Aye well, so it is; and the brat is yours now. Take and do what you will with him.'

A few moments later he had gone striding from the room, shouting for his squires, and Herluin rose and stretched until the small muscles cracked between his shoulders, looking down at Randal where he stood gazing dazedly up at him, the torch dribbling unheeded in his numb hands. 'What a thing is life, that it can be changed by moving a few carved ivory pieces on a chequered board—or even by dropping half a fig on a horse's nose, eh, Imp?'

A squire came running to clear the chess board, and the minstrel swung round on him, saying with a flick of one long forefinger towards Randal, 'I have just won this from your Lord; will somebody take and feed it, and put it in whichever of the wall chambers has been made ready for me.'

The squire looked startled and resentful, and muttered something about the wall chambers being for the family, and sleeping in Hall like everybody else.

Herluin's brows drifted upward. 'But then I am not "everybody else", and it pleases me not at all to sleep with the common herd of squires and the like. I am de Bellême's minstrel, my good boy. If no chamber has been kept for me, then I fear, I greatly fear, that you must dispossess someone else, even as your Lord has dispossessed his saintly stepmother . . . Meanwhile I am away to snatch a mouthful of fresh air before sleeping time.'

And so in a while, without any clear idea of how it came

about, Randal found himself, his stomach full of bread and cold sucking pig, lying curled at the foot of a bed of skin rugs and piled rushes in a narrow chamber in the thickness of the wall, opening off the guardroom stair. It was pitch dark, for there was no window to see the white star through, and a curtain of some heavy stuff hung over the entrance. The darkness itself was like a curtain—a black curtain that hung close before Randal's face as he lay staring into it, and made the air thick to breathe. He heard distant sounds, a snatch of song from the guardroom below, the murmur of movement and voices from the Great Hall where those who slept there would be settling for the night, the scream of a hawk. But they were all muffled and far off. Here in the darkness there was no sound at all, no familiar stirring of hounds in the straw; nothing but his own breathing. And quite suddenly he began to be frightened again. A new fear now. So much—a whole life-time of things—had happened to him since he lay on the gatehouse roof at noon, that now, alone in the dark, dazed and bewildered by the rush of events, he was not sure whether any of it had happened at all. But if it had been a dream, was he awake now, or still tangled in it like a fly in a cobweb? And if Hugh Goch was a dream, then Herluin must be a dream too. He could not bear that Herluin should be only a dream. Panic was rising in him, and he began to whimper a little, threshing about on the piled rugs of the bed. His outflung hand found the corner of a soft, thick leather bag with something hard inside it; he reached out farther, exploring in the darkness. Herluin's harp that someone had brought in—he remembered now—and laid on the bed. He could feel the shape of it inside the thick, soft leather of the bag, and the raised scratchiness where the leather was enriched with gold and silver threads.

Comforted, he must have fallen asleep on the instant, for he heard no footsteps on the guardroom stair, but between one moment and the next the curtain over the entrance was thrust back, and light flooded into the narrow chamber, and Herluin was on the threshold holding up a rushlight that glimmered like a star.

Randal crouched up in the straw, the harp held against his

23

knees, blinking at the tall man as he came in and let the curtain fall again behind him.

Herluin crossed the little chamber and set the rushlight on its pricket in a niche high in the rough stone wall, then turned, stretching and yawning, to look down at the small figure on the foot of his bed. The long, wide sleeves fell back from his up-spread arms, revealing the brilliant lining like the blink of yellow on a goldfinch's wings.

'Now why did I never bethink me before, that I should keep a guard-dog?' Herluin said, his gaze taking in the harp that Randal held against his knees. 'Have you kept it safe for me all this while?'

Randal nodded.

Herluin sat down on the carved stool that, save for the make-shift bed, was the only piece of furniture, and stretched his long, loose legs all across the narrow space.

'By what name do they call you? Or do they only whistle?'

'Randal—I'm called Randal,' the boy said hoarsely; and without knowing that he did so, crept close against the bony black knees, his gaze fixed on the minstrel's face.

'Randal. Hy my! What a man's name for such a small imp,' Herluin said, his face cracking into its winged and twisted smile, and put his hand on the boy's rough head. 'Aye, well, you'll grow to it one day. Meanwhile I shall call you Imp.'

# 3

# THE WATER STAIR

In the world outside the strong walls of Arundel, things were stirring that autumn; a muttering of unrest from end to end of the Kingdom, a sudden flare of revolt in Wales. And in October, the King being too deep in his war with Brother Robert to handle any other troubles himself, Henry of Coutances, his younger brother, landed in England, to deal with the disturbances.

Randal heard of these happenings, as he heard the autumn wind siffling over the ramparts, and with as little thought. Indeed, he had not much thought to spare for anything, just then, from the strange experiences of belonging to somebody for the first time in his life.

Soon, before winter closed the seaways, de Bellême would be sailing to take up his heritage in Normandy, and Herluin with him, and Randal with Herluin. Any day now, Hugh Goch would ride with Henry of Coutances, back to his Welsh wars; but meanwhile, it was glorious hunting weather, and both brothers remained at Arundel while the Wealden Forest flamed gold and russet in the October sunshine.

The fine weather broke at last, some days after they heard of Henry's landing, and a gale came booming up from the southwest, salt with the taste of the sea, and the grey, driving rain blotted out the downs behind its trailing curtains of nothingness. And at dusk the storm blew to the gates of Arundel a drenched and weary man on a drenched and weary horse.

He was brought into the torch-lit Hall where half the folk and hounds of the Castle were gathered, waiting for the trumpets to sound their Lord in to supper; a tall bony man in an old leather gambeson black with the wet, who stooped a little as though from a lifetime of wearing heavy mail. And at sight of him, Herluin, who had been singing for them beside the fire—one of the songs of Roland—ceased his singing and laid down his little

bright harp between one note and the next, and came to his
feet in a kind of lazy bound.

'D'Aguillon! Why, Sir Everard, by all that is most wonderful!
And what do you, de Braose's man, here in the Honour of
Arundel?'

The crowd had parted to make way for the newcomer, as he
came through them to the fire, and Randal, looking up from
where he squatted at Herluin's feet, saw the knight's very dark
eyes lighten with pleasure.

'Ohé, Herluin the Minstrel! I thought it was your voice. But
I need not have doubted finding you here, knowing that de
Bellême as soon moves without his minstrel as without his
shadow . . . I have been up to Henry's camp at Portsmouth,
with words from de Braose about the Bramber levies—the old
man grows too gouty for war; young Philip must lead them if
they are called out. And now I am on my way home—or was,
when the storm caught me.' He was putting back the coif of his
gambeson as he spoke, and the thick, badger-grey hair flattened
under its pressure sprang slowly erect. 'Grace of God! What a
storm! Already the ford is impassable and so I come to claim
shelter until the floods sink and I can get across the Hault Rey
and be on my road again.'

'What word from Henry's camp?' someone asked.

'That Mowbray of Northumberland has plundered four
Norwegian trading ships, and is likely to make trouble when
the King calls him to account for it,' d'Aguillon said briefly.

There was a little silence, then someone said with a reckless
laugh, 'Well, with matters as they are at present, that's as likely
a thing as any other to set spark to stubble.'

D'Aguillon bent to hold cold, rain-wet hands to the blaze, the
steam already wisping up from his sodden gambeson, while one
of the squires hurried to fetch him a cup of wine. No one com-
mented on the last speaker's words.

For two days more the storm raged. The gale beat wild wings
about the Castle, and the rain fell spitting and sizzling into the
fire; and they lived by torchlight with the shutters drawn across
the high Hall windows slamming and rattling in the gusts, be-

cause with the windows open they would have been flooded as well as blown inside out. As it was, they would have been smothered with the smoke that billowed down the smoke-vent, if it had not been for the draught that wailed along the floor stirring the dusty rushes. Randal could have lain much more snug in his old corner of the kennels, tucked down under the shelter of the curtain wall, but now that he belonged to Herluin, and had the right to sit in the rushes and the icy draughts at the minstrel's feet, nothing would have induced him to sit elsewhere.

On the third morning they woke to broken skies and a sunrise laced with thin, watery fire, and by evening the sky was clear save for great sheep's-wool clouds trailing their shadows across the valley from one rim of the downs to the other. And Herluin said to the stranger knight, laying aside his harp in its bag of embroidered leather, and stretching as he rose, 'Come away on to the downs for a mouthful of air before supper. We have been too long mewed in the dark like moulting falcons.'

'Say rather like smoked hams hung too long in the chimney corner. Surely I will come.' Sir Everard scuffled his feet in the rushes, and got up also, hitching at his sword sheath.

Randal, squatting in the rushes, cleaning Herluin's spare pair of shoes, sprang to his feet and tugged at the minstrel's wide-falling sleeve imploringly. 'I also! My Lord, take me too, and Bran and Gerland!'

And so a while later, with Randal and the great feather-heeled hounds flying ahead, the minstrel and the old knight passed out through the castle gates, and turning northward, set their faces to the long slope of the downs.

The wind was not as strong as it had been, but up on the downs behind Arundel it still came booming up through the oak woods, and the seagulls whirled overhead like blown leaves. On the edge of the oak woods a great dyke, blurred by time until it was curved and gradual as the trough of a wave, cut across the shoulder of the downs, made—but Randal knew nothing of that —by the Bronze men, two thousand years before, to guard their turf-banked fortress where Arundel Castle stood now. And by

29

and by the two men fell to walking to and fro along its lip, while Randal, scrambling down into it, found a spot that was warm as summer, with the westering sun spilling down the bramble-choked slope at his back, under the wind that whirled the flocks of brown leaves overhead and laid the long grass at the edge of the dyke over all one way; and squatting down there, began to pick fleas out of Gerland's brindled coat, while the old hound lay and groaned in ecstasy. Leaving Bran and Gerland —the other hounds too, but Bran and Gerland most of all—was the one thing that he was going to hate in leaving Arundel. Would anyone bother to pick the fleas out of Gerland's coat when he was gone? The thought made him extra thorough now; but between fleas he watched the two men walking to and fro, the one lithe and loose-knit, his mantle flying like black wings about him, the other stiff and soldierly in his old gambeson, with his sword gathered in his arms as he walked. He wondered what they were talking about, and wished that the wind were the other way so that he might hear. He was not at all sure that he liked the strange knight, who had a mouth like a trap and the kind of eyes that you could not lie to.

From the seaward end of their walk, where the land began to drop too steeply for comfort, Herluin and Sir Everard could look down over the marshes and the estuary, and see where the Hault Rey came looping out through the downs, round the last sinking shoulder of the hillside on which the town and Castle stood. The river was still in tawny spate, but already it did not reach so far up the half-drowned alders as it had done that morning, and the wind-ruffled water that spread in great lakes all across the marshy valley seemed shrinking almost while they watched.

'Truly, it has been a most noble storm,' said Sir Everard, as they checked as by common consent, and stood looking down. 'But from the speed that the floods are sinking, I think that it cannot have broken far inland. If not tomorrow, then surely at the next day's low tide, I shall be able to get Valiant across the ford and go on my way.'

Herluin said slowly, 'Since the wind blew you into Arundel Great Hall three nights since, I have been thinking—a little.

D'Aguillon, will you do something for me, for your Richard, his sake?'

'What would you have me do?'

'Take the Imp with you when you ride from here.'

The old man looked quickly at the younger one, but nothing was to be read in the cool, faintly bitter face, the pale eyes, in the windy, westering sunlight. 'Why?' he demanded, after a few moments.

'Because I have known you—somewhat—since Richard and I learned our book together at Bec Abbey, and I would liefer give him into your hands than those of any other man I know.'

'Surely you honour me,' d'Aguillon said, deep in his throat. 'That was not my meaning, however, as you know full well. Why give the boy into any man's hands, out of your own?'

'Hy my! For a number of reasons. Firstly, because the life of minstrel or jester is a chancy thing, as all men know—playing with fire was never yet a safe pastime, though amusing; and—' his light tone hardened—'if ought should happen to me, I would not have him left in the hands of the Montgomery brood.'

They had turned inland again, with the wind over their left shoulders, and Sir Everard nodded, his gaze on the wooded crest of the downs ahead. 'Aye, bad men, both of them . . . It is sometimes in my mind to wonder——'

'What?' said Herluin gently.

'No matter. I was going to say that I sometimes wonder you still hold to de Bellême yourself. But to each man the secrets of his own heart.'

Herluin shrugged, the slow expressive shrug that showed him for no Norman but French to the bone, and rolled his eyes heavenward. 'I am something of a fool as well as a minstrel . . . But we are talking of the Imp, not of me. I have given you one reason concerning him. For a second—I am fool enough to care that he should have a chance in life more suited to him than any I can give. It would be different if I saw the least likelihood of making a minstrel of him, but there is no music in the Imp. Mercy of God! There is *no* music in the Imp!' Herluin shuddered as a shrill tuneless whistling reached them down the gusts. 'If

I keep him with me, he will find no place of his own, ever; he will strike no root, and he needs to strike root, greatly. You could give him that. Will you take him?'

'What as?' Sir Everard said, twenty paces farther along the dyke.

'As a fellow for Bevis. You were saying only yesterday that the boy was growing up too solitary; that you feared you did wrong to train him up yourself, instead of sending him to one of the great houses.'

'And that is true enough.' Sir Everard gave a quickly suppressed sigh. 'But Richard was my only son, and he is Richard's, and when Richard was killed . . . I am a selfish old man; I delight in the boy's company, but he—he needs company of his own age, and not merely that of the villeins' children.'

'Give him Randal to be varlet with him, and squire with him when that time comes,' Herluin said. 'He'll make a good squire. He has lived so long with hounds that along with most of their faults he has learned the hound's chief virtue of faithfulness.'

The old man did not answer until they had turned seaward again, the wind snatching at his words. 'And in ten years or so, Bevis will be made a knight however unworthy, because he is my grandson and gently born and it is the custom. What place for your Randal then?'

'A squire's place at all events, which is none so ill a thing. Give him his chance, d'Aguillon.'

They paced on in silence a little farther, then Sir Everard said, 'You have, I think, some fondness for the child.'

'It is easy to grow fond of a stray dog,' Herluin said lightly.

'And the child has some fondness for you.'

'Because mine was the first hand that ever touched him in kindness, no more. He is a small cub; he will soon forget.'

Sir Everard looked round at the man strolling beside him, and the grim gash of his mouth that Randal liked so little had unexpectedly gentle corners. 'And you? Will you also forget so soon?'

'I?' Herluin flickered up his eyebrows and laughed, lazy, light, mocking laughter into the wind, that seemed echoed by the sea-birds' crying. 'I shall have forgotten him in three days!

I am Herluin, de Bellême's minstrel; any man will tell you that I have no heart to remember with!'

And Randal, pulling a tick from behind Bran's left ear, thought, 'It cannot be anything that matters, after all. It must be something funny, or Herluin would not laugh like that.'

The men had come to the seaward end of their walk again, and halted as before, looking down to where the Hault Rey swirled the colour of heather ale over its paved ford.

'I'll take him,' Sir Everard said abruptly. 'And this I promise you, that save for knighthood, which is beyond my hands, he shall have what Bevis has, both of the kicks and the honeycomb.'

Not that night, but the next, when it came to sleeping time, and he had propped his harp in its usual corner of the narrow wall chamber, Herluin lounged down on the roughly carved stool, and crooked a finger for Randal. 'Come here, Imp.'

Randal, who was spreading his own rug just within the doorway, where he had slept ever since Herluin had objected to his sleeping across his feet, came and stood against the minstrel's black-sheathed knees looking up at him inquiringly.

'Tomorrow, when the river ford is passable at low tide, Sir Everard goes home to his own place, across the downs,' Herluin said.

Randal was glad, and showed it as clearly as a pup wagging its tail; but his gladness lasted for only a heartbeat of time.

'And you,' said Herluin, 'you go with him.'

Randal stared at him, startled, and beginning to be afraid; and then burst into a flurry of words. 'Why? I do not understand—for how long? I must be back before we sail for Normandy.'

'You are not coming with me to Normandy, Imp.'

'But you said—you promised——' Randal was sick and breathless now, staring at Herluin with dilated eyes.

'Did I so? Then it must be that I am breaking my promise.' Herluin's voice sounded faintly bored. 'Never trust a minstrel. Hy my! Anyone will tell you that de Bellême's minstrel changes his mind as often as a swallow changes course.'

'But I don't understand!' Randal protested frantically. 'Have I made you angry? Tell me, and I'll never do it again— only don't send me away.'

There was a little silence and a queer smile rather like a shadow flickered across Herluin's face without ever touching his eyes. 'Na na, there is naught amiss. Never think it, Imp.' For the moment he had dropped something of his usual drawl. 'It is in my mind that here is a better way for you, that is all. It may even be that when you have as fine a beard as Sir Gilbert the Steward, you will think so too. Or it may be that you will not. A fine thing it would be if a man might foretell how the moves in life will turn out, as clearly as the moves in a game of chess.' Then, with a deliberate return to the cool, affected drawl that his world knew, he yawned hugely, stretching with his fantastic winged shadow stretching on the wall behind him. 'So—I change my mind; the thing is settled. Sleep now, Imp. They tell me that low tide is at some barbarically early hour in the morning.'

Randal stood back a little, still staring at him, breathing short and quick. 'Yes, I will go and sleep,' he said thickly, through the sob in his throat. 'But not here! I will sleep with the hounds as I used to do. *They* do not change their minds!' And he turned and stalked out with his nose in the air and his mouth tight shut on the grief within him.

He went down the spiral stair, past the entrance to the guardroom where the men-at-arms were settling in for the night, and down again, slowly, his hand on the great stone central core of the stairway. Half-way down, he checked altogether, not quite able to believe, even now, that Herluin would not call him back or come after him. But the moments dragged out long and thin, and no lazy voice called, no step sounded on the stair behind him, and he went on down, into the darkness. The man-at-arms on duty at the stair foot passed him through without trouble, thinking that he was on some errand for Herluin, and he came out through the archway into the courtyard in the midst of the great shell Keep. He knew that the gate to the outer bailey would be shut now, and certainly no one would open it again for the likes of Randal. That was no matter; in the

34

flying autumn moonlight another archway opened like a black mouth; that was the entrance to the water stair that led down to the Castle well, outside the Keep, and in normal times it was not kept guarded.

Randal oozed his way along the wall to it, taking advantage of every blot of shadow. There was no reason why he should not have walked boldly across to it, no law against his sleeping in the kennels again as he had used to do, though it might have meant answering questions that he did not want to have to answer, if he were seen. But before Herluin came, his night-time comings and goings about the Castle had mostly been furtive affairs, and now that Herluin was gone from him again, he returned without thought to his old, secret ways. He reached the dark mouth of the stairway unseen, and slipped into the pit of blackness that it made, as an otter slips into the water without a splash. The hollow feel of the tunnel was all about him, and the cold, green smell of water coming up from below.

There was another smell too, that brought him up on the third step, sniffing delicately and cautiously like a hound. A very faint scent, it wafted up on the stronger water smell, seemed to whisper in his nostrils, and then before he could lay hold of it, was gone. He stole down two more steps, and now he had it again, more strongly this time, more surely. Once, a great lady had walked close by him, and her mantle had given out a strange scent that was heavy and warm and sweet, but animal. He had asked someone what made the lady smell like that, and been told that it was musk; and now he knew the scent again, infinitely thinner and fainter, but the same. But why was the scent of musk creeping up the water stair? One of the Lady Adeliza's women meeting in secret with someone among the knights or men-at-arms? He thought he caught the murmur of voices in the darkness far down the stairway; but it seemed to him that both voices were men's, and even in the midst of his misery, a little stir of excitement shimmered through him. He crept nearer, slipping his feet silently from step to step. Near the foot of the steps was a recess where a narrow doorway led to some chamber deep in the foundations of the Keep, and

35

just below that, the stairway turned a corner before it ran out
into the vaulted well-house. It was from below this corner that
the murmur of voices came. Randal gained the recess safely,
and flattened himself against the slimy stonework, listening
with all his ears.

The voices were close below him now. One of them spoke in
low-toned, fierce impatience, and he knew it for the voice of
Hugh Goch.

His carefully held breath caught in his throat in a cold
moment of terror. He knew that he was in deadly danger.
Whatever it was that Hugh Goch did here, whoever he met in
dead-of-night secrecy, he would not welcome eavesdroppers.
He knew that if Hugh Goch caught him, he would kill him here
in the dark; and he longed to turn and run, leaping upward to
the silver moonlight at the head of the stair. But as before, when
the Lord of Arundel had looked up at him as he leaned over the
parapet of the gatehouse roof, he seemed turned to stone and
built into the wall.

The other man was speaking in his turn, answering Hugh
Goch's impatient words.

'It is too late in the year to start anything now, more especially with Brother Henry playing watch-dog.' It was a curiously
smooth voice, a hairless voice, with a faint suggestion of a lisp.
'De Lacy sends you word to go to Shrewsbury, as many of your
knights with you as maybe, and hunt your Welsh forests towards
winter's end, that you may be ready in the Marches before
spring. The King will summon Mowbray to appear before his
Easter Court on the matter of the Northman's trading vessels;
Mowbray will refuse, and then——'

'The revolt will flare up as at a signal.' Randal heard Hugh
Goch's soft, snarling laugh in the darkness. 'A fine signal for our
purpose, and one that can be relied on to bring in the whole
of the Marches. We Marcher lords, we're all pirates and reivers
to a man—but at least we do our reiving openly and not under
cover of self-made laws as the King does!'

'Be ready when the time comes, and before high summer we'll
have done with Red William and his self-made laws, and mount
Stephen of Aumale in his place.'

'Bid de Lacy to have his own weapons sharp,' Hugh Goch said scornfully, 'and never doubt that I'll have mine!'

Randal heard the formless sound of movement, and a soft footfall on the water stair. The two voices sank to a mumble, mingling with the brush and pad of stealthily retreating footsteps, dwindling away. The sounds had quite died now, nothing left of what Randal had overheard but his own wildly drubbing heart, and the faint, lingering echo of the scent of musk. The boy drew a great gasp of air, the first full breath that he had drawn in all that while, and gathered himself together to run. But even as he did so he heard one of the men coming back. He had just time to flatten himself again into the embrasure of the door behind him, before the man, whichever it was, swept by.

The heavy folds of a cloak actually brushed Randal, but no scent of musk came from them. The dark figure swept on and up, taking the water stair two steps at a time. He saw it silhouetted for an instant in the stairhead arch; even the bleaching moonlight could not quite drain the red from Hugh Goch's hair. Then it was gone.

# 4

# RIVER OF NO RETURN

RANDAL waited awhile in the darkness, his heart hammering. But he could not stop there for ever. He must go forward, or back, and he was not going back. The man with the hairless voice must be well out of the way by now. . . . He crept on down, round the corner of the stairway, the last faint traces of the womanish scent dying into the cold smell of the water strong in the enclosed spaces. He saw the well-house empty in the backwash of reflected moonlight, and the whiteness of the night hanging beyond the arched doorway, and flung himself at the steps up to it as though at this last instant hands that smelled of musk were closing on the back of his neck, and shot out into the thick moon shadows at the foot of the Keep mound.

There were still people about in the outer bailey, which always kept later and more uncertain hours than the Keep, and Lovel, long since well of his fever, his battered old lantern in his hand (it was only Gildon who took a naked torch among the hounds, and then not if Lovel was there to see him) was just snibbing the door of the kennels, after his nightly prowl round, as Randal came darting across the bailey.

Randal flung himself against the door, tearing at the latch under the huntsman's surprised hands. 'Let me in! You let me in!'

'So, so? I thought that you were Herluin's man these days,' the other grumbled, peering at him in the light of the lantern.

'Na!' Randal spat the words between his teeth. 'Tomorrow I go with the old knight he is for ever talking to—him with a mouth like a trap—but tonight I sleep with my own again!'

Lovel grunted, not interested enough to ask questions, and let him through, rattling the door to again behind him.

Randal stumbled forward into the familiar rustling and snuffling, dog-smelling darkness. He knew the place so well that it was as though his feet could see the way for themselves. But there was light at the far end of the place; a silver sword of moonlight slanting down from the high window; and at the foot of it, Bran and Gerland lay outstretched, their brindled hides bleached to cobweb grey in the shadows, frosted silver where the moonlight fell.

They greeted Randal with softly thumping tails, and he crawled in between them as he had done on so many nights, and lay down with his back against Gerland's flank and his head on Bran's shoulder, and his face hidden under his arm from the white, fierce sword of moonlight. He was shaking from head to foot, and it seemed to him that he could smell musk everywhere, and hear the nightmare smoothness of a voice that lisped a little, in the darkness. But already he was not quite certain what he had overheard; the whole incident seemed to be dissolving as an evil dream dissolves when the dreamer wakes from it, leaving only a sickly taste of the evil behind. Gradually his heart quietened from its pounding and his breath that had been coming in little, whistling gasps grew steady again. But as his terror ebbed away, the furious misery that it had almost driven out for a time came back and engulfed him.

'Tomorrow I go away,' he told Bran and Gerland in a small, cracked whisper. 'I will never forget you—do not forget me, old Bran—old Gerland . . . I told him hounds did not change their minds. I told him—I told him . . .'

Bran licked his face sleepily.

Next morning at low tide, so early that it was not yet full daylight, and the white mist lay across the marshes, Randal left the great Castle of Arundel that had been the only home he knew in all his first ten years, mounted before Sir Everard on his tall roan stallion. Herluin strolled down with them to the paved ford, but Randal would not look at Herluin again, at which the minstrel grew mocking-merry under the alder trees.

Randal had crossed the Hault Rey often, when they took the hounds to run on the marshes, but this time, as Sir Everard gentled the horse down into the swift, brown water, and he saw it swirling and boiling mealy with foam about the great brute's legs, it seemed to him that this was more than just the Hault

Rey; this was something strange and terrifying, wild water sweeping between the unknown world that he went to, and the old familiar one that, with all its badness, was the only world he knew.

'Up, my Valiant, come up!' said Sir Everard's voice above him, and he saw the strong, dark hand on the reins, and felt the upward heave, the slipping scramble of the great horse under him, as Valiant lifted his hind quarters clear of the swirling flood. And they were across, with the old life left behind on the far side, the good and the bad of the old life, Bran and Gerland, Hugh Goch with his bird of prey face under the flaming hair, and the queer, evil, musk-scented dream—it really did seem like a dream now—that he had had last night on the water stair, and Herluin, standing among the alder trees.

But Randal did not look back.

He never afterwards remembered much about that long day's ride. Indeed, it never seemed to be part of his life at all, but just a kind of bridge between one thing and the next. Usually it would have seemed, to the boy who had never been on a horse before, both splendid and terrifying to sit so high above the world, feeling the liveness and the willing strength of the great roan surging under him, and hear the drub of the strong round hooves on open turf or miry track spooling by so far beneath. But afterwards he could scarcely remember it at all.

Late in the day there was a town of reed-thatched houses under the downs, that Sir Everard said was called Steyning, and a little later still there was suddenly a familiar thing; a grey, stone-built castle on the last low shoulder of the downs, with a river casting a bright loop through the marshy valley about its foot. 'That is Bramber,' Sir Everard said. 'De Braose holds it from the King as Hugh Goch holds Arundel—as I hold Dean from de Braose.' And almost as he spoke, the roan turned aside of his own accord through the dusty wayside tangle of bramble and seeding willow herb, heading southward, where the downs fell back to let the broadening river through. Sir Everard chuckled deep in his throat, a contented sound. 'Valiant knows the way home, you see.'

It was not yet dusk, but the 'tween-light was blurring the

outline of all things, when they came at last, two or maybe three miles down-river, to the ford of a stream brawling down from the high chalk, and saw through the smoke-soft screen of willows and alders the gleam of a firelit doorway reflected in the glossy darkness of a mill leat. 'Yonder is the Manor Mill,' Sir Everard said, as he steadied Valiant down to the ford and they splashed up on the farther side. 'And now—does the wind smell different? We are on Dean land;' and a while later still, pointing, as the woods fell back, 'See, up the valley yonder. There is Dean. That is your home, Randal.'

Looking where the finger pointed, Randal saw a straggle of deep-thatched huts and bothies strung along the track where it wound upwards towards the downs, the faint, irregular pattern of field strips striping the valley, and at the upper end of the straggle, set about with hawthorn and old fruit trees, a long low hall with its byres and barns around it. Beyond, only the steepening coomb winding upward, and the whale-backed ridge of the downs against a sunset that was like the echo of a brighter sunset somewhere else. Soft blue wafts of evening woodsmoke lay across the village, and the sunset looked as though there were trails of smoke across it, too. And as he looked, a queer thing happened; for it was as though something in Randal much deeper and older than his ten years, said softly and with certainty, 'Yes, this is home.'

A man crossing the track from the woodwright's shop with a new ox-yoke on his shoulder, turned to greet his returning Lord with a welcoming growl; a couple of women, one with a squalling baby on her hip, heard the clop of hooves and came to cottage doorways, and a scattering of children appeared from nowhere and ran grinning at Valiant's feathery heels, until their mothers called them in to supper. And all of them stared at the strange boy with the fair hair and dark skin, whom d'Aguillon carried before him. And tired as he was—it was a long ride from Arundel to Bramber, farther still from an old life to a new one—Randal felt their interest and curiosity, and stared back at them under his brows, wondering about them as only somebody whose chief experience of people is that they kick can wonder. But all the while, unwillingly, rebelling

42

against it because he did not want to be happy in this new life that Herluin had betrayed him into, the queer sense of home-coming was with him.

They were half-way up the village street when, with ears and tails streaming, three great hounds came bounding to meet them.

'Ohé, Luath—Luffra! Ohé, Matilda lass,' Sir Everard greeted them as they came yelping and weaving about him. 'Sa, sa! Here's a clamour! You will let them know through half Sussex that the Lord of Dean comes home!'

They did not jump up, having been trained like all good hounds not to leap upon a mounted man and startle the horse; but Luath, who was the tallest of them all, reached up and nosed Sir Everard's foot in the long Norman stirrup, while Valiant dropped his head to touch muzzles with the bitch Matilda, and Luffra, who was little more than a puppy, skirmished about them with tail and ears flying.

A big, half-wild pear tree, gnarled and twisted with age, hung over the gateless gap that led from the village street into the Hall garth, the little brown pears showing among the rusted leaves, and as they drew near, something that was not the wind made a sudden frowing and flurrying in the branches, and Randal, looking up, saw a long, thin leg in loose, russet-coloured hose appear from among the leaves. It was followed by another, and next instant a tall boy dropped lightly into their path almost under Valiant's nose, making the horse snort and sidle, and came to Sir Everard's stirrup as the knight reined in to a trampling halt.

'Bevis! That was a fool trick!' Sir Everard growled, patting Valiant's neck. 'Softly, softly my Valiant. Have you never seen the boy before? Have you no more sense, Bevis, than to come dropping out of nowhere under a horse's nose to startle him half out of his wits?'

'He's not really startled, only a bit surprised,' the boy said, with a breathless laugh in his voice. 'And I didn't drop out of nowhere. I was up in the pear tree, watching for you.'

'So? And how did you know that I should come home this evening?'

'Ancret said you would. She said she heard Valiant's hoof-beats this morning in the wind, and you would be home by dark.'

He was a tall boy, maybe a year or so older than Randal, with a thin, eager face that looked white in the twilight, under a feathery tangle of dark hair; and as he spoke, his gaze flicked from his grandfather to the boy riding before him, lingered, frowning a little, and flicked back again.

'Who is that?'

'A boy called Randal. Herluin, de Bellême's minstrel, who was your father's friend, sends him to you for a fellow varlet. For the rest—doubtless he will tell you himself, whatever he wants to tell you, by and by.'

Bevis turned his gaze again to meet Randal's, which had been fixed upon him since the moment that he dropped out of the pear tree. And they looked at each other, both frowning, a little wary, like two young dogs who walk round each other on stiff legs, uncertain whether they are going to be friends or fly at each other's throats.

'How long is he to be here?' Bevis said at last.

'That is as God wills. He will be varlet with you, and squire with you when the time comes.' Sir Everard sounded a little stern.

'I don't mind that'—Bevis spoke with a faint challenge, after a moment's silence—'so long as he remembers that it is *I* who have the right to be your body squire when *that* time comes, grandfather.'

Sir Everard laughed, deep in his throat, his sternness forgotten, and set Valiant in motion again. 'Since you have already been my varlet for two years, and so he must be two years behind you all the way, you may surely sleep secure on that score, unless of course I decide that your manners are too ill to fit you to be any decent knight's body squire—in which case I shall send you up to de Braose to herd the Bramber swine.'

The boy Bevis gave a crow of laughter, apparently completely reassured by this dire threat, and padded along at his grandfather's stirrup, with the hounds flowing all about him, as they headed for the long, low Hall that was already shedding dim, saffron firelight through high windows and open doorway to greet them.

A sharper note of light, ragged and jaunty like a dandelion, came round the end of the Hall, and a little man, knotted like a tree root, came with a stable lantern swinging in his hand, to take Valiant as they clattered to a halt.

'Not washed away by the floods, you see, old Wulf,' said Sir Everard, and dropped stiffly from the saddle, lifting Randal down after him.

Randal was so tired and stiff from the long journey that his legs buckled under him, and he stumbled and all but fell before he got his balance. The lantern light swam round him for a moment, or he round it, like the autumn moth that had come fluttering out of the dusk to circle about and about the candle flame, beating soft, spread wings against the horn panes. Ever after, when he thought of that first coming to Dean, he remembered old Wulf's brown, toothless face lit from below by the lantern, and the powdery white moth turned to silver in its airy circling.

'Take him with you to help Wulf stable Valiant.' Vaguely he heard Sir Everard's voice above him. 'If he is to be varlet with you, he cannot begin too soon.'

And then, a little behind the boy Bevis, he was stumbling after the swinging lantern and Valiant's feathery heels, into the new life that was waiting for him to learn its ways.

# 5

# RED AMBER

THE Hall was the heart and centre of the Manor, a long, low timber-framed building deep-thatched with reed that was bee-brown save where the new reed of a mended place shone pale as honey, with its fire burning on a long hearth down the centre of the floor, and the smoke-blackened beams showing still where firelight or torchlight touched them, the red and blue and saffron paint that had made them gay for a Saxon master before the Normans came. D'Aguillon had made little change in the place, save that for comfort he had built on a small solar at the far end, raised up a few steps over an undercroft where they stored farm implements and spare bee skeps at one end and the Manor's quota of war bows and leather jacks in great iron-bound kists at the other.

The byres and barns huddled about the Hall, all within the tangled hedge of hawthorn and the little half-wild fruit trees. Below the Hall garth, the reed and turf and bracken-thatched bothies of the villeins straggled downhill, each with its kale and herb plot, its tethered cock among his clucking hens, its woodpile beside the door, its bee skep at the back; and beyond the village stretched the three great arable fields, each divided into long narrow strips, lord's land and villeins' land all mixed up together, with the long, communal pasture lying between it and the high, wind-haunted stride of the downs above, where Lewin Longshanks kept the Manor sheep. It was all Dean land, from the river in the east where the trading ships passed up to Bramber or down to the open sea, away up to the whale-backed ridge of Long Down, a mile and more to the westward; from the ford by the mill where the Manor corn was ground, down-river until the Bramble Hill thrust half across the valley, and, so they said, the King of a forgotten people slept with his golden treasure about him, in the heart of the green grave-mound against the sky.

This was the share that Sir Everard's sword had earned him thirty years ago, when he was young and followed de Braose who followed Duke William from Normandy. A knight's share of English land, held for the usual knight's fee, five mounted or ten foot soldiers to follow his Baron in time of war, and in war or peace alike, for the Lord of the Manor himself, a month in every year spent on Castle guard duty at Bramber.

A small, self-contained world that, as the years went by, had woven itself very closely into the fibres of d'Aguillon's being. And it was the new world to which Randal woke, on his first morning, lying in the deep fern beside the fire, with Bevis and the hounds and the rest of the household; stiff and sore, bewildered, bruised and aching in heart as well as body, and yet still with that unwilling feeling on him of having come to the place where he belonged.

But in the next few days he lost something of that feeling. The new life that he had to lead now was so very strange to him. and it irked him like a too-tight garment. In the mornings, until ten o'clock dinner, he must go across to the small, thatched church just outside the garth, and sit with Bevis at the feet of Adam the Clerk who looked after the souls of Dean and kept the Manor Rolls, sniffing the smell of mice that always clung to the little man's rusty gown, and struggling to make sense of the marks that he scored on wax tablets and then smoothed out and scored again. He must learn to handle light weapons, and to tend old Valiant and Hector, Sir Everard's second horse, and to handle hawk and hound; and all that part he liked. (He knew already, of course, more about hounds than Bevis was ever like to do.) But at meal times in the smoky Hall he must bring water for Sir Everard to wash his greasy hands, and help to serve him as Bevis did, for Bevis might speak with his grandfather as man to man, but that let him off none of his duties, and he served the old knight on bended knee as the varlets and squires served Hugh Goch in his Great Hall at Arundel. He was quick to learn all these new things—his old life had at least taught him to be quick-witted—but they still irked him because he could see so little sense in them. And these were only the surface things, for underneath there were others even more bewildering. Different ways of living inside oneself and treating other people from any that he had known before, things that he could only guess at, feeling in a confused and half-painful way that they might be good to know about, but not even beginning to understand.

Bevis might have helped, but Bevis and he were still watching each other from a long way off. They did their work together but when they were free, each went his separate way, and Randal was left to his bewilderments.

It was more than a sennight after his first coming to Dean, that the change came about. It was the day they started cider-making—perry-making would follow after when the later-ripening little brown pears had had time to go part rotten—and half the folk of the Manor were gathered at the top end of the Hall garth, where the cider press stood among d'Aguillon's apple trees. The cider press, like the mill and the dovecot, belonged to the Lord of the Manor, and everybody brought his own pears and apples to it for crushing. Randal and Bevis had been pressed into service with everybody else, fetching up the willow baskets of apples that the two villeins in charge tipped into the press, and though this also was new to Randal it was something that he liked wholeheartedly. The whole cheerful, crowded scene under the apple trees, centred about the great stone press with the plough-ox treading his patient circle harnessed to the pole, the sweet, heady scent of the half-fermented apples, the clear, amber stream of juice trickling down the narrow trough into vat after vat, had all the feeling of holiday that he loved.

So much so that presently he had forgotten that he was supposed to be working at all, and was standing on the outskirts of the throng with a basket of apples dumped at his feet, watching a flock of small birds busy among the seeding thistles in the corner of the garth. He had seen their like before, on the downs above Arundel when he was helping to run the hounds, but had never wondered about them. They were very beautiful little birds, and as they flittered from thistle head to thistle head, he saw the golden bars on their wings, and the patch of chestnut crimson on their foreheads. And then a gleam of sunlight woke

under the apple trees—it was a grey, drifting day of broken
lights and shadows—and suddenly they were feathered jewels.

Delight sprang up in Randal, and he said to Bevis, who happened by at that moment with an empty basket, 'What are
they? Oh, they look as though they had rubies in their foreheads!'

'Goldfinches,' Bevis said checking in his tracks. That was all;
they didn't even look at each other, they were both watching
the gold-touched and jewelled finches among the pale, silky
thistle heads. But for the moment their delight leapt between
them, making a bridge from one to the other.

Next instant, as though at some signal, the goldfinches burst
upward in a puff, a flurry of little birds. They swept right overhead, the brief sunlight striking through their pulsing and
quivering wings to touch them with fire, before they wheeled in
a cloud and flittered out over the hawthorn hedge. Randal took
a quick step back to follow their flight, caught his heel in something and sat full in a vat of apple juice that had been set aside
under the hedge.

Amber juice sluiced over the edge of the vat, deluging Bevis
who stood nearest, as with a breaking wave. And Randal, kicking
and spluttering, saw the other boy's usually grave face above
him, splintering into helpless laughter even as he grabbed his
hands to pull him out. A splurge of voices had broken out all
round them, half grumbling, half richly satisfied, according as
grief for the loss of so much good cider or joy at seeing someone
sit heavily and unexpectedly in a vat of apple juice was uppermost in this man or that. And in the midst of it all, Randal and
Bevis stood dripping with sticky, golden juice, snatching at
their breath and crowing with laughter and trying not to, because with Reynfrey the Steward, who had been one of d'Aguillon's men-at-arms, bearing down on them, they had a feeling
that it might be no laughing matter.

'You young devils!' said Reynfrey, towering on them, his
thumbs in the belt that held up his big stomach. 'I'll teach you
to go playing the fool with the year's cider, that better folk than
you have had the work of pressing!'

'But we weren't—we didn't—I stepped back into Randal

without seeing he was there, and Randal stepped back into the cider vat,' Bevis spluttered helplessly. 'Oh Randal, look out for that bee, you'll have it down your throat. It thinks you're a foxglove full of nectar or something!'

Reynfrey caught them each by an ear and banged their heads together, just to sober them a little, then turned them round in the direction of the Hall.

'Pull up your roots, and march, my fine young foxgloves, and don't let me see either of you again today.'

By the time they reached the Hall they were more or less in their right minds again, and Bevis said, 'If we can slip in quietly without Sybilla catching us, we can snatch a clean tunic each, and go and wash off in the stream, and no fuss.'

But Sybilla caught them just as they were letting themselves into the storeroom under the solar, where, among all the other things, the clothes kists lived, threw up her fat hands in horror and also decreed clean tunics and washing, but not in the stream and not without fuss.

Sybilla oversaw the household and the cooking, and Bevis and his clothes so far as he allowed anybody to do that. Now she shooed the boys into the storeroom as though they were chickens, and dared them to disappear again while she fetched the water that she had been heating for kale broth over the Hall fire. And they stood in the middle of the beaten earth floor, not daring to move for fear of where their drips might go, exchanging rather hesitant grins and rubbing one foot over the other, until she came back, lumbering from leg to leg and panting as she always did, for she was very fat.

'Ah, now, I did think at least you'd have had the sense to take off those sopping rags while I was away!' she scolded, setting down the great crock. 'Dear o' me! However am I to get these stains out? And me with my hands full enough already and naught but those lazy sluts to help me——'

It was when they were stripped that Bevis, standing a little behind the other boy, said suddenly, in a tone sharply drained of all laughter, 'Randal—let's look at your back.'

It was the first time that he had seen Randal stripped, for they slept in their shirts, and it was too late in the year for river bathing except when one was really uncomfortably dirty.

'Why—what is amiss with it?' Randal asked in a small, guarded voice.

'It's all stripy. Did they—beat you a lot at Arundel?'

'Lovel beat me sometimes, like the other hounds.' Randal screwed his head over his shoulder in an attempt to see his own back. He had not been beaten since Herluin won him from Hugh Goch, and that was more than two months ago now. 'Does it still show, then?'

'Didn't I say? It's all stripy.' Bevis sounded almost angry. And then in quite a different tone, thoughtful and a little wondering, 'I never saw anybody with their backs all stripy before . . . Yes I know, Sybilla, I'm *coming*.'

Sybilla clucked and scolded all through scrubbing them, and seeing them into fresh shirts and clean woollen tunics smelling of the herbs they were stored with to keep out the moth, then threw the dirty water out of the door, where it deluged a flurry of indignant hens; and finally surged away, leaving them to follow or not as they chose. There was no question of locking up, too many people had things in the storeroom that they might need to get at, and the door was not secured in any way save by a stout pin to keep out the hounds; things such as the war bows that had to be kept close were locked in the great armoury kists against the wall.

Randal was hitching at his tunic, pulling it up through his belt in the Saxon way; it was Bevis's and too big for him, but he had not a second tunic of his own until Sybilla or one of the other women found time to make him one.

'Bide a moment,' Bevis said, rooting in the little carved kist that held his clothes and belongings. 'Something to show you.' He straightened and turned round, holding whatever it was in his hand, gently and carefully, as though it were alive. 'Look, now.'

It was an irregular lump of something roughly the size and shape of two walnuts joined together, and of a dark, dusty, greyish-reddish colour that looked as though there was some other colour underneath.

'Take it in your hand,' Bevis said.

Randal took the thing, puzzled; he had expected it to weigh like a stone, but it weighed like a feather. 'What is it?'

'Red amber—a piece of very old red amber. A man called Laef Thorkelson who goes long voyages to the other end of the world gave it to me. It's a sort of magic; when you warm it, a sweet smell comes out, and when you rub it very hard in your hands something wakes up in it that pulls things towards it— threads and flakes of chaff and things. There isn't anything in here, but I'll show you another time. Laef Thorkelson called it the Gold of the Sea.'

'Gold?' Randal said, still staring at the dark lump.

'Hold it up and look at the light of the doorway through it.'

Randal, with a puzzled, half-frowning glance at the other boy, did as he was bid, and instantly caught his breath in wonder and delight, the same delight that he had felt in the goldfinches, but somehow sharper because the thing was more strange. For as the light struck through the dark lump in his hand it was transmuted. It became a thing of flame, like a flower when the sun strikes through it, shadowed and dimmed at its edges, burning with all the fires of life at its heart. Herluin had said that Randal had no music in him, and nor had he, not so much as would serve to set two notes together in their right order; but something in him answered to the smoky flame in the heart of the amber as the music-maker and word-weaver in Herluin might answer to a new song of Roland that no one had ever heard before.

'It is beautiful!' he whispered. 'It's so beautiful it's as though it would burn your hands! It's—it's Sea Fire, not Sea Gold.'

'Sea Fire,' Bevis said consideringly. 'Yes, that's what it is! Oh, I knew you'd like it, Randal.'

They looked at it together a few moments in a shared silence of delight. Then Randal gave it back into the other boy's hand.

It was a mere lump of dusty darkness again, the fires quenched, as Bevis stowed it away once more in the bottom of the kist. 'I keep it hidden under my shirts and don't show it to everybody, but you can see it whenever you like. Now come on, let's take the hounds and run them up to Long Down and talk to Lewin and old White-Eye before supper.'

From that time forward, with nothing spoken on either side, Bevis and Randal began to hunt in couples, and Randal's feeling of having come to the place where he belonged returned to him.

And then a few days later he was lying up in the barn where the barley was stored to wait for threshing, and the big oxcart stood with its shafts pointing toward the rafters. Bevis had been captured by Reynfrey, who took the boys for sword and buckler practice, and set to hacking at a stake in the ground as though it was one of Duke Robert's men. Reynfrey, standing by, would call out the different kind of strokes that were to be used, and it was good practice, but not exciting. More fun, Randal thought, stretching all out like a hound, to lie hidden among the gold of the stacked barley and the sharper yellow of the drying beans that filled the barn even on this grey and blustering autumn day with something of sunshine, listening to the wind soughing across the thatch, when you should be doing something else.

A speckled hen appeared in the barn doorway, looked round her with a bright purposeful eye, and strutting across to the loose pile of bean stalks in a dark corner, settled herself to lay an egg. She had three there already, but Randal, who had a fellow feeling for her, and might himself one day need not to be betrayed, had not betrayed her. Presently Cerdic the Ox-herd came in and began to work tallow into the axles of the oxcart, which needed greasing, whistling as he worked, and all unaware of the boy peering down from the shadows between the unthreshed barley and the roof, and the little speckled hen watching him with an alert, gold-rimmed eye. It was all very pleasant and peaceful.

But Sybilla with a big rush basket on her hip surged into the doorway just as the hen arose with a triumphant cackling from the fourth egg. Sybilla pounced, with a speed surprising in anyone so fat, sent her streaking for the barn door with an outraged squawk, and gathered up the eggs, adding them to those already in the basket.

'As if I hadn't enough work already, without the hens laying in every corner of the garth!'

Cerdic laughed, rubbing the back of a tallowy hand across his nose. 'Reckon you'd expect them to come and lay their eggs in rows on the Hall doorsill, then?'

Randal, unseen in the barley straw, grinned with delight. Sybilla snorted. 'Get on with your greasing, and don't try to be more of a fool nor you are already!'

'Sour as a crab-apple,' said Cerdic, reflectively.

She hitched the egg basket higher on her hip. 'Well, 'tis enough to make anybody sour. The nicest little sucking-pig all dressed for d'Aguillon's supper, I turn my back on it for so long as it takes to go pull a few leaves from the bay tree, and now where is it? Gone!'

'Gone?' echoed Cerdic.

'Stolen! And if you were to ask me who stole it, I should say that scrawny little ferret d'Aguillon brought home with him from Arundel! The boy hadn't a-been here three days when I caught him stealing honeycomb!'

Randal, who, honeycomb or no, had seen Luffra behind the woodpile with the remains of a sucking-pig, on his own hurried flight from Reynfrey, was not grinning now.

Cerdic, who was big and patient like the oxen he worked with, had returned to his axle greasing, and said quietly over his shoulder, 'Be there all that harm, in a child stealing honey-comb?'

'Maybe not, so long as it *is* but honeycomb. But what d'Aguillon should want to bring him here for . . . Oh I'm sorry enough for the child. God be thanked there's no child in this Manor has marks on its back the like of those there are on his—though I make no doubt he earned them with his thieving ways. But if I'm never to leave my kitchen for a breath of time with an easy heart . . .'

'I'd not think too hardly of the boy. He and the young Master seem good enough friends.'

'Aye—since young Master saw his back.' She shrugged with a kind of fond exasperation, and her voice grew faintly doting. 'Soon as he saw Randal's back, a' course Bevis would do ought

55

in the world to make it up to him. Dear o' me, the soft little heart he has—I mind me how when he was scarce four year old, he would ha' given the little Sunday shoes off his own little feet to old Horn down at the mill because he'd cut his foot on a bramble root.'

Cerdic grunted, his head between the wheel and the side of the oxcart, and Sybilla hitched up her basket again, saying, 'Ah well, I can't stand here chittering to *you* all day with the pottage only half made,' and surged out.

Cerdic returned to his whistling, finished his greasing, and went out too, leaving the barn alone to the boy who lay with his head on his arms, hidden in the stacked barley.

Randal lay quite still for a long time. Once he thought he heard Bevis calling him, but he did not answer. He hated Bevis, he hated the whole world, but Bevis most of all. There was a feeling of black betrayal on him, worse even than when Herluin had changed his mind. He lay there while the long hours passed and at last the light began to thicken and grow mysterious in the great barn, as it does before twilight, telling himself that he didn't care. Presently he knew that it must be near supper time, and he was hungry; and because he didn't care, of course he didn't care, he slithered down out of his hiding place, shook himself like a dog, and stalked out and across the Garth where the evening mist was just beginning to rise among the old crooked apple trees, towards the Hall.

If the storeroom door had been shut, he might not have done it, even then; but some careless soul had left the storeroom door ajar. It gaped, a little cramped oblong of darkness, in the angle made by the solar's outside stair, as Randal came by. And he checked, half moved on, and checked again, staring in. The low undercroft was full of crowding shadows, but he could just make out, among the great armoury kists and new axe heads and spare bee skeps, the corner of Bevis's little carved kist: the corner in which the lump of red amber lay, with its fires quenched in the dark, waiting for the light to waken it again.

He glanced round quickly. No one was in sight, though he could hear the voices of Sybilla and the other women at their cooking in the Great Hall. Then he slunk down the four steps into the narrow doorway. He was crying a little, though he did not know it, crying with a desperate sense of loss, as he eased up the lid of the kist, and thrust his hand inside. His fingers explored down through layer after layer of Bevis's clothes and belongings, and at last, at the very bottom, met the lump of amber. He pulled it out with a gasp, and without waiting to look at it—there was not enough daylight left to wake the fire, anyway—stowed it inside his tunic and shirt where it lay, not cold like a stone but light and oddly living against his skin. Then he shut the lid of the kist again, and stole out, as secretly as he had come.

Just outside the postern door to the Hall, which opened from the foot of the solar stairs, Bevis all but ran into him.

'Randal! I've been looking for you half the day! Where away have you been?'

'Out,' Randal said, and followed the other boy back into the Hall with his shoulders hunched and his head down.

That evening he was very clumsy in serving d'Aguillon at table. He spilled the salt, fell over Matilda, upset a cup of wine, and finally had his ears boxed by Reynfrey to teach him to attend to what he did; and when Bevis whispered to him, 'I tipped a whole wheatear pie on the floor the first time *I* served at table,' he turned his back on him. All evening he would not look at Bevis; had he done so, he might have been surprised at the puzzled and hurt look in the other boy's face.

For the past three nights they had spread their sleeping rugs and straw-filled pillows close together beside the fire, but tonight, when the time came for sleep. Randal waited until Bevis had spread his bed, and then took his own rug and pillow round to the far side of the hearth. Bevis had given up trying to talk to him by that time and so said nothing about this new arrangement. And Randal lay down and rolled over with his back to everybody.

As he did so, he felt the lump of amber against him. Tomorrow, before Bevis went to his kist and found it missing, he must find a safe hiding place for it. A very safe place where Bevis would never find it; Bevis, who had everything, who, from his secure world could give the shoes from off his lordly

57

feet to someone below him in the mud because they had cut their foot, who had shown him the red amber with fire in its heart, as the Lady Adeliza scattered largesse to a beggar, just because he was sorry about the stripes on his back.

But Bevis would not have the red amber any more; everything else, but not the red amber. Randal would have that; all the fire and beauty of the red amber for himself, because he could never have any of the other things.

# 6

# THE WISE WOMAN

WHEN he woke in the morning he had thought of the perfect hiding place in his sleep.

All he needed was the chance to slip off on his own for a while, but at first it seemed that he was never going to get it. For after the early morning spent as usual over the writing tablets and trying to read Latin from a book with Adam Clerk, and after dinner in the Great Hall, Sir Everard summoned both boys to walk out with him to see how the autumn ploughing was going on in the South Field. Alfwine was ploughing with the big wheeled ox-plough that the whole Manor shared, his boy far ahead leading the patient, wide-horned oxen, and the cloud of gulls wheeling and crying in his wake. At the head of each furrow, where the field ran up towards the downs, the earth that turned up from the shear was mealy pale, but as the furrow went valleyward, the soil grew richer, until just above the edge of the River Woods it was deep, leaf-mould brown, with a glint of almost harebell colour where the light touched it.

That lovely and unexpected sheen of colour waking on the slabby darkness of newly turned earth made Randal think again of the flame springing up in the red amber where there was no flame before. He pressed his hand secretly against his stomach above the belt, and felt the light hardness of the amber lying there. He must find a chance to take it down to the hiding place before Bevis found that it was gone . . .

Both the chance and the need were upon him sooner than he expected, for when they came into the Hall garth again Reynfrey was waiting for a word with d'Aguillon about the choice of beasts for the autumn slaughtering, and Sybilla called to Bevis from the Hall doorway. 'Master Bevis, Master Bevis! *Where* is your shirt with the blue chevron bands?'

'In my kist,' Bevis called back.

"Tis not, then, for I've looked all through.'

'It must be!' Bevis said—they had closed in from shouting distance now.

'Go you and find it, then.'

'I will,' said Bevis, and he disappeared in the direction of the storeroom.

D'Aguillon was deep in discussion with his steward, and with a little sick lurch of the heart, Randal caught his chance, and disappeared in the opposite direction.

There was no time to be lost. Any moment now, Bevis would find that his treasure was gone. He wriggled through the weak place in the garth hedge that Bevis had shown him, and ran. He was making for the woods that licked in a long tongue up the steeply-winding coomb following the course of the chalky stream. They were mostly of stunted oak, hazel and hawthorn and elder, but in one place an ancient pollarded ash leaned out across the stream, and it was for this ash tree that Randal was making. A faint honey scent and a humming sound like the song of bees round the hive on a summer evening reached him even before he pushed his way through the tangle of dry hemlock stalks and seeding willow herb, to emerge on the bank where the ash leaned out over the water. It was the same scent, the same sound that had first drawn him to the place, days ago; for the stunted shape of the old tree was mantled in ivy and the ivy was in flower, though the oaks and alders were brown with autumn and growing bare, and the bees and wasps and drone flies had gathered to this last harvest of the year.

Randal reached up, and pushed aside a hanging swathe of ivy, pollen-powdery and sticky wth the nectar of the green-gold flower balls, disturbing a painted butterfly as he did so, and felt underneath. Yes, there it was, a little hole in the ash trunk, just large enough to take four fingers. It was dry and tindery inside so that one could easily scratch it bigger with a bit of sharp stone. He had meant to show it to Bevis. . . . In frantic haste he searched about, found a bit of flint of the sort he wanted in the stream bank, and set to work. The hole had to be big enough to take his hand holding the amber, so that he could get the treasure out again as well as pushing it in. Fungus-speckled flakes of rotten wood crumbled away and fell, light almost as dust, to the foot of the tree, and he got a splinter under his thumbnail and had to stop to suck it; and then at last the hole was big enough. He fished the lump of amber up through his neck-band, and thrust it into the crumbling, rough-edged hole, and settled it inside. Presently he would plaster up the opening with earth and moss, and it would be quite in the dark again. He had not looked to see the fire wake in it since he stole it out of Bevis's kist. Stole, stole, stole! He chanted the word inside himself. He was Randal the Thief; very well then . . .

There was a sudden swift brushing through the undergrowth behind him, and he let the ivy swing back over the hole and spun round just as Bevis came thrusting through the tangle of willow herb. Bevis's face had a queer pearly whiteness and his mouth looked exactly like d'Aguillon's as he halted and stood looking at Randal.

Randal gave a kind of whimpering yelp, like a puppy that is very frightened, and then stayed quite still. And so they stood, staring at each other.

'I thought something was amiss, ever since last night,' Bevis said at last. 'Where is my red amber?'

'I didn't—I don't—I don't know what you mean,' Randal stammered. 'I—oh *no*!'

For Bevis had taken a quick step towards him with fist up-raised. '*Don't* you?' he said. '*Don't* you?' and there were queer little lights flickering in his eyes. And then the movement of the ivy that had not quite ceased swinging caught his eye and he looked beyond Randal, and saw the powdery trail of rotten wood and fungus powder down the bark of the old ash tree and lying at its foot. He looked at Randal once more, then reached out and thrust the ivy aside and saw the little hole with its freshly enlarged edges. He put in his hand and took out the piece of red amber. He stared at it, and then at Randal, his eyes wide and bright and his nostrils flaring above the clamped mouth. Then, still without taking his gaze from the other boy's face, he thrust the thing down the front of his own tunic. And all the while there was no sound but the sucking of the stream under the bank and the deep song of the bees in the ivy bloom.

Then Bevis cried out at him in a strange voice full of furious

63

grief, 'Oh, Randal, why did you do it?' and flung himself upon him like a wild beast.

In any ordinary fight, Randal would have held his own against Bevis, though the other boy was nearly two years older than he was, simply because Bevis had learned to fight fair, and he had not. But this was not an ordinary fight. Bevis seemed possessed of a devil. It was as though he did not even feel the blows which Randal, sobbing as he fought, drove into his white, furious face. He knocked Randal down and when the younger boy scrambled to his feet knocked him down again. Randal's nose was bleeding and his right eye was full of jagged stars; he was dazed and dizzied by the blows that seemed to come at him from all directions at once, and when he kicked or struck out his blows no longer found Bevis at all. He was down on the ground now, with Bevis on top of him panting in his face; they were rolling over and over together in a vicious flurry of arms and legs; his head was being banged on the hard, exposed ash roots, and everything was going dim and blurred and far off...

And then suddenly it seemed that it was over, and the devil was out of Bevis. Randal waited for more blows, but they did not come. Slowly he humped himself on to his knees and crouched there, one shoulder leaned against the ash trunk, his head hanging, and the blood from his nose dripping *splat—splat—splat*, like the ripe mulberries that he had once seen dropping from a tree at Arundel and making crimson stains on the flagstones. Bevis stood over him, drawing his breath in a queer, whistling way.

'Why did you do it?' Bevis said again at last; but whereas the first time it had been simply a cry, this time it was a question that demanded an answer.

Still crouching against the ash trunk, Randal looked up at him slowly, and saw with fierce satisfaction that there was a broken bruise on the other boy's cheek bone. 'Because I hate you!' he said hoarsely. 'I hate you, Bevis d'Aguillon, you and your old bit of red stone that you go round showing to people like—like a king giving something to a beggar! I never asked you to tell Reynfrey you pushed me into the cider vat when I fell in all by myself! I never asked you to be sorry for me and—

and *kind* to me because of my back! I don't mind my back—I
don't *mind* being beaten.' His furious torrent of words fell over
itself and his voice cracked into a wail. 'And all the while I
thought—I thought——'

Slowly, the white rage in Bevis's face gave way to bewilderment. 'Randal, stop talking gibberish—I don't understand. I
don't know what you're talking about.'

'Oh, yes, you do, because it's true—it's all true, isn't it?'
Randal flung at him, sniffling through his bleeding nose.

'No it's not, then!' Bevis shouted. 'You're a horrible boy to
think such things.'

'I'm not so horrible as you are!' They were both shouting
now, shouting and glaring and ridiculous; but to them it was
not ridiculous. 'You're the most horrible boy in all Sussex, for
all that Sybilla thinks you're so wonderful!'

There was a little silence, and then Bevis squatted down on
his haunches, close to the other boy. 'Did Sybilla fill you up
with all this?'

Randal nodded. 'At least—she was talking to Cerdic; it was
after Luffra stole the sucking-pig, and she thought I'd done it,
and I heard——' He choked. 'I heard all she said.'

'Sybilla is a fool,' said Bevis as his grandfather might have
said it. 'She's a *fat* fool—and you're a worse one for paying any
heed to her.'

Randal did not answer. They squatted staring at each other
among the tangle of the past summer's willow herb. Far off
across Muther-Wutt Field they heard someone whistle to a dog,
the low of a plough ox, the ring of hammer on anvil from the
smithy, and above them the bees were busy in the ivy bloom.
At last Bevis said, 'Well, of course I was sorry about your back;
wouldn't you have been sorry about mine? It—it made me feel
I wanted to hit somebody. But it wasn't anything to do with
that, my showing you my bit of amber.'

Randal scowled at him out of the one eye he could still use.
'Why did you, then?'

'Because of the goldfinches, I suppose. And then you fell in
the cider vat and we all started laughing; and after that everything was friendly, until—until——'

His voice trailed away, and the bee-haunted silence settled on them again. Strange things were happening in Randal. Something swelling up big and painful in his chest. So Bevis had wanted to be friends after all, and he had spoiled everything by stealing the red amber, spoiled it before it was well begun.

'Bevis,' he said in a small cracked whisper, 'oh, Bevis,' and could say no more, because there did not seem anything more to say, and because his throat was full of tears as well as the taste of blood.

And then the wonderful thing happened; for Bevis suddenly reached out and laid an arm across his shoulders and began to shake him, the small, easy, companionable shake that means friendliness as well as exasperation. The queer, pearly look had quite gone from his face.

'Don't you ever go listening to people like Sybilla again!' he said. 'Do you hear me? Don't you ever——' He stopped shaking. 'I've made a wicked mess of your face! Come on, let's wash off the worst of the blood, and then we'll go down to Ancret and ask her to salve it. Sybilla's hands are heavy, and besides she asks too many questions.'

They dropped down by the twisted alder roots on to the tiny spit of shingle, and set to work to clean up, in the swift, icy, downland water that smelled of watercress.

When they had got rid of as much of the blood as they could, both from themselves and the front of Randal's tunic, they set off to visit Ancret—the same Ancret who had heard Valiant's hoof-beats in the wind, on the morning of the day that d'Aguillon came home. Randal had heard stories about Ancret, queer stories, and he knew that she was herb wise, and doctored all the ills of the Manor. He knew that she had been Bevis's foster-mother after his own mother died, and that Bevis loved her, and he had seen her in the distance, about the village and the Manor lands, but he had not gone to see her in her own place before.

The shadows were lengthening as they crossed the familiar driftway that led up from the ford to the village, and headed southward, for Ancret lived withdrawn from the rest of the Manor folk, away beyond the cultivated land, within the fringe

66

of the woods below the Bramble Hill. A thrush flew out of a
hazel bush as they stepped out from the trees into the little
clearing that was Ancret's herb plot; nothing else moved, not
even the air. In that first moment Randal would not have
thought that there was a cottage there at all, save for the dark
oblong of a doorway in the side of a little green mound in the
midst of the clearing, and the whisper of woodsmoke, curling
out through a hole in the top to mingle its blue tang with the
wet wood and fallen leaf and coming frost smells of the autumn
evening. Certainly he did not see anyone besides himself and
Bevis in the clearing, until there was a movement by the door,
under the elder tree that grew there, and he saw, in the way that
a sudden movement will show a herd of fallow deer where there
was only dappled sunlight the moment before, that there was a
woman standing there. A woman in a faded, grey-green kirtle
exactly the colour of the bothy's turf roof behind her, who
looked as though she had known that they were coming, and
was waiting for them.

She was a small woman, slight and narrow-boned, but standing there under the elder tree she looked tall. Randal was to
find later that she always looked tall, that if she wore her rough,
homespun cloak with the great earth-coloured patch where she
had torn the hem, it fell about her like a queen's mantle. All
he saw now was that she had dark eyes—dark and full and
bloomed with light like a deer's, in a narrow, work-worn,
weather-browned face; and that her hair, hanging in thick
braids over her shoulders, had cloudy lights in the darkness of
it, the colour of the ripe elderberries, and was much younger
than the rest of her, like a girl's hair.

'Good fortune be to you, fosterling,' she said.

'Good fortune come with me, Ancret my foster-mother,'
Bevis returned, as they halted before her.

'You have come, then.' Again it was as though she were expecting them. She looked from Bevis to Randal and back
again. 'So, there has been the fine blood-letting. How did that
come about?'

'I hit him,' Bevis said, and shut his mouth exactly like his
grandfather.

Ancret looked at the bruise on his cheek, and the laughter shimmered at the back of her dark eyes. 'It is in my mind that he hit you also.'

'Well, of course he did.' Bevis rubbed the place and then hurriedly stopped as he found how sore it was. 'But mine's only a bruise and 'twill mend quickly enough on its own. I've brought him to you to put his face to rights, Ancret.'

She stooped, and took up a pitcher that stood beside the door. 'Then go you and draw me some water from the well,' and as he took the pitcher from her and went to do her bidding, she turned full to the younger boy for the first time. 'And you, come your ways in with me, Randal.'

She must have heard his name long before this, from the other Manor folk, but it made him feel a little queer all the same, to hear her call him by it, with her strange dark eyes upon him, and for a moment he was not sure that he wanted to go into the bothy that was like a little green mound; he had always heard that the fairy kind lived in mounds. But he remembered that she was Bevis's foster mother, and the laughter was shimmering again behind her eyes. So he nodded, and followed her down the three earthen steps through the low, dark doorway.

Inside it was not so dark after all, for the bothy faced west: the evening light came in down the steps and the smoke hole was so big that he could see a patch of milky sky and the shadow-flash of a bird's flight across it. The fire burned on a raised hearth in the centre of the round house-place, and little barley cakes were baking on the hot hearthstone, adding their own friendly, new-bread smell to the heavy smell of earth and the blue reek of woodsmoke and the aromatic tang of nameless herbs.

Ancret made him sit down on a stool at the foot of the steps where the light from the doorway fell strongest, and taking the pitcher from Bevis, when he brought it dripping from the well, she poured a little into a bowl and set it to heat in the hot fringes of the fire. Then she fetched a bundle of leaves from somewhere in the farther shadows, where it seemed to Randal that there were many strange things hanging that he could not

68

quite see, and took seven leaves from the bundle and set them
to seethe in the water. And all the time she spoke no word.
Randal had hoped that Bevis would come in too, when he had
brought the water, but Bevis had gone out again, and he could
hear him hammering something, a sound like a woodpecker but
sharper, *tap-tap-tap*, all the while they waited, he on his stool
and Ancret standing withdrawn into herself beside the hearth,
for the water to boil. *Tap-tap-tap, tap-tap-tap.*

When the steam rose and the surface of the water crept and
dimpled, Ancret took the bowl from the fire with a piece of
cloth wrapped round her hand, and broke other herbs into it,
and shook cold water into it from her fingers until it was cool
enough to use. Then she stripped back Randal's tunic, and with
the leaves themselves bathed the bruises on his arms and body
and face. She bathed his black eye, which was the sorest of his
hurts, last of all, and then laid her hand over it, and said in a
tone of authority, as though to someone or something that he
could not see,

> 'Out fire and in snow,
> In weal and out woe.
> Sorrow of flesh bid you go.
> In the name of St Luke of the Ox's Horns.'

She kept her hand there a long time, and it seemed to Randal
that a lovely coolness flowed out of her fingers, soothing away
the fiery throbbing that had been there before. And when at
last, with a long sigh as though something had gone out from
her, she took her hand away, he saw, squinting out of his usable
eye, that the palm and finger tips were reddened as though she
had scorched them.

It seemed that the thing was finished, and he got off the stool,
and stood looking up at her with a vague idea—he was too
battered by all that had happened both within him and without, to think of anything very clearly—that he should thank
her. But before he could find the words she took his damaged
face between her hands and bent to look into his eyes, holding
them with her own, so that he could not look away. 'You're no
Norman, like Bevis my fosterling and no Saxon either, despite

your hair. What are you, that Sir Everard brought home with him?'

'My mother was a Saxon lady, and my father was a Breton man-at-arms,' Randal said.

'Breton? So—the old blood comes back,' Ancret said musingly. 'Breton–Briton, Briton–Breton . . .' Then as Randal looked at her, frowning in bewilderment, she smiled. 'The Saxons drove out your kind, many and many of your kind that fled across the narrow seas and took refuge in the place they called Brittany; but when the Saxons' time was done, the old blood came flowing back, at the heels of Count Alain of Brittany, to Hastings over the chalk yonder, on the day that Harold died.' It was almost as though she were singing now, crooning to herself rather than to him. 'But we, who are an older people still, who were an old people when they raised the grave mound on Bramble Hill in the days when the world was young, we see the conquerors come and go and come again, and marry and mingle, but we know that all things pass, like a little wind through the bramble bushes. There are few of us, of the pure blood, left now, but something of our blood runs dark, dark like the veining in an iris petal, through all the people that come after. Even through you, under your thatch of Saxon hair.' How dark her eyes were, so dark that you felt as though you might lose yourself in them as in the stillness of deep water. 'Aye, the old blood runs strong, and comes into its own again; you should know that, you that Sir Everard brought home on his saddle bow.' In another moment, he felt, the dark, still water would close over his head and he would know something— something that he did not want to know. Then, in the very instant before it happened, she let him go, turned him to the little doorway that was mostly in the roof, and said, 'Out, after the other one.'

When he climbed up into the last of the sunset, Bevis was sitting on the sloping turf edge of the roof, with his knife in one hand and a heavy flint in the other. He stuck the knife back in his belt and sent the flint skittering away into the bushes, and drew his legs up with his arms round his knees. Randal scrambled up beside him—the roof came down so low that he only

70

had to put his hands on the edge and give a little hop—and settled himself with his legs swinging. He was not quite sure what they were waiting for, but he was content, with a content like the quietness after a storm, to be with Bevis and do whatever Bevis wanted. And in a few moments Ancret came out after them with two of the barley cakes hot from the bakestone and dripping with some dark, sweet, pippy mess which Randal had never met before.

'There,' she said, giving one to each of them, 'never say that Ancret sent you away hungry—though indeed it must be near your supper time, up to the Hall.'

Bevis looked at her contentedly, already licking the dribble of dark sweetness round the edge of his cake. 'I wish you still lived up at the Hall, Ancret.'

She stood with one hand on the branch of the elder tree that arched above them all, smiling a little secret smile. 'I lived for years up to the Hall, herded among other folk, for your sake, little fosterling, because I love you. Now I live my own life again in my own way, and when you want me, it is you who must come to find me. I shall always be here for your finding—while you need me.' The smile that had been secret flashed open in her dark, narrow face, 'I—and my bramble syrup.'

So that was what it was, this dark, sweet, pippy stuff. Randal took a bite of barley cake and chewed, then licked a blob of the syrup from his thumb, his tongue enjoying the sweetness even while the deeper part of his mind was still full of the things that had happened between himself and the boy beside him. Through the berry-laden branches of the elder tree he could see the Bramble Hill against the sky, and the turf hummock on its crest that Ancret said 'they' had raised when the world was young, and the other hummock of brushwood and furze roots that the Manor folk had been raising for days now, ready to be lit on All Souls' Eve, Reynfrey said, as the fires had been lit up there every All Souls' Eve and every May Day Eve since before the memory of man. All bloomed with shadows now, shadows crowding among the bushes and the bramble domes, quiet under a windy sky that was suddenly flying with the manes and tails of wild horses.

71

He licked up another blob of the stuff, crushing the pips between his teeth. 'It is good!'

'In all the Manor—in all this reach of the downs,' Ancret said, 'there is no bigger and sweeter fruit than you may find on the Hill of Gathering.'

'The Hill of Gathering?' Bevis said, questioningly.

'Did I say the Hill of Gathering? It is an old name; folk do not use it any more.'

Bevis swallowed the last of his barley cake and sucked his fingers. 'Maybe they called it the Hill of Gathering because of the great gathering that there must have been when they raised the barrow on the top—or maybe it's because of the gatherings when they make the fires and the Sun Dance on All Souls' Eve.' They were all three looking up towards the hill, through the elder branches, seeing it withdrawn into its own shadows, its own secrets, dark against the sunset.

'I wonder if it's true,' Bevis spoke again in a little while. 'I wonder if there *is* a king buried up there with all his treasure about him; gold cups and crowns and arm rings under the bramble bushes.'

Randal said without knowing why, 'It might be just a champion, with his sword.'

'Whatever there is,' Ancret said, sweeping round on them almost, for the moment, as though she were angry, 'you let him sleep. There's never aught but sorrow come yet to mortal man from the gold of the Hollow Hills. Now let you be off, for it's time and more than time that you were home to your supper.'

It was twilight as they came up towards the Hall, not by the driftway but over the fields, and just outside the weak place in the hedge, Bevis halted, holding out something that he had just fished from inside the front of his tunic.

'Here,' he said, shamefaced all at once. 'Take it, Randal.'

All Randal could see in the 'tween light was a dark lump about the size of a walnut, but the moment he touched it, his fingers knew it by the light, live feel. So that was what Bevis had been doing with his knife and the pebble outside Ancret's bothy: splitting his treasured piece of amber in two.

He stood with the thing in his hand, looking from it to Bevis

and Bevis and back again. Then he shook his head. 'You don't
—have to do that, Bevis.'

'No,' Bevis said. 'That's why I'm doing it. Not because I have
to—because I want to.' Suddenly he was in desperate earnest.
'Then we shall both have a piece of red amber—don't you see?
Please, Randal.'

There was a long pause before Randal said gruffly, 'All
right,' and then the moment after, in a small, hoarse rush, 'I
shall carry it with me always.' And he thrust it into the front of
his own stained and filthy tunic. Sybilla was not going to be at
all pleased when she saw that tunic.

Sir Everard looked at their faces with interest when he saw
them at supper, but made no comment. And that night Bevis
and Randal spread their sleeping rugs and hard, straw-stuffed
pillows alongside each other again.

# 7

# THE CUSTOM OF THE MANOR

ALL Wales went up in flames that winter and they heard that Hugh Goch had called out almost every knight in the Honour of Arundel to follow him on a new, bloody campaign into the mountains. So the Lord of Arundel would have a better excuse than hunting in his Welsh forests, to account for being in the Marches when spring came. But de Braose was not a Marcher Lord, and so in the Honour of Bramber all was quiet as that winter went by.

The river woods that had been softly dark as smoke all winter broke out into the mealy gold of hazel, and the curlews were crying over the downs. D'Aguillon rode away to render his thirty days' knight's service at Bramber, leaving the boys in Reynfrey's charge; and by the time he returned, the spring ploughing was upon them. The swallows came back to the great Manor barn, and soon after the swallows, a wandering friar, who said, 'Have you heard the news? The news about Mowbray who sacked the Norwegian trading ships last year? Since the King summoned him to face his trial at the Easter Court, he has come out into open revolt! Arundel and de Lacy and William of Eu have all joined him, and most of the Marcher Lords. May the sweet Mother of God have mercy on us, for we are all sinful men!'

Randal went away by himself after that, and thought about the voices on the water stair that he had shut his mind to and managed not to think about for months, and would not tell even Bevis what was the matter.

Haymaking came, and then barley harvest. And a wandering minstrel came to sing for them at the boon feast afterwards, when the whole Manor supped with d'Aguillon in the Great Hall.

'You'll have heard that the King has marched north?' said
the minstrel, tuning his harp. 'Oh yes, almost three months ago.
Fé! Don't you ever hear *anything* in this corner of Sussex? He's
got Mowbray, they say—captured him by a trick outside his
own walls, and made his Lady yield up the castle to save her
Lord's eyes. Very fine eyes, so I've heard, but they'll not be
much use to him now, save to show him his prison walls or
maybe the shadow of the noose dancing.'

Autumn came, and the nights were full of droning dor-
beetles, and they brewed the year's perry. Winter came and
went, and Sir Everard rode for Bramber again, to return thirty
days later with the news that the King had brought Mowbray
and his rebellious Barons before his Christmas Court at Glouces-
ter. 'Aye,' he said, kicking his spurs beside the fire, and shaking
the rain from his heavy war mittens, 'it seems that the loyal
Barons dealt out hanging and mutilation with generous hands
—the more so, maybe, because for the most part they would
have been on the rebel side themselves, had they been more
sure of success.' He generally spoke to his varlets as though they
were grown men. 'Arundel? Arundel got off with a fine, being
maybe too powerful even for the King.'

So it was finished, Randal thought, finished and done with
as though he had never heard those voices on the water stair;
and he felt as though he had escaped from something. He was
wrong, quite wrong, but it was to be years before he knew it,
and meanwhile, life was good.

He and Bevis were up on Long Down one wild evening not
long after Easter; the second Easter of his life at Dean. They had
been hoping to take out Bevis's new sparrow-hawk and fly her
at starlings—Randal had no hawk of his own yet, but Bevis was
going to help him catch and train one next spring, when Sir
Everard judged that he would be old enough—but the wind
had got up since morning, a wild wind with flurries of rain and
bursts of sunshine on its wings, that set the cotters' geese scurrying and stripped the early fruit blossom and roared like a fur-
nace in the river woods. Hopeless weather for hawking, but not
the kind of weather when one could bear to remain indoors; and
so they had come up to Lewin the Shepherd, their particular

friend, on Long Down where he had just brought the sheep up to their summer pasture, now that the lambing season was over.

They were huddled one each side of him in the shepherd's cave that he had made for himself in the heart of a thorn clump. He had two or three caves in different parts of the Dean sheep runs, but this one up on Long Down was the best. From outside there was nothing to be seen at all but the blackthorn tump, greyish white now with its fleece of blossom, but crawl under the low branches and you were in a sort of lair, part hollowed out of the ground, part out of the blackthorn tangle overhead. lined with straw and old skins, snug from the wind and the rain that drove across the shoulder of the down, yet with the whole countryside open before you.

And what a countryside, from up here on Long Down! Craning forward, Randal could look southward to the sea, northward to the Weald, Andred's Weald far below him, rolling away into the distance—the vast oak forests that cut this high down country of Sussex off from the rest of England far more surely than the sea cut it off from Normandy. Ahead of him the world fell away into the sweeping whorls and hollows of the river valley, then rose again like the waves of a slow sea gathering themselves to the crest of Thunder Barrow full four miles away, with nothing between him and it, but the emptiness of wind and rain and flying sunshine, and the wings of a sailing gull. Far below, and a mile or more away, he could make out the huddled roofs of Dean with its three great fields running to the river woods and the marshes seaward. And on the long curved slopes of the coomb-head below them, sheltered somewhat from the wind, Dean's sheep grazed in a quiet, grey crescent, watched over by Lewin and his dogs.

There were three dogs in the shepherd's cave, for beside Lewin's two, Bevis had brought up his new hound puppy, Joyeuse, one of Matilda's last litter. With three dogs and three humans in it, the little cave was somewhat close quarters; but to Randal it seemed to have a deeper feeling of shelter than a proper house could ever have, shelter as a wild thing in its lair might feel it. And when the sunshine that for the moment had been all about them fled on, and suddenly the next shower was

77

hushing overhead, with never a drop coming through—three days of steady rain, Lewin had once told him, before it came through the roof of a properly built cave—he shivered luxuriously and pressed his shoulder closer against Lewin's in its oily-smelling sheepskin cloak.

'It is good up here! Better than sitting round the fire in Hall, cracking last year's nuts!'

'Why so late in the day to come up, then?' Lewin Longshanks said in his deep, gentle, grumbling voice, never taking his gaze from the sheep below him in the coomb-head. ''Tis a'most time to be going home again, before you've well come, I'm thinking.'

'We couldn't get off earlier,' Bevis said, sitting with the puppy's leash twisted round his wrist. 'It's the day for the Manor Court, and grandfather likes us both to be there in Hall while he gives his judgements—he says it's part of our training. And such a lot seems to have piled up while he was at Bramber. Alfwine and Gyrth squabbling about their boundaries again, and Cerdic wanting leave to graze two more geese on the common grazing, now that he has another son, and Gudram claiming the Custom of the Manor that he should be forgiven six boon-days' work because the gale before Easter blew down his best apple tree. Quite a lot of them were things that Reynfrey could have dealt with just as well but——' his voice was suddenly thoughtful. 'They won't go to Reynfrey if they can help it, they save it all up for grandfather.'

Lewin turned on him a pair of very blue eyes that were wrinkled at the corners as the eyes of seamen and shepherds often are, though he was still quite young. 'Reynfrey is a Norman,' he said simply.

There was a little sharp, surprised silence, and then Bevis said, 'So is grandfather.'

'D'Aguillon is d'Aguillon, and Reynfrey is his paid man.'

'Reynfrey is kind enough, and just,' Bevis said hotly. 'Grandfather wouldn't have him for his steward if he was not.'

'But d'Aguillon is d'Aguillon of Dean,' said Lewin, and somehow the argument was unanswerable.

Nobody spoke for a while, and then Lewin broke the silence again. 'I mind my grandfather claiming the Custom of the

Manor from Wulfthere, our Thegn, when his apple tree blew down, the year before Hastings's fight.'

Hastings again. The Senlac that Reynfrey talked about sometimes, if you could get him into the right mood, stripping up his sleeve to show the long, white, puckered scar on his forearm. Senlac to the Normans, Randal thought, Hastings to the Saxon kind. 'Lewin, were you at Hastings fight?'

'I?—I was six years old on the day that Harold died. I remember Wulfthere riding off with his sons and house-carls, their weapons keen for war . . . I remember the women weeping. And then later came d'Aguillon your grandfather, and Reynfrey with a bloody clout round his sword arm, but never the old Thegn and his sons again.'

'I'm glad grandfather forgave Gudram his six boon days,' Bevis said, after a while.

The rain had swept on now, and the sun was out, dazzling the wet blackthorn blossom. 'The shadows are growing long,' Lewin said. 'Time you were away home, and the flock gathered in.' He drew his long legs under him and ducked out from the cave, the boys and dogs behind him, and cupping his hands about his mouth, sent the long-drawn folding call echoing down the valley.

'Coo-oo-oo-o-up! Coo-om along! Coo-oo-o-up!'

They knew that he would have no more time for them today, and took their dismissal in good part, for they were used to being sent packing by Lewin whenever he had had enough of them. Besides, it must be drawing on towards supper time. So they took their leave, doubtful if he even heard them, and set off for the distant huddle of roofs that was home. They walked quietly until they were through the flock, keeping Joyeuse on the leash, but once clear of the sheep, Bevis slipped her free and they ran, boys and hound puppy, laughing and shouting with the wind behind them, racing the long cloud shadows that swept along the shoulder of the downs.

When they burst into the firelit warmth of the Hall, with sticks and dead leaves and wet, torn-off petals of pear blossom and the first spatterings of the next rain squall clinging about them, they found the household already gathering for supper,

79

and a stranger there with Sir Everard. At least he was a stranger to Randal; a fat man with pale blue eyes in a round, weather-beaten face, who wore his sandy hair in braids like a woman over the shoulders of his stained and greasy leather tunic, and had beads of red coral round his neck and copper rings on his bare arms. But Bevis greeted him as Laef Thorkelson, and asked if his ship was at Bramber.

Laef Thorkelson! Randal's ears pricked at the name. So this was the man who went long voyages to the other end of the world, and had given Bevis the piece of magical red amber. Almost without being aware of it, his hand went up to feel the little bag hung round his neck under his tunic, in which he always carried the half of the red amber that Bevis had given him. And the huge, sandy stranger standing in the firelight seemed just a little larger than life, as he gazed up at him.

Laef Thorkelson stood with his feet planted wide apart as though they gripped the leaping deck of a ship, and grinned down at Bevis. 'Aye, safe and fast in the lea of the downs, under the Castle. And maybe tomorrow I shall sell de Braose a pipe of wine or a damascened blade; but meanwhile here come I to warm myself at the Dean hearth fire again—and find you a good span taller than when I saw you last.' His small, bright eyes, wrinkled at the corners as Lewin's were, turned from one boy to the other, and he said to Sir Everard standing beside him, 'It seems that your household has increased; I mind me there was but one whelp when last I came this way.'

It was Bevis who answered, before his grandfather could do so, flinging an arm across Randal's shoulder. 'He came to us from Arundel, more than a year back, and his name is Randal and he is my friend and will be squire with me by and by.'

After supper in the Great Hall, which Laef Thorkelson with his great laughter made to seem as full as it did when the whole Manor supped with d'Aguillon at Christmas or Easter or the boon feasts between, the Lord of Dean and his guest settled before the fire in the solar. Bevis and Randal had been allowed to come too, and now they squatted in the firelight, Randal busy oiling and burnishing Sir Everard's sword, while Bevis, with Joyeuse asleep against his knees, did the same for the nut-

shaped helmet. For some time now it had been their task to keep
d'Aguillon's war harness in good order, and it was a task that
they loved, for it made them feel as though they were squires
already.

Randal was glad that he had got the sword this time. It was
a huge and beautiful sword, forged by the armourers of Sara-
gossa, who were the best armourers in Christendom or beyond
it; the firelight played on the blade like running water, and
d'Aguillon's seal was cut into the fine reddish stone of the
pommel. D'Aguillon sat on the foot of the low sleeping bench,
with Matilda between his knees, the bitch crooning with half-
shut eyes as he gentled her ears; and Laef Thorkelson, merchant
and sea captain, sat in d'Aguillon's carved chair, with his great
feet stretched to the fire. And so, sitting with the flicker of the
burning logs on their faces, the two men talked companionably,
the talk of old friends. They were very old friends, and it seemed
that Sir Everard had even made one voyage to the far north
with Laef Thorkelson in their early days. 'That was in the beginning of time,' he had said, speaking of it at supper, 'when I
was young and not bound by wife or bairns or holding of English acres.' But just now they were discussing the news of the
outside world, which was disappointing to Randal who had
hoped for adventures and marvels and sea dragons, from the
man who had given Bevis the red amber with fire at its heart.

He turned Sir Everard's great sword over to come at the
other side, laying the wave-rippled blade across his knee, and
set to work again with the oily rag, huddling closer to the fire as
a fresh gust boomed against the house. The shutters rattled and
the smoke drove down the chimney in a billowing cloud that
made them all cough. Then the smoke cleared, and Bevis
leaned forward over the helmet in his lap and flung another log
on the fire, and the flames leapt up, reaching even to the corner
where Tyri, Sir Everard's Norway goshawk, sat on her bow
perch with her black and white mutes striping the wall behind
her.

And at that moment, out of the quiet rumble of voices that he
had long ago ceased to listen to, the name that even now could
make Randal's heart lurch unpleasantly, caught his ear.

81

Hugh Goch!

'The King would have done well to remember that de Lacy and Hugh Goch are Marcher Lords.' It was Sir Everard who spoke. 'And that the Marches are ever the quickest part of his Kingdom to spark into revolt.'

Laef Thorkelson chuckled. 'Lucky for Hugh Goch to get out of that affair with no more than a fine, when William of Eu paid for his part in it with his ears and most of his fellows found their way to the Tower or the scaffold.'

'Aye, our Red King was lavish enough with the noose and the branding iron,' d'Aguillon said, drawing Matilda's soft ears out like wings on either side of her head. 'A stronger hand for dealing with his own Barons than he has for Normandy, seemingly.'

Laef grinned in his sandy beard. 'Maybe he'll not need to take Normandy with the strong hand, after all. There are more ways than one, so I've heard, of killing a cat.'

'So-o?' D'Aguillon's hands checked on Matilda's twitching ears. 'And what might you mean by that?'

Laef Thorkelson looked round at him, his elbows on his knees. 'Last November, Pope Urban, being taken with a vision, preached a Crusade at Clermont.'

'And?' said Sir Everard.

'Long before Christmas, Duke Robert was chafing to take the Cross. The thing is veritably cut to his measure, fighting, adventure and the hope of plunder besides—and all in God's sweet name. But to take the Cross, he must first come to some sort of settlement with Brother William. Also, he must have money. So—it is beautifully simple—they meet and come to terms. Robert has pledged his Duchy to William for ten thousand marks. So William has Normandy while Robert is away smiting Saracen's heads from their shoulders; and if Robert comes not back, he has Normandy still, and if Robert comes back—why then, William is within the gates, and it is Robert, even if he can raise the ten thousand marks again, who must drive him out.'

In the silence that followed, a burned log fell with a rustle into a red hollow on the hearth. Joyeuse whimpered in her sleep, chasing dream hares, her paws and muzzle fluttering, and

Bevis stroked her tawny flank, then went on burnishing the heavy, nut-shaped helmet.

'And all this is sure?' Sir Everard said at last.

'Have I ever brought you news that was faulty?'

'Not so far as I remember.' The corners of the knight's grim mouth quirked a little ruefully. 'It is news that concerns all England and much of Christendom somewhat closely; but the thing that I am chiefly wondering at this moment is—how are the ten thousand marks to be raised?'

'Not out of Red William's pouch. By you and de Braose and le Savage of Broadwater . . . All England is to pay another Dane Geld, so they say. Glad am I, and give thanks to Thor and the White Kristin, that *my* plough cuts its furrow in the salt sea, and no King may tax my acres.'

Sir Everard sat a moment staring into the fire, while Matilda whimpered and nosed at his hand, wanting to have her ears pulled again. Then he said, 'Ranulf Flambard must be taking great pleasure in life. I hope Red William is sufficiently grateful to his Chancellor who squeezes England for him like a ripe fig. Aye well, if 'tis more than three shillings the hide, we must do without the new yoke of plough oxen for a while.'

'Pass it on to your villeins and make them pay for their own field strips,' suggested the sea captain.

Sir Everard looked up from the fire, with the odd gentleness at the corners of his wolftrap mouth that came there sometimes, but not often. 'Who have had the same poor lambing season as my own . . . I've held Dean for half a lifetime, friend, but not in *that* way.'

And in a while they returned to an earlier part of their talk, and the knight was asking, 'What of young Henry? Does he take the Cross with Robert, or join William to help him reive away Robert's Duchy?'

'So far as I have heard, neither, but bides him quiet in his own Castle of Domfront, which is about all that the other two have left him.' Laef Thorkelson let out a harsh bark of laughter like the bark of a dog-seal on a foggy night. 'Na na, you cannot blame the young one for the times that he has joined whichever brother offers the best chance for his sword, against the third, since whenever they make common cause it is to turn against *him*. Munin and Hugin! What a brood of wolves, these sons of the old Conqueror! Brother ready to tear brother's throat at a word!' And then, with a sudden change of mood, he leaned across and brought down a hand like a hammer on d'Aguillon's bent shoulder. 'Not such brothers were we, in the days of our hot youth, eh, old lad?'

And now at last they were away into the sort of talk that Randal had hoped for. Wonderful talk of steep green northern seas, and icebound lands where the sun never set all the summer long nor rose in the winter days; of hunting great white bears for their skins, and the strange flickering lights that played across the northern sky like a vast diadem of flame in the winter nights, and made a sound like the rushing of mighty wings overhead. Strange, heady talk that flashed and flickered like the northern lights in the small, firelit room where the rushing of wings was the spring gale roaring in from the sea over steep miles of English downland.

Randal's head was still singing with it, like the echo of harp song, when at last it was time for bed, and he went with Bevis to bring up the little dried apples and late night cups of wine for Sir Everard and his guest. But under the singing, the thing that he was really thinking about, was the old Norman knight in his Hall saying, 'I've held Dean for half a lifetime, but not in *that* way'; and Saxon Lewin, in his shepherd's cave on Long Down, saying, 'd'Aguillon is d'Aguillon of Dean'; and the six days' boon work that Gudram had been forgiven because it was the Custom of the Manor. He thought about those things, which were really one thing, a good deal.

# 8

# ALL SOULS' EVE

THEY had been down in the river woods, helping Lewin Long-shanks to make hurdles for the lambing pens, and now they were on their way home. The woods were very still, with the still-ness of an autumn day drawing on towards evening, frost-scented, leaf-mould-scented, woodsmoke-scented where they had been burning scrub, and the boys, with Joyeuse running ahead like a tawny shadow, loped along through the stillness without dis-turbing it save by the occasional contented cracking of a hazel nut. The blackberries were over, but there were still nuts in their green-frilled cups to be found on the hazel bushes, and Bevis and Randal gathered them as they went along and cracked them in their teeth, picking the milky, brown-skinned kernels from among the broken shell shards, and crunching happily.

Two and a half years had gone by since Gudram claimed the Custom of the Manor when his apple tree blew down. Good years, and very full ones. And this one the best yet, Randal was thinking, remembering bitter cold night-time visits to Lewin at the lambing pens, hot summer evenings spent lazy by the river with nothing stirring in all the valley save the plop of a water rat under the bank, the joy of the first time his hawk came back to the lure after making its kill . . . Bevis had been made a squire at summer's end, on the very same day that they had heard of Hugh Goch's death in Wales, shot through the eye in a skirmish with Norse raiders.

'The Old Lion led the Norman centre at Hastings,' Lewin said softly into his golden beard, when that news came. 'Now the cub dies of an arrow through the eye, as Harold Godwinson died.' And he gave one of his own ewe lambs to Steyning Priory as a thank offering.

So Hugh Goch was dead, and de Bellême was Lord of Arun-del after him, and Randal wondered whether perhaps now he would see Herluin again. But de Bellême had been campaigning with the King all this while, helping secure the Marches of Normandy, and had not yet come to take possession of his English lands. Maybe later he would come—there was a rumour that the King was returning in the spring—and Herluin with him. It was not so very far from Bramber to Arundel . . . It would be good to see Herluin again. He had known that for quite a while now. Little by little through the four years since it happened, he had come to understand that it had not, after all, been betrayal, when de Bellême's minstrel changed his mind.

They had reached the place where the woods opened, and slowed to a halt, turning as by common consent to look up at the Bramble Hill that Ancret had once called the Hill of Gathering. There was a little wind stirring on the Bramble Hill, though down here on the edge of the river woods the air was still. Randal could see the shivering and frowing of the bushes and bramble domes that crowded thick about the long green barrow up there against the sky, and on the level space before the barrow, the dark, beehive shape of furze branches and piled brushwood, for once again it was All Souls' Eve. Tonight, as soon as dusk fell, the fire would be lit, and almost every soul on the Manor, and as many as could get away from the Manors round, would be up there dancing with home-made torches kindled at the blaze, making of themselves a great spinning wheel of light in the autumn darkness.

'I wish d'Aguillon would let us join in the Sun Dance,' he said suddenly, using the name for it that he had heard Ancret use, and Bevis after her.

Bevis nodded, still staring upward with eyes narrowed into the westering light. 'So do I, in a way, but they wouldn't really want us up there. It's—a thing you have to be part of, not just join in from the outside.' He laughed. 'And poor old Adam Clerk would nigh on throw a seizure, I'm thinking. He is upset enough ever year, as 'tis, because grandfather will not stop the fires altogether.'

'Yes, but I don't see why,' Randal said seriously.

'I suppose because he's a Christian priest and thinks it is his duty to stamp out all that has to do with the Old Faith. But the trouble is that there is such a lot of the Old Faith, and he's such a very gentle stamper!'

Joyeuse, who had been foraging to and fro in the under-growth, came trotting up with a piece of rotten wood in her mouth, rippling with proud delight from her moist, mushroom-pink muzzle to the tip of her sweeping, golden tail. They had taught her to retrieve for them when they went hawking or shooting, and retrieving for Bevis—it was always Bevis she brought the fallen birds to, even when it was Randal's arrow or hawk that had made the kill—had come to be so much a part of her that when there were no dead birds, she brought him sticks and flints and anything else that she could find. Bevis took the bit of wood from her, laughing; it was part of a rotten birch branch, with fungus that looked like a scatter of red-hot sparks clinging to it, and stooped and caught her muzzle in his hands and shook it, while she danced about him with lashing tail, and a few moments later they were on their way again, the matter of the Sun Dance quite forgotten.

Presently they came over the shallow neck of the woods that ran up between North and South Fields, and saw in the distance their own Mill, and the ford of the Dean stream above it. The few elm trees by the Mill stood up tall and stately golden, the hazels and alders by the ford kindled to a more russet fire by the setting sun: the whole wide, wooded valley wound its way up to Bramber touched with apple colours, bonfire colours, as though the woods too made their Sun Dance, and the faint mist of the frosty evening was already rising blue as bonfire smoke under the trees. Among the hazel scrub that half hid the track from the ford, there was a flicker of movement, and a glint of sharp emerald colour that was alien to the tawny hues of All Souls' Eve.

'Look, Bevis,' Randal said, 'there's someone coming up from the ford.'

Bevis looked in the same direction. 'Stranger, by the look of him. I wonder whether he's for us, or only heading down the river for Durrington or Broadwater—come on, let's go and see.'

They whistled Joyeuse to heel, and went swinging down

through the hazel scrub at top speed, for in their world strangers
were always an event.

The man whom they met on the river track rode a fine bay
palfrey, and his tunic, with its long, trailing sleeves turned back
with fur, showed lizard green under the darkness of his cloak. A
man with a plump, smooth face and brilliant, colourless eyes on
either side of a surprisingly thin, high-bridged nose. But his
voice, though smooth like his face, and with the barest trace of a
lisp in it, was pleasant enough when he spoke, reining in his
horse as the boys and hound reached him.

'God's greeting to you. I am a stranger in these parts. Can
you tell me if I am on the right road for Shoreham?'

Bevis shook his head. 'You are on the wrong side of the river
for Shoreham, sir. You should have crossed over at Bramber.'

'I had a feeling that was the way of it. I was misdirected by
some fool of a villein. Would I had the flogging of him.' The
man showed his teeth for a moment, then turned the furious
grimace into a smile, and shrugged. 'Assuredly this is not my
fortunate day—which comes, maybe, of journeying on All
Souls' Eve. If I turn back now I shall not be in Shoreham, if 'tis
as far as they say, until long after dark, and to crown all else,
Grisart here is working loose a shoe. Who's Manor am I on
now?'

'This is Dean, sir,' Bevis said. 'My grandfather, Sir Everard
d'Aguillon, holds it from de Braose. In his name I bid you most
welcome to all that the Manor can yield, both for yourself and
your horse.'

'Ah, a cup of wine, maybe, while your Manor smith sees to
Grisart . . .'

Bevis smiled, with the quick back-toss of the head which was
so much a part of him. 'I am very sure that my grandfather will
not be content to lose your company before morning, if your
business in Shoreham will wait until then.' He set his hand on
Grisart's bridle. 'Come, this track to the right leads up to the
Hall.'

Randal had said nothing all the while, looking up at the
stranger knight under his brows. There was something he had
known before about the man, and yet he was sure that he had

never seen the plump, smooth face until this moment. The half-memory made him uneasy, because mingled with it was a queer feeling of evil, a feeling of a shadow falling across him, across all Dean.

The man had wheeled his horse into the track that led up towards the village, Bevis walking at his stirrup and Joyeuse running ahead, and Randal fell in behind them, still frowning. He never took that track, even now after four years, without remember the first time, and feeling again something of that lovely, unexpected sense of home-coming. He felt it now, so sharply that it hurt him.

Ancret, who had come up to tend old Wulf for the ague, was crossing the Hall garth with a crock in her hand as they came in through the gate gap under the ancient pear tree. She turned to look up at the stranger, herself aloof as a shadow, drawing back her skirts a little as the horse went by. It was a strange, deep look, and when they were past, the man made the sign of the Cross, saying half-angrily, 'That's a darkling look to meet at the day's end! I wonder you care to keep such a bird of ill-omen about the place.'

'That is Ancret, my foster-mother,' Bevis said quickly and a little hotly. 'She is herb wise and heals all our ills hereabouts. I don't think she would waste her magic putting the Evil Eye on anyone.' But he too made the sign of the Cross, not for any fear of Ancret, but because it was not good to talk of the Evil Eye, especially towards dusk on the eve of All Souls.

The sound of horses' hooves clattering to a halt before the Hall door brought Sir Everard from the storeroom, where he had been checking over the Manor's stock of war-bows with Reynfrey. He greeted the stranger with the grave and somewhat stiff courtesy that he had for all guests, as Bevis held the stirrup for him to dismount. And a little later, while the older boy went indoors to help the stranger wash off his dust and see to the lay-ing of an extra place at table, Randal was leading Grisart down through the village again in the direction of the smithy.

He waited, sitting on the horse-block outside, while Cissa, the little black-browed Manor smith, dealt with the loosened shoe; then he brought the big bay palfrey up to the Hall again.

By now it was the time of the evening that Lewin called owl-hoot, and in the long, thatched stable where all the Dean horses had their stalls it was already deep dusk, filled with the good scent of the horses and the evening hay in the mangers, and the lazy sound of champing. Randal called for Elli the stable boy, and bade him light and bring the stable lantern and hang it in the spare stall, then fetch water and fill the empty manger, and while the bay, having drunk as much as he judged good for him, grew busy with the hay and beans, he fell to rubbing him down. Bevis came in before he was half-way through and set to work beside him. In public they were careful to keep up their relative position of squire and varlet, but in private they did all things together, as they had always done. Elli had gone off again to his supper, and they were alone with the horses.

'What is amiss, Randal?' Bevis asked suddenly.

'Nothing,' Randal said, shaking out the big horse rug. 'Have you heard what his name is yet?'

'Sir Thiebaut de Coucy. Why? Do you know something about him?'

'I? No I——' Randal stumbled; 'I don't think so. Bevis—I don't like him.'

'I don't like him either,' Bevis said after a moment. 'But he'll be gone in the morning.'

They finished rugging Grisart, then turned towards the door, Randal carrying the lantern. At the next stall he checked, and went in for a good-night word with Swallow, his own horse. Swallow was grey; not the hard, iron colour of most grey horses, but a soft, smoky grey, deepening almost to black at ears and muzzle. Randal had loved him even before he was old enough to manage anything bigger than a pony, when the tall grey was just one of the Dean horses. It still seemed to him a wonder that Swallow was his, and just as the old sense of home-coming had hurt him earlier that evening, so now his joy in possessing Swallow was suddenly so piercing sharp that it hurt him too. He put his arm over the arch of the grey neck, as the horse whinnied softly and swung his head to greet him, and pressed his face a moment against the horse's cheek, holding to him as though for comfort against this queer feeling of a shadow having fallen across them all, that he could not shake off.

Bevis had strolled on, pausing for a word with his own Durandal, and with the old war-horse Valiant in the end stall. Now he checked again in the doorway to call, 'Come on, Randal. We shall be late for supper.'

And Randal gave Swallow a parting pat, and went after him.

The household was already gathered when they entered the Hall; d'Aguillon and their guest sitting at the high table, and the rest of the household, Ancret among them this evening, at the lower tables set up on trestles in the body of the Hall. It was a fast day, but with thick fish soup flavoured with saffron, and eel pies and kale and good, dark barley bread, and baked pears stuck over with sorrel and rosemary for the high table, nobody felt the lack of meat. And when the meal was over, and Bevis and Randal with the house churls to help them had cleared the tables and stacked the trestle boards away, they drew the benches to the central hearth, and settled with the Lord of the Manor and his guest and the hounds about the fire.

It had been autumn out in the woods, but it seemed full winter now, and they put up the shutters and huddled close about the hearth, stretching out their feet among the dogs who lay blinking at the flames. Often after supper Sir Everard played chess with the boys, as part of their education, or sometimes Adam read to them from his treasured *Lives of the Saints*. But tonight they had a guest, and instead of chess or reading, they turned to him for news of the outside world.

And so, sitting with his back propped against the blackened kingpost of the Hall, his face with its pale, brilliant eyes now lit, now lost, in the flare and fall of the firelight, Sir Thiebaut talked. He talked well and interestingly, telling them the latest news of the Crusade that was now sweeping to the very gates of Jerusalem, speaking the great names, of Duke Robert himself, of Raymond of Toulouse and the bold Tancred, talking of the sieges of Nicaea and Antioch, the battle of Dorylaeum (the names sang themselves like a charm, like the runes on a Norseman's sword). And all the while Randal, heel-squatting against Luath's warm, rough flank, watched his face in the red light of

93

the fire; that queer half-memory still teasing and tugging at him with the certainty that somewhere he had known Sir Thiebaut de Coucy before.

He talked of London too, of the splendours that were to be found there, a little condescending in his manner, while the Sussex draughts set the rushes eddying on the floor and blew the acrid smoke into one's eyes.

'If Saxon Harold could rise from his grave now, my Faith! His one eye would start clean from his head to see the change that Norman power and skill has wrought in London.'

Randal, still watching the man's face, felt the Saxon half of him stiffen, the hair rise a little on his neck like a hound's when it is angry. One did not speak so of Harold Godwinson here in this corner of Sussex where so many of the Manors had been his own. And Sir Everard seemed to feel the same, for as though to cover the other man's slip of courtesy that had set the house churls bristling, he said quickly, 'Doubtless London is a fine city, these days. To us, with all Andred's Weald between, it seems like a city of another world. But even here in our remoteness, we hear things from time to time. Is it true that they have built a stone bridge across the Thames?'

'Aye. That is Ranulf Flambard's handiwork. These two years past he has been raising for our Red William such a city as no King in Christendom can better.' He laughed at the back of his high-bridged nose. 'Indeed, 'tis so that I am in these parts—on Flambard's behalf, to beat up your Sussex Barons into providing me more drafts of craftsmen to work your Sussex oak for the roof of the great new Hall at Westminster . . . Say now, have you any skilled woodwrights or trained dressers of stone on the Manor?'

Sir Everard's stern gash of a mouth quirked a little at the corners. 'Edda who can build and patch a flint wall, and Wilfram who can make a wagon wheel with any man in Sussex, but not such, I think, as would serve to work the roof of the King's Hall. Why do you need more workmen suddenly at this stage of the work?'

'To hurry it to its finish. You will have heard the rumour that the King comes again in the spring? Red William has as good as

94

finished his campaigning in the Norman Marches; and what is there, once Normandy is safe, but to return to England? Aye, and once returned, there are those who prophesy that he is to be crowned again—and where but in his own new Hall? That would mean a bishopric for Ranulf Flambard, and Ranulf Flambard knows it.'

'But why crowned again?' Sir Everard said. 'Once knighted, one does not kneel a second time for the accolade.'

The stranger shrugged. 'He has been crowned before, yes; with the crown of England alone; but see you, now he has made all again as it was in his father's day, he is King of England and Count of Maine and Duke of Normandy.'

'Only Duke of Normandy until Robert rides home from his Crusade.'

'Why as to that, there may be two thoughts concerning the matter: Brother Robert's and Brother William's.'

The two men looked at each other in silence, and then, as though to change the subject, Sir Thiebaut glanced about him at the faces in the firelight, and said in a tone of faint amusement, 'You have a strangely shrinking household, Sir Everard. Surely there are fewer of us round the fire than rose from supper a while since.'

For a moment nobody answered. Randal thought of the brushwood pile that he and Bevis had seen on the Bramble Hill. For some while past he had been aware of one after another of the household folk rising and melting away after Ancret into the darkness, and he was sure that Sir Thiebaut had been aware of it too.

Adam Clerk broke the silence, twisting his thin hands together in deep distress. 'I do try—I do most humbly and truly try to bring them with a whole heart to Christ, but they come to Mass on Sundays and Saints' Days, and turn at all other times to their Horned God, no matter how hard I strive to make them see that he is the Devil. And Ancret is the worst of them, for all that she gives the wax from her bees to make candles for our little church. It is my fault—I am sure that it is my fault—but really I do not see what more I——' His eye fell on Bevis raking in the hot ash with his dagger, and he shook his head. 'Even the

95

boys burn nuts in the fire to read their futures when they should be thinking, on this night of all the year, of their immortal souls!'

'So?' The amusement deepened in Sir Thiebaut's silken voice. 'I had thought it might be that. Do you dance round a sacred thorn tree? Or is it a Fire Festival, hereabouts?'

Sir Everard rose, touched the little clerk's drooping shoulder kindly in passing, and turned to the lower end of the Hall. 'Come to the door and see what we do hereabouts.'

Bevis and Randal had risen too, the hounds all about them, and slipped ahead to raise the heavy doorpin and have the door open for the Lord of Dean and his guest; and a few moments later they were all outside in the darkness of the foreporch. It was very cold, with the tang of frost sharp in the air, and a little mean wind that had risen with the coming of dusk; and below in the darkness of the river woods the owls were crying. Southward, upward of two miles away, the Bramble Hill rose blackly against the crackling brightness of the stars; blackly, but wearing a feathered crest of fire. And even as they watched, flecks of light brilliantly and deeply coloured as the heart of the red amber seemed to break off from the main brightness and go circling and swooping about the dark shoulders of the Hill.

The Sun Dance had begun.

Randal was standing very close to Sir Thiebaut, and as the man moved, huddling his cloak around him, it seemed to the boy that a faint, sweet, animal scent stole out from under the dark folds. It was very faint, the merest ghost of a perfume put on days ago. The warmth of the hearth fire must have woken it, but in the Hall it had been masked by the stinging tang of woodsmoke that blunted one's nose. There was no woodsmoke out here, and instantly Randal knew it for what it was, the animal sweetness of musk.

Even as he realized it, Sir Thiebaut spoke again. 'So—a Fire Festival indeed! Doubtless the sun will be greatly encouraged to return in the spring, thereby.'

And now that it had no face to it, now that Randal was standing in the dark with the scent of musk in his nostrils, the voice did the rest; a smooth voice with a trace of a lisp, so smooth that there was about it an odd suggestion of hairlessness. The voice that he had heard on the water stair at Arundel, four years ago!

His heart began to race, and the scent of musk suddenly made him want to retch. He pressed back against the doorpost behind him, telling himself that it didn't matter now, it couldn't matter. The plot to kill the King and set his cousin in his place was three years dead, and though, seemingly, this man had been one of the lucky few to slip through the net afterwards, his being here could not matter now, could not possibly bring any harm to Dean. His sense was telling him all that, desperately, over and over again, but far down below the level of sense, he was struggling like a fly in a spider's web, caught in horrible dark, sticky strands that reached out to him from the old life behind him, struggling but unable to get free. It only lasted a moment; then he took a deep breath and told himself not to be a fool, and straightened from the doorpost.

Sir Thiebaut must have asked some question while he was not listening, maybe something about the Hill itself, for Sir Everard was saying, 'It has been in some sort a sacred hill, and the Manor has made its fires there since before the memory of the oldest man in the valley and his grandfather before him. There's a legend of a king buried in the green howe up there, with all his treasure about him, and whether that was aught to do with the thing, I would not be knowing, I who am mere Norman. I doubt if they know themselves.'

De Coucy made a small, abrupt movement, and the smoothness of his voice sharpened a little, as he took up the one word that really interested him. 'Treasure! It would be gold, think you?'

'Gold, I imagine, and fine weapons which have ever been the treasure of the fighting man—if indeed it be not merely the gold of legend.'

'But do you tell me that you have never taken measures to find out?'

'I have never felt the smallest desire to find out,' Sir Everard said simply.

'Ah, you are wasted on this greedy world. You should be in Steyning Priory,' said the smooth, faintly-amused voice. 'Faith!

If it were on my land I'd have every villein on the place to work, and the whole barrow laid open to the sky.'

'It would have gone hard with our fields the while. Besides, if men that we have forgotten laid a king's treasure there with their dead King, it was not done that men of a later year might dig it out and put it to their own uses. If it is only the gold of legend, then 'twould be a pity to rob it of its shining.'

'Such niceties are beyond me,' Sir Thiebaut said impatiently, then deliberately lightened his tone, and shrugged, half laughing, and shivered. 'But to each man his own affairs . . . It is cold out here, my friend. In Heaven's name let us go back to the most pleasant warmth of your fire.'

Randal took his chance as the others turned back to the fire-light, and slipped out into the night, and round the end of the Hall towards the stables. His heart was still beating uncomfortably fast, and the palms of his hands were sticky despite the cold, and he knew that he was running away from something; but he always ran away from things.

Bevis found him squatting in the dark, safe shadows of Swallow's stall a while later, and demanded with worried exasperation, 'Randal, what *is* amiss with you tonight?'

Randal shook his head. He had never kept anything from Bevis except this one thing. But if he told him about Sir Thiebaut he might feel that he must tell Sir Everard, and Sir Everard might feel it his duty to tell de Braose, and who knew where the thing might end. He was afraid, desperately afraid of what might happen if the old evil were woken up and dragged into the daylight.

'I felt sick,' he said. 'I ate too much eel pie for supper, and I felt sick.'

And that was a kind of running away, too.

# 9

# THE HAWKING PARTY

SIR THIEBAUT rode off next morning, leaving behind him a feeling like an evil taste lingering in the mouth. But little by little the day to day life of the Manor closed over the whole incident, and at last even Randal almost forgot about him.

The King returned in the spring, and at Whitsun he was crowned a second time. Crowned in his great new Hall at Westminster, under the roof of Sussex oak. And Ranulf Flambard duly received the Bishopric of Durham. 'King of England, Duke of Normandy and Count of Maine' ran the Red King's titles. But with the first autumn gales came the news that Brother Robert was on his way home from Jerusalem.

Christmas came, and then it was New Year; a new year and a new century.

'An old world has passed and a new world stepped into its place in the last hundred years,' Sir Everard said to Bevis and Randal as they walked back from Midnight Mass in the tiny, flint-walled church, ice crackling in the ruts underfoot, and checked to watch the winter fires of Orion swing low above the Bramble Hill. 'And what this new, untouched century holds for men, God, He knows. But I think that before it is half spent, there will be no more talk of Saxon and Norman, but only of English. I shall not see that, my children, but you may—you may.'

'You—don't think the world is going to end this year, as they say?' Bevis said, as though the words stuck a little in his throat. So many people believed that, but somehow it had not seemed so near until the New Year was actually upon them.

'No,' Sir Everard said simply. 'I do not. It seems to me that so many things are beginning now, and I cannot believe that God would let them spring, only to cut them down before they come to flower.'

At the end of January Sir Everard received the usual yearly

summons to Bramber. In the earlier years, before Bevis was a squire, he had gone unattended on his month's knight's service, and then last year he had taken Bevis. And now Randal, miserably grooming Valiant until the old war-horse's flanks shone like copper, was facing the prospect of being left behind alone once more.

'Next year you will be a squire, and then you'll be coming too,' Bevis said wretchedly. He was more wretched about it even than Randal. And Randal nodded, and went on grooming Valiant's tail, and said, 'I shall have a fine time while you are away. I shall help Lewin with the lambing.'

But they both knew that next year would not be quite the same. For one thing, old de Braose's son was being married this February, and though the wedding would of course be at the bride's home, he would be bringing her back to Bramber, and there would be feasting and revelry, harpers and jugglers and merchants from foreign parts, hunting and hawking, and Randal would have loved the clash and colour and swarming life of it all. For another, at the back of everyone's mind there was the thought, whether one believed it or not, that the world might indeed be coming to an end this year. That there might never be another February to be a squire and ride to Bramber behind Sir Everard.

Bevis said suddenly, as though he was thinking the same things, 'I could not bear it to happen before grandfather makes you a squire.'

The two boys looked at each other across Valiant's hind quarters. Randal didn't think he could bear it either. 'I don't believe the world is coming to an end, not really,' he said. 'I'm sure Lewin doesn't, or he would not have planted that new elder sapling in the sheep fold for sheep-medicine. No, I'll get to be a squire, sure enough, and then—you'll be a knight.'

There was a little silence while they both thought about that. And then, propping his shoulder against the side of the stall, Bevis said, 'Randal—if you were to get your chance of knighthood too—say that one day we were to fight Duke Robert, and before the battle de Braose thought to make some more knights, and he sent for you and said, "Randal of Dean, I would that you receive knighthood of me this morning," what would you do?'

'Refuse,' Randal said simply. 'I have no land. I couldn't furnish my helm.'

'Not every knight holds land.'

Randal did not answer at once. He had turned his head, the harsh liveness of Valiant's tail still under his hand, and was looking out through the stable door, across the garth where the hens were scratching after dropped corn, to the familiar tawny lift of the downs beyond the still bare branches of the pear tree by the gate, and suddenly he was wondering what it would be like to hold Dean. He had never, after the first baffled and rebellious days when he stole the red amber, envied Bevis his foster brother for the things he had, only for the things he was; he envied him for being the sort of person who did not run away from things, but not because his grandfather was d'Aguillon of Dean. He did not envy him that, now, only he wondered for the moment what it would be like.

'A landless knight is no better than a man-at-arms,' he said at last. 'I should not mind being an ordinary man-at-arms like my father, but I should hate to be a man-at-arms wearing a knight's sword, having to sell it to whoever would feed me, maybe even my helmet my Lord's property and not my own; sitting in my Lord's Hall, looking for insults from the very dogs, and seeing them everywhere.'

It was Bevis's turn to be slow in answering, while Randal finished his task and put away the brushes and currycomb, and all the while outside they heard a green woodpecker laughing his first derisive laughter of the year. Then he said, standing away from the side of the stall, 'I'm rising two years older than you, but sometimes you make me feel like a babe in swaddling bands, Randal.'

'You haven't run with the hounds in Arundel bailey with your eyes and ears open,' Randal said. And then as though in some way their positions were reversed, and he was trying to comfort the other boy, 'I don't at all mind that I shall never be more than a squire, you know—so long as I'm your squire, that is.' Something swole up in his throat and made him sound gruff, although his voice had only just finished breaking. 'I shall like being your squire—and I'll be the truest squire to you that ever knight had to carry his shield for him.'

And then that evening when they were both at work in the solar, burnishing Sir Everard's ring-mail hauberk—it was always bright as a salmon skin, but they could not risk a speck of rust now—the old knight's tall shadow fell upon them from the doorway.

'Let me look,' he said, bending down to watch them with the silver sand. 'Sa, sa, the work is well done. But it is work for a squire. Why do you make Randal do half your work for you, Bevis?'

'I wanted to,' Randal said quickly, and looked up in reproach. 'I have done squire's work for you for as long as I have been your varlet, d'Aguillon.'

D'Aguillon nodded, his dark eyes narrowing into a shadow of a smile, and sat himself down in his carved chair, leaning on one elbow to watch the boys still. When he spoke again, it was to Bevis, but clearly his words were for Randal as well.

'I have been thinking, these past few days: Bevis, do you remember how when first he came among us, you bade him understand that you and not he were to be my body squire when the time came, and we decided that since he must always be two years behind you in his training, there could be small risk of his forgetting that?'

Bevis flushed like a girl. 'I was a jealous puppy!'

But Sir Everard took no notice of the interruption. 'His full time is not up until the autumn, but how say you, shall we forgive him the last few months, this Randal of ours, and give him his squirehood tonight?'

And so, when Sir Everard rode for Bramber next morning, not one squire but two rode behind him.

The south wind was booming in the elm tops, and the cloud shadows were sweeping up the valley and over the downs like a charge of cavalry, and as they brushed by the hazel bushes at the ford, the yellow pollen-dust clouded the sunlight for yards around them. It seemed to Randal that winter had flowered into spring overnight, and he did not care if the world ended tomorrow, he was a squire with Bevis, riding behind his knight today.

The life of the great Castle was both strange and familiar to Randal. He knew as he knew the feel of his own skin, the talk of the men-at-arms in the crowded bailey, the baying of hounds from the kennels and the scream of hawks in the mews, the sour smell of the Great Hall and the richly greasy one of the kitchens: all the teaming, furtive, sweating, laughing, brawling life of the place. It was the life that had bred him and been part of him until he was ten years old. But now he was seeing it all from a different level, and so came the strangeness. It was odd and disturbing, like being two people at once. It was not only that the dog-boy had become a squire; but that the Randal who had slept with the Montgomery's Irish wolfhounds had become a different Randal altogether. The change had come on him so gradually through the years at Dean that he had not noticed it until now, and it made him feel a little strange inside his own skin.

It was eight days before the return of young de Braose and his bride, when Sir Everard and his squires rode in to Bramber, but already there were many more people in the Castle than usual, guests invited and uninvited, for the door stood open to all comers at such a time. Priests and jugglers, merchants to spread their wares in the courtyard, knights and squires, a Saxon harper, a wild-eyed Welshman with sure tidings of the end of the world, a horse dealer, a goldsmith, a seller of charms against colic and the Evil Eye. More and more they came, and all the while, among the in-swarming of new faces, Randal was looking out for Herluin, de Bellême's minstrel. He knew that de Bellême was campaigning in Wales, but he might send his minstrel to the wedding festivities, just as a man might lend his cook to a neighbour for a special occasion. But the days went by and Herluin did not come.

Instead, on the very day before young de Braose was expected, Randal came out of the stables where he had been overseeing the Dean horses at their evening fodder, just in time to see Sir Thiebaut de Coucy clattering into the bailey on his bay palfrey. He drew back instinctively at sight of the man, fancying even at six spear-length's distance that he could catch the scent of musk, and the queer dark smell of evil that de Coucy seemed always to carry with him. Then he told himself not to be a fool, and turned off about his own affairs. And in the days that followed there was so much happening, so much to do, that he managed for a while to thrust Sir Thiebaut out of his mind.

Next day Sir Philip de Braose rode in with his bride. The King had made the marriage, as he made all the marriages among his nobles, for his own advantage, mating this great house with that, as old Lovel had mated his hounds. But in spite of that, Sir Philip and the Lady Aanor, riding with his young knights and her ladies behind them, looked as though they might do well enough together. Randal, pressing forward with the rest of the crowd about them, saw a tall girl with a grave face that had laughter and eagerness somewhere at the back of it, who rode her fine white mare with the ease and freedom of a boy, despite the graceful, hampering folds of crimson silk that hung down on either side of her almost to cover her feet in the silver stirrups. But he looked with a quicker and deeper interest at the young man beside her, who would be Lord of Bramber one day. A thick-set young man with brown hair and a square, steady face, who might have passed easily enough for one of his own men-at-arms but for something of mastery in the level, iron-grey eyes. Sir Philip de Braose would not be an easy lord to serve, but Randal thought that he would be very well worth the serving.

After Sir Philip's coming, life at Bramber seemed even more crowded than it had done before, and it was three evenings later before suddenly Randal had bitter cause to think of Sir Thiebaut again.

That evening there had been much harping and merry-making in the Great Hall, and when the company split up and the fires were smoored for the night, Randal's head was still full of the bright harp music and the jewelled, bird-like flash of the juggler's cups and balls, as he huddled himself in an old cloak to lie down with the squires and hounds and lesser folk about the hearth. Bevis had gone after Sir Everard to the closet above the guardroom where the old knight was housed, to help him disarm and take charge of his harness; but it seemed that he had scarcely left the Great Hall before he was back beside Randal, saying quietly and quickly as he bent over him, 'Grandfather wants you.'

Randal looked up in quick anxiety from the warm nest he had been making for himself in the rushes. 'What is amiss? He is not ill?'

'No. I don't know what it is. He told me to fetch you, that's all.'

Randal nodded, and turned with him and they slipped out together, down the steep spiral stair to the guardroom, then up again and along a narrow passage in the thickness of the wall, groping their way in almost total darkness, until a bar of light shone to meet them down three steps from the chink in a leather curtain over a doorway.

Sir Everard was standing beside the narrow shot-window, making—or rather pretending to make—some adjustment to the buckle of his sword belt. He had lately come from guard duty, and still wore his hauberk, though he had slacked off the lacing of the coif and let it slip down so that it lay about his neck like a monk's cowl of glimmering mail. And as he turned from the window at their coming in, Randal thought that his face in the light of the candle on its ledge was grimmer and more sternly set than he had ever seen it before, his mouth an even straighter gash.

He gestured them to come and stand before him, but did not speak for a long moment.

'Bevis, Randal,' he said at last, 'I have something that it is in my mind I should tell you both—you, Bevis, as my grandson, and you, Randal, because I know that in any case Bevis has no secrets from you, and because I think that to you, also, Dean is very dear.'

Randal's heart gave a small, sick lurch. His eyes on d'Aguillon's face, he waited for what was coming next.

'I have been with de Braose this evening since coming off duty. He sent for me to give me warning that Sir Thiebaut de Coucy has cast hungry eyes on the Manor.'

There was a long, stunned silence, and then Bevis said, 'You mean that Sir Thiebaut de Coucy has cast hungry eyes on the gold that he thinks to be buried on the Manor land.'

'Undoubtedly. But that makes little difference so far as we are concerned.'

Randal said in a thick, hot rush, 'But Dean is yours! Sir— sir it can make no odds what de Coucy thinks; Dean is *yours*!'

D'Aguillon smiled, a smile that made two hard lines run from his nose to the corners of his mouth. 'That was your Saxon mother speaking, Randal. By our Norman custom, all land is the King's. The Barons hold from the King, and we lesser folk from the Barons. Have you forgotten that? I pay knight's fee for Dean, as all men pay for their manors, though, like most other men, I have come to look on the Manor, both land and folk, as mine—have come to love it very dearly.' He looked up into the darkness of the shot-window, and fretted with his sword belt. 'Bone of my bone, it has become, flesh of my flesh . . . But Sir Thiebaut has the ear of the new Bishop of Durham, who owes him something in the matter of the roof of the new Hall at Westminster, and the Bishop of Durham has the ear of our Red William. And Red William is ever joyful at any excuse to change about the holders of his fiefs, lest with passing from father to son the bond between lord and land should become too strong, and something of the King's power be lost thereby.'

Bevis shook the dark hair back from his forehead in that swift, defiant way of his. 'What are we going to do?'

'So far as I can see—and I have given some little thought to the matter already—there is nothing under heaven that we can do.' Sir Everard sounded unutterably weary. 'There is no appeal save force of arms against the King's decision in such a matter, and we can scarce expect de Braose to raise his banner and bring out the Honour of Bramber in revolt against the King and the rest of the Kingdom, in the cause of one knight's fee.'

In the silence which followed, Randal carefully traced out with his eyes the shape of a greenish damp-stain that made the likeness of a grotesque face on the wall behind d'Aguillon. Then Bevis said very gently, 'If we lose the Manor, what will you do, sir?'

'De Braose will yield me another fief, out from among his own manors. If I were a young man, I think that I should not take it, but turn my back on Sussex and my face towards Constantinople and the Emperor's Varangian Guard. But I am old, my children . . .'

Bevis said quite quietly, and quite seriously, 'Would it help if I killed him?'

And Sir Everard swung round from the window, and looked at him with a queer mingling of expressions on his stern face. 'No, Bevis. When there is killing to be done, I kill for myself, and do not delegate the task to a squire scarce seventeen summers old. How shall it avail us that you are hanged or made Wolf's head? And even though by some miracle the deed were not brought home to you'—he leaned forward a little, his dark eyes holding the boy's gaze—'I will not hold Dean by right of murder in cold blood, *and nor shall you!*'

And all the while Randal said nothing, and all the while he was thinking—thinking that there was one weapon that might save Dean, and he held it in his hand; if only he had the strength and skill, and the courage, to use it properly.

Sir Everard slipped free the buckle of his sword belt, and crossed to the sleeping bench and laid it down. The tiny golden roses that diapered the worn and scuffed red leather of the scabbard caught the candlelight, and made a pattern in Randal's mind that he did not see at the time, but that powdered the darkness for him all night, afterwards.

'No use that we talk more of the thing tonight,' Sir Everard said, and raised his arms slowly above his head. 'Come and aid me out of this lizard skin of mine, Bevis, for tonight it weighs as heavy as the whole world on my shoulders.'

When Randal got back to the great Hall, somebody else was of course asleep in the warm corner he had marked out for himself, but he had a heavy heart and too much to think about to trouble with turning him out. He crawled in among the hounds for warmth, and lay down with his head on the flank of an old wolfhound. But there was no sleep for him that night. Instead he lay going over and over in his mind the words that he had overheard on the water stair at Arundel. He had almost

forgotten for so many years, but now every word, every inflexion
of the smooth voice, the snarling softness of Hugh Goch's laugh,
were clear in his inner ear again, as though he had heard them
not an hour ago. 'Be ready when the time comes, and before
high summer we'll have done with Red William and his self-
made laws, and mount Stephen of Aumale in his place . . .'

If he went to Sir Everard or straight to de Braose with his
accusation against de Coucy it would be only his word, the word
of someone who had been a child at the time, against that of the
knight; and having tried and failed, there would be nothing
more he could do. But perhaps the threat might serve where the
actual deed would not . . .

He was coldly afraid. He had always been afraid of things
and people. Men had put that fear into him with many kicks
when he was so small that it had become a part of him. But
when he tumbled up with the rest before it was daylight, shaking himself like a hound and rubbing the dusty feel of the long
night's wakefulness out of his eyes, he knew exactly what he was
going to do, and the only uncertainty in his mind was how he
was going to get word with de Coucy alone.

But that was to be made easy for him, for on his way down to
feed and groom Valiant, he was overtaken by a fellow squire in
a kind of cheerful ill-humour, who demanded of him, 'Does
your knight ride with the hawking party this morning?'

Randal shook his head. 'No.'

'Neither does mine, but I'm lent to de Coucy to tend his horse
and saddle the brute for him. If a man comes travelling without
a squire, he should saddle his own horse or leave it to be done
by the stable churls, say I,' and he darted on.

Randal followed more slowly. So there was a hawking party
planned for this morning, and de Coucy was riding with it.
Well, that might be his chance. He turned into the long, thatch-
roofed stables that were already alive with grooms and squires
hard at work, and went to Valiant's stall. He brought down hay
from the loft and filled the manger, then set to work to groom
him. While he was still at it the horses for the hawking party
were already being led out, and he heard the falconers gathering, men's laughter, and the baying of a hound in the still frosty

air; and the trampling of hooves dying away as he turned from
Sir Everard's horse to his own. Swallow greeted him with a
whinny of pleasure, thrusting a soft muzzle with delicately
working lips against his shoulder, but Randal had no time to
give the grey more than a hurried pat, and a couple of handfuls
of fodder in his manger while he saddled up. He was not worried
about the hawking party being away ahead of him; they would
ride slowly and he could easily overtake them. But at any
moment Bevis might be here to groom his own Durandal and
there would be the need for explanations. And any explanations
that there had to be would be much better left until later.

He was done now and ready to be off. He led Swallow out
into the bailey, where the fowls were beginning to scratch
around the garbage pile and the breath of hurrying men hung
in little puffs of cloud on the grey air that was turning silvery as
the sun rose; he swung into the saddle and headed for the gatehouse, settling his feet in the long Norman stirrups as he went.
He had a story all ready for the gate guard in case of need, about
having been sent after one of the hawking party with a message;
but the men-at-arms lounging in the guardroom doorway
seemed to assume, despite the lack of any hawk on his fist, that
he was one of the party who had overslept, and made no
attempt to check him.

'Up river, or down?' he asked of one man-at-arms leaning
against the wall and idly picking his teeth with an old goose
quill.

'Up,' said the man, pointing with the feather and returning
to his pastime as Randal, with a word of thanks, clattered out
over the bridge.

Swallow was fresh and eager to be away and broke forward
into a canter, shaking his head and scattering foam over his
breast as they headed down the steep track that curled about
the Castle mound. Once past the thatched huddle of St Nicholas'
Church and College among the willows at its foot, Randal
turned him up-river, into the marshy country that ran in a
long, watery tongue far into the Weald, and settled down to
overtake the hawking party.

Presently he saw them, through a screen of still bare alders and crack-willow. The hounds had been slipped from leash and were working the rushes and dank tangle of last year's hemlock and willow herb on the river bank, while the horsemen, falcon on fist, gentled their horses to and fro on the fringes of the tangle, watchful for the heron to break cover. Randal drew rein among the alders, looking for de Coucy among the rest, and found him without much trouble, some way farther down the bank. The party was a large one, and well scattered. No one was likely particularly to notice his coming.

After a few moments he urged Swallow out of the thicket, and rode forward at an amble. The hounds, who had been working in silence, gave tongue at that instant, and amid a flurry of baying and shouting, a heron broke from cover of the rushes and leapt upward in swift, spiral flight. Three of the knights loosed their falcons at her, and the chase was on. The heron climbed desperately the blue circles of the upper air, striving to gain height to use her own weapon, her dagger bill; and behind her the falcons mounted steadily, dark-winged death on her track. Randal could hear the hawk bells ringing, a shining thread of sound as thin as lark song, as they climbed, and narrowed his eyes to follow the deadly chase. Up and up and up into the sun-lit blue and silver of the February sky, until at last the foremost falcon, soaring like an arrow from a bow, overtopped her and stooped, avoiding the despairing dagger thrust of her beak, and made his kill.

Randal brought his dazzled gaze down out of the sky as the falcons dropped, and while the hounds were searching the river-bank cover for the fallen heron, and everyone seemed riding here and there, brought his horse up beside that of de Coucy.

'God's greeting to you, Sir Thiebaut.' His mouth felt uncomfortably dry.

Sir Thiebaut looked round, his plump face startled for an instant, then covered as with a mask. 'D'Aguillon's varlet, is it not?' he said after a pause, and there was something guarded in his voice as well as his face.

'D'Aguillon's squire.'

'So—— Have you some message for me?'

'No message. I came to speak with you on my own account,' Randal said. 'When the rest move off, fall behind a little, that we may talk the more easily.'

Sir Thiebaut sat his bay palfrey and looked at him, his brows rising a little over those brilliant, colourless eyes. How assured he seemed, in his dark gown turned back with fox fur, the peregrine on his fist unhooded and made ready for flight: how coldly formidable. Randal was aware to the depth of his being that he was a boy of fifteen, and had been less than two weeks a squire; he felt very small and naked to be challenging such as de Coucy.

'Surely your new squirehood has gone to your head like too much cider,' de Coucy said contemptuously. 'But I am not used to that tone from an equal, let alone from a mere squire. Thank your patron saint that I am a patient man, and go away, my good lad, and cool that hot head of yours in the river.'

'I will go when I have said what I came to say,' Randal told him. 'If you like I will speak it before these others.' He glanced about him. 'There's more than one within shouting distance. But I think that maybe what I have to say, you would as lief not hear cried aloud to the world.'

He watched something flicker far back in the man's eyes, and wondered whether he was remembering the water stair at Arundel, or whether there were other matters.

Then the knight shrugged, still with a show of contemptuous good humour. 'What man that is flesh and blood and no cold saint has not something that he does not particularly wish his world to know? Nay then, I'll hear you, since you seem so set on it,' and he wheeled his horse as he spoke, and began, Randal beside him close as a shadow, to separate from the rest of the hawking party. The falcons had returned to their lords' fists by now, the heron had been recovered and the hounds leashed again, and the whole company were drifting off up-river towards the next patch of cover.

Randal and Sir Thiebaut dropped farther and farther behind, until the hawking scene grew small and bright with distance as it had been when Randal first saw it through the screening alders. Finally, in the lee of a tump of still bare blackthorn, they reined in and turned to look at each other.

'Well?' Sir Thiebaut said. 'Now, before I lose all patience, what is the thing that you would say to me?'

Randal's heart was suddenly banging against his ribs.

'Firstly, Sir Thiebaut, by way of sweetening what comes after, to pass on to you some words I once heard from that Ancret who dared to look at you in a way you did not like, when you came to Dean a year and a half since. "There's never aught but sorrow come yet to mortal man from the gold of the Hollow Hills." Remember that, if you think, by gaining Dean, to gain also a king's fortune from the crest of the Bramble Hill.'

'So you have heard tales,' de Coucy said after a moment, dropping pretence.

'Yes, I have heard tales. Maybe you can tell me that they are not true?'

Sir Thiebaut smiled. 'Come to think of it, why should I?'

He was hatefully sure of himself. Randal longed to smash his fist into the plump face and take some of the sureness out of it. He steadied his voice with an effort, terrified that even now it might betray him with an unbroken squeak.

'You have some influence with His Grace of Durham——' How pompous that sounded! He felt that his enemy was mocking him for it.

'A little, I hope. And His Grace of Durham has—have you heard it?—some influence with the King.'

'Then, if you have not already spoken of this matter of Dean, let you leave it unspoken. If you *have* spoken, then let you use this influence that you have with His Grace, that he give the words back to you as though they had never been.'

'And why?' said de Coucy again, pleasantly.

'Because five years ago last October, I, who was then a dogboy at Arundel, overheard what passed between you and the Lord of Arundel on the water stair of his castle.'

Sir Thiebaut made no sign, save that his eyes narrowed a little, but the peregrine on his fist suddenly bated wildly, filling the silence between them with her scream and furiously clapping wings. When the bird was quietened, the knight said gently, 'Yes, and how do you know me again?'

Something clicked in Randal's brain, and he saw the danger.

Many men might wear musk, and a voice was such a small thing to swear to—to those who had not heard it as he had done.

'It was dark in the stair-way,' he said, taking a risk, 'but once outside, the moon was very bright.'

The knight inclined his head as though giving him best on that point, but smiling, because he could afford to. 'You were then, perhaps, ten years old? Whatever you heard, whatever you dreamed you heard, who, think you, is going to take your word against mine? The word of a boy scarce yet a squire, and at the time only a child, and it appears a mere dog-boy at that, against the word of a knight?'

'In these days even a knight cannot afford to have suspicion fall upon him,' Randal said, thinking out his words as he went along. 'The King is half mad with suspicion—all men know it— and loves not those who are even whispered to have plotted against him. And'—his voice did shake a little then, but he steadied it instantly—'I am ready to take my story before the Bishop of Chichester and offer myself for trial by ordeal to prove that I speak the truth!' (What would they do? Make him plunge his hand—his sword hand—into boiling water? That was the most usual ordeal. He must cling to the faith that, whatever it was, the God that Adam Clerk had taught him about would strengthen him and bring him through unscathed to prove that his accusation was a true one.)

'So, a fighting cock indeed!' Sir Thiebaut said softly, and then, 'Have you not thought that it might be no very hard matter to have such a troublesome boy—cleared from the path?'

Randal had thought of that, but not the answer. His quick wit furnished him with that now, in the moment of his need. 'Yes; and therefore I have set a written and sealed report in the hands of—someone, to be opened and acted on, if any harm comes to me.'

He watched the odd little flicker behind de Coucy's eyes again. He did not think the man believed him, but saw that he could not be sure; and he knew that while he could not be sure, de Coucy would not dare to risk it.

Something from the long-ago night when Herluin had won him with a game of chess came into his mind.

'Checkmate, Sir Thiebaut,' he said.

Sir Thiebaut seemed to be watching the distant hawking party, but after a moment he looked round once more at the young squire. And Randal, meeting the narrowed gaze of the pale, bright eyes, found himself looking into sheer hate. A personal hate that went far deeper than the question of Dean.

'No, only stalemate,' he said, very, very gently. 'And I think that one day you shall weep blood for this day's work, my kennel-bred squire.'

# 10

# THE FLOWERING FLINT

RANDAL rode back to Bramber, stabled Swallow, and went in search of Sir Everard. At the head of the Keep steps he met Bevis, looking very white and taking his position as senior squire heavily—the more so, perhaps, because of last night—who caught him by the shoulder, demanding, 'Randal! What in Satan's name do you mean by skulking off without leave like this? Where have you been?'

'I went after the hawking party,' Randal said. 'Where is Sir Everard?'

'Well, next time you think to run off to play——' Bevis began furiously; and then something that he saw in the other boy's face halted him. 'Randal, what is amiss now?'

'Nothing,' Randal said. 'No, I think—everything is going to be well enough. But I must speak to Sir Everard.'

Bevis dropped his hand. 'Go along and make your peace with him then. He is in the armoury with de Braose, and I warn you, he's angry.'

The armoury was on the ground floor of the Keep, with the dungeons and storerooms, beneath the guardroom; a kind of undercroft with its low, barrel-vaulted ceiling supported on short, immensely strong piers, so that the place was like a church that had gradually sunk down squat and bow-legged under the immense weight of the great Keep above it. There among the pike stands and stacked shields and iron-bound armour-kists, with a couple of torch-bearing squires to light them—for though the armoury was above ground it had no windows nor outer door—Sir Everard and the old Lord of Bramber were looking at several sword blades laid on a kist top between them.

Sir Everard glanced up as Randal came clattering down the steep, curling, guardroom stair, and looked at him a moment, deliberately, his black brows drawn together.

'Ah, Randal, wait there,' he said, as though there had been

no question of his squire being absent without leave, and turned his attention back to the sword that de Braose was holding to the light. His mouth was at its grimmest, and the frown lingered between his eyes, but clearly he did not intend to take his squire to task before onlookers.

Randal waited, standing stiffly in the archway at the stair foot, while the two knights bent their heads over this weapon and that. They were old friends, old comrades in arms; but it was hard, Randal thought, seeing the Lord of Bramber, fat and gout-ridden, with his pouchy, used-up face in which only the eyes still seemed really alive, to think of him, young and strong and maybe much as Sir Philip was now, leading his squadrons to the charge, at Senlac, over the downs: he was so long past his fighting days, though he could be no older than d'Aguillon. But, past the use of them though he might be, he had kept the same passion for fine weapons that another man might feel for horses and a third for jewels. Now, smiling a little, he passed to his old companion a damascened blade on whose dark surface the torchlight played changeably as on a stormy sea.

'Feel. Is not the balance sweet? I had to have a new hilt made for it: the Saracens have narrower hands than ours, seemingly, and the grip was too small.'

'From Laef Thorkelson?' Sir Everard said, making the blade sing as it cut the air.

'Ah, I forgot that you were a friend of Laef Thorkelson's. He has brought me more than one of my best weapons; fine Arab blades that have no equal in the North.'

'It is a lovely weapon'—Sir Everard felt the balance again and squinted one-eyed along the blade—'though a little light, to my mind, maybe because I have carried a heavy sword all my life . . .' He gave it back, and took up another from the kist top. 'This has more the weight of my own sword that I carried at Senlac, and that Bevis will carry after me.'

Clearly, since it seemed that there was nothing to be done about Dean, they had set the matter behind them for the time being, in cleanly and civilized fashion, to take pleasure in their old companionship and the keenness of damascene sword iron.

And still, at the stair-foot, Randal waited.

At last the time drew near to noon—dinner had been set back two hours to suit the hawking party—and de Braose bade his squires to wrap the blades again in their oiled linen swathings and lay them away in the open sword kists, before they all climbed back into the dim daylight of the guardroom above. When the Lord of Bramber had ambled away leaning on the shoulder of one of his squires, Sir Everard gestured Randal to follow him up on to the rampart that cut the inner from the outer bailey.

Randal followed the tall old man as he descended the Keep stair, crossed the inner bailey and went tramping up the rampart steps with the chape of his sword ringing on the stones beside him. The rampart walks, not greatly used except in time of war, for the look-out was kept from the roof of the Keep itself, were good places to be safe from interruption or unwanted listeners.

'Randal,' Sir Everard said, strolling a little ahead, his shoulders hunched in his old, rust-stained leather gambeson, 'you know the duties of a squire. If you have any excuse to give me for going off this morning without first asking my leave, give it to me now.'

'I went after the hawking party,' Randal said to his stooping, leather-clad shoulder. 'De Coucy rode with them, and I had to get word with him alone.'

Sir Everard stopped in his tracks so abruptly that Randal all but bumped into him; then he turned round quite slowly, and stood looking at his squire.

'If I had come to you for leave first, you might have asked me why I wanted word with him,' Randal urged, to the stern uncompromising face.

'Randal,' said Sir Everard in a voice that grated a little. 'What have you been doing?'

Randal leaned against the side of a crenelle, surprised to find that he was shaking. But he had been shaking without knowing it, ever since he left de Coucy and the hawking party.

'Sir—I knew something about de Coucy that I thought I could maybe use as a weapon against him.' He checked, stumbling for the right words. He could not tell d'Aguillon the whole story. For himself, his only loyalty was to Dean, but d'Aguillon's loyalties were wider and he might feel it needful to go to de Braose . . . But something he must tell him. 'When I was in Arundel, I overheard de Coucy once, in a place where he had no right to be, with a man he should not have been with, and they made a plot that—would not have pleased the King. I think that he will leave Dean alone.'

There was a long silence. The little February wind hummed through the crenelles of the rampart, and below in the courtyard the hawking party was returning, and folk beginning to make their way towards the Great Hall for dinner. Sir Everard brought up both hands and set them on Randal's shoulders, and looked at him very straight out of those dark eyes that would be so hard to lie to. 'Tell me the truth, Randal; this plot you speak of, is it finished, a thing altogether of the past, or does anything of it reach out to the future?'

'It is altogether of the past,' Randal said, 'but the King loves not those who plot against him, even in past years.'

'True,' Sir Everard said slowly. 'So be it, then, I will ask no other question. A bargain is a bargain, even with such as de Coucy.' And then, as Randal heaved a sigh of relief. 'No. One more question. How did you contrive to make such a bargain— your word against his, and you were a child at the time?'

'I—reminded him of how half-mad with suspicion the Red King is; I said I would take the thing before the Bishop of Chichester and submit to being proved by ordeal. I—oh, I know it was a weak enough weapon, but it was all I had, and— and it worked!' Suddenly there was a great swelling in his throat and he could say no more. He was aware of the warm trickle of tears on his face, and he stuck out his tongue like a puppy to lick them up.

D'Aguillon was shaking him very gently, very kindly. 'You young fool! You very valiant young fool! Fifteen is too young to be making yourself a deadly enemy!'

Next day Sir Thiebaut de Coucy was gone, seemingly forgetful that he had ever looked in the direction of Dean. A week later, Sir Philip de Braose took his wife away to his own Manor at the northern end of the Honour; and the great Castle guarding the pass through the Downs settled to its usual way of life again. The month of Sir Everard's guard service drew to a close once more, and on a day of soft rain sweeping in from the sea, the old knight and his squires rode home.

The alders were dropping their little dark catkins in the water of the ford, and the elm trees below the Mill wore their brief purple mist of blossom, and as they drew towards home the babble of the young lambs came down to them from the lambing pens. Bevis let the reins drop on Durandal's neck, and stretched his arms wide above his head.

'Oh, it is good to be back. We have been away too long!'

Randal, with his head up into the soft rain that tasted a little of the sea on his lips, heard the babble of the lambing pens, and the deep content welled up in him because Dean and the Dean sheep would not suffer a change of master this year.

'There'll be a-many lambs come already by the sound of it,' he said, and he and Bevis looked at each other as they rode, sharing the contentment. He had told Bevis the whole story. That was a different matter from telling Sir Everard, though he would have been hard put to it to find words for the difference.

Sir Everard glanced back over his shoulder. 'You have run in strict leash all these past thirty days, and it is time that you were slipped. Bide for supper, then away with you up to Lewin and his lambing pens. It is in my mind that you would liefer spend the night there than lying decently by the Hall fire, at this time of year.'

And so, when Sybilla had done fussing over them, and supper was finished, they left Sir Everard to talk over the Manor affairs with Reynfrey and Adam Clerk, and took Joyeuse who had been bringing Bevis all that the house had to offer, including the best kitchen ladle and a hen's egg warm from the nest, and set out for the lambing pens on the sheltered skirts of the downs. It was still raining, the fine, soft rain that seems at any moment ready to turn into mist. The branches of the old pear tree dripped and splattered on them as they went out through the gate gap and turned uphill for the open downs, and away to their right they could hear the voice of the little winter bourn that began to run when the springs broke in November and would dry up again by May. It was not very dark for there was a moon behind the clouds, and in a little they saw the dark mass of the lambing pens on the sheltered southern slope of the little coomb, silent now, save for the occasional bleat of a lamb waking to find itself separated from its mother. A dim flicker of firelight shone from the opening of the bothy through the mizzle rain, and as they drew nearer, there sprang up a gleam of paler and stronger yellow that spoke of a lantern, and a great baying broke out, at which Joyeuse pricked her ears and whined, pulling against the leash.

Then Lewin's voice sounded, quieting the dogs. He was standing, big and peaceful, beside the opening of the bothy, his old battered lantern half shielded under his sheepskin mantle, when they came up.

'The thirty days are finished, and 'twas in my mind to wonder whether you would be up tonight,' he greeted them.

'It seems more than thirty days,' Bevis said. 'Oh, *Lewin*, it is so good to be back! How goes the lambing?'

'Well enough. Aye, well enough this year. I was just going to take my look round the pens now. Coming with me?' It was a question that he had asked often before, and he knew the answer so well that he did not even wait for it. 'Tie up the bitch then, and come.'

Bevis made her fast by her leash to the elderwood doorpost, and the great hound sat down quite unprotesting, for she was used to being tied up there. She was friends with Ship and White-Eye, and friends with the sheep, but no dogs save their own were allowed among the ewes at lambing time. She licked the hands of both boys, and lay down nose on paws with no more than a liquid whimper of protest as they turned away after the shepherd.

Lewin heaved back the hurdle at the entrance to the big lambing fold, and they followed him in, Randal fixing the hurdle in place again behind them. He had spent many hours up at the lambing pens every year since he first came to Dean, and the scene was as deeply familiar to him as any other part of the Manor's life; yet tonight, all at once, he was seeing it differently, with a new awareness that was almost painful, as though he had one skin less than usual: the deep bracken litter underfoot catching running gleams of light, coppery gold, from the lantern under Lewin's rough cloak, the man-high hurdle walls laced thick with furze branches to keep out the wind, the huddled, woolly shapes of the waiting ewes through which they waded knee deep, feeling the faint, live warmth rise from them like the mist of their breath. Ship and White-Eye moved ahead, running quietly among the ewes, looking, just as surely as Lewin, to see that all was well; and the rest followed. Every now and then Lewin halted and stooped to feel a woolly body, or to let a meagre beam of light shine on to one of the ewes from the lantern that he kept so carefully shielded. 'There's some fools that goes swinging a lantern round among the ewes and then wonder that the lambs get trampled on,' he said in that soft, caressing growl of his. 'And there's some, not much wiser, that reckons 'tis the light that terrifies them.'

'And it isn't?' Randal said, bending with him over one of his charges.

'Na, 'tis the shadows that the light casts . . . 'Tisn't often, save in the hardest winters, that we get wolves on the hill nowadays, but a light carried heedless sets the shadows leaping and prancing and running—ah, just as the wolves must have come leaping round the folds in the winter nights way back; and the sheep remember.'

The next ewe was standing head down to nuzzle at something on the ground, and as he let a careful gleam fall on her from the lantern, two little damp, sprawling shapes flashed out of the shadow into sharp-edged reality on the trampled, russet bracken. 'Sa, sa, here's one for the side-pens. Bravely done, my girl!' Lewin gave the lantern to Randal, and scooping up the two limp creatures, turned towards the small hurdled-off pens round the sides of the fold, where the ewes were housed with their new-born lambs for the first day. The mother followed, bleating distressfully and sniffing at her nearest lamb, and Randal brought up the rear with the lantern carefully shielded under his own cloak.

When they reached the pen, he uncovered the lantern at a

word from Lewin, while the shepherd made sure that all was well with the ewe and persuaded the lambs to suck; and the fine rain that drifted across the top of the hurdles caught the gleam of it and became a spitting, golden smoke. Ship came thrusting into the pen, and his shadow, running sideways from him before the lantern, was suddenly the shadow of a wolf. Hurriedly Randal spread his cloak to shield the light, and the shadows came crowding in, jagged, leaping shadows of wolves that prowled beyond the corner of the eye; and Lewin's crook lying beside him might have been a spear.

Lewin glanced up from the ewe, and his eyes met Randal's. 'You see?' he said.

Perhaps it was remembering, as Lewin meant it when he spoke of the sheep remembering. It was gone now. Come and gone in the time that it took for the shadow of the boy's cloak to swing across the little hurdled pen. And the shepherd got up, and held out his hand for the lantern, stowing it again beneath his thick sheepskin mantle. 'She'll do well enough,' he said, and turned back to the main fold where Bevis was waiting with White-Eye.

They finished the round of the lambing fold, found another lamb newly born, but nowhere any sign of trouble. 'Looks like an easy night,' said Lewin in rumbling content. They went into the big enclosure beside the other, where the ewes that had given birth within the last few days were folded at night with their lambs. Here, too, all was quiet. And in a while they went back to the bothy, where Joyeuse greeted them with softly thumping tail, before them the prospect of warmth and shelter, until presently Lewin would take down the lantern that he had just hung from the roof, and start the same round all over again. There was little rest for the shepherd folk at lambing time.

Now he shook the rain from his shoulder, and drew the old sheepskin rug across the opening of the bothy that was built of hurdles like the folds, and thatched with furze; and blew up the fire of crackling thorn branches in the hearth, made of a few stones, in the corner, and propped a pot of water to heat over it. Often there would be a motherless or ailing lamb before the fire, but not tonight. They huddled close, for the wind seeped through the hurdles for all the lacing of furze branches, Ship and White-Eye and Joyeuse lying nose on paws among their feet. Randal sat with his hunched shoulder leaning against Bevis who leaned companionably back, and stared a little sleepily into the fire, where a red hollow like the gaping mouth of a dragon had opened under the crackling thorn branches, and listened to the soft rush of the wind across the thatch.

'And all the time, the wind blows over,' he thought. 'Ancret's people, and the Saxons, and Harold dead at Hastings over yonder, and now the Normans: and all the while the wind blowing over the downs, just the same.' Half asleep as he was, he was suddenly aware of the new life in the lambing pens, the constant watchful coming and going of the shepherd and dogs and lantern, as something not just happening now, but reaching back and back, and forward and forward, into the very roots of things that were beyond time.

Something of the same mood must have been upon Lewin also, for when he had brought out the meal bag and tipped barley meal into the birchwood bowl, thrusting away the dogs' soft, expectant muzzles, he rose—but he could not stand upright in the little bothy—rooted in the willow basket hanging from the roof, in which he kept his few personal belongings, and brought out something wrapped in a rag of yellow cloth.

'I'll show you a thing,' he said to Randal. 'Sitting here at nights I've had it in my heart to show you, a good while past. Showed it to the young master when he stood no higher than my belt,' and as Randal looked up expectantly from the fire, and Bevis watched with the interest alight in his thin, eager face, he unfolded the yellow rag, and put into the boy's hand a thing somewhat like a double axe-head made from flint, mealy grey and tawny with the outer weathering that flint gathers through the years—an axehead, but with no hole to take the haft, nor any flanges for binding it on.

Without quite knowing why he did so, for he was not left-handed, Randal put out his left hand for it, and felt his fingers close over it as something infinitely familiar. But he had never seen such an object before.

'What is it?' he demanded.

'What it is called I do not know, but with such things it is in my mind that men fought the wolf-kind, and maybe each other, very long ago. I have seen others turned up on the downs, but never one to equal that one. I found it up on Long Down, years ago, and kept it because it was made for a left-handed man, even as I.'

Randal shifted it to his right hand, and found that it was true. One could use it perfectly well with the right hand, but it did not lie there happily, as in the left.

'Left-handed, or one-handed.' He did not know what made him say that. He leaned forward, looking at it in the light of the fire. And then, maybe because of the strange mood he was in, maybe because he was half asleep, maybe because of that dark thread of the old blood that Ancret had recognized, running in his veins, an odd thing happened. Once, in the outer bailey at Arundel, he had watched spell-bound while a wonder-worker who made live pigeons come out of an empty basket, had made a striped pebble picked up from the dirt where the fowls were scratching, grow in his hand without any visible change, into a yellow iris flower. He could see now the shimmering, silken fall of the petals, the dark, hair-fine intricacy of the veining that sprang from the slender throat, the sheer, singing strength of the colour. And as the pebble had become a flower, so the thing he held was suddenly warm as though fresh from the knapper's hand, and the outer crust of the centuries all gone like a little dust, leaving the beautiful, dark blue flint in all its newness. It was as though the thing flowered between his hands. He had an extraordinary sense of kinship with the unknown man who had first closed his fingers over that strange weapon, who had perhaps seen the wolves leaping about the lambing folds as he, Randal had almost seen them for an instant tonight; and extraordinary feeling of oneness with Dean, of some living bond running back through the blue, living flint, making him part of other men and sheep and wolves, and they a part of him.

This was the true seisin. He had the oddest feeling that because he had earned some right that he had not had before, because, coward that he was, he had set out with the only weapon he had against Sir Thiebaut de Coucy, Dean itself was letting him in . . .

The water in the pot began to bubble, and Lewin took it off and poured it into the bowl of barley meal, stirring with a stick as he did so, until he had a good steaming, porridgey mess, and added a lump of honeycomb—Ancret gave him a honeycomb from time to time—saying, 'That is in honour of the day that you come back from Bramber. 'Tis not every night that White-Eye and Ship and I have our stirrabout sweet.'

And Randal shifted, rubbing the firelight and the dust of sleep out of his eyes with his free hand, and grinned at Bevis who grinned back, and returned the strange flint weapon into the hand that Lewin held out for it. The warmth in it was only from the fire after all, and the flint was covered with the grey and tawny weathering of the years.

But the feeling of being given seisin, of being let in, remained with him.

# 11

# WITCH HUNT!

LIFE at Dean went on in its usual way. The swallows came back to the great barn. They dammed the stream and dipped the sheep, Bevis and Randal taking their turn to stand waist deep in the cold water, heaving the terrified and struggling beasts off the hurdle jetty. Hay harvest came and went, and the barley in Muther-Wutt Field was almost ripe to the sickle.

But under the surface of things, there was an uneasiness like thunder in the air, gathering ever more thickly as that spring and summer went by. People whispered together that maybe the end of the world was indeed coming. Strange things happened; omens and marvels. Last winter there had been strange lights in the northern sky; now a calf with two heads was born up at Durrington. People had queer, unchancy dreams and talked about them at half-breath afterwards; and as always when people were afraid, they turned back to the old gods. The Prior of Steyning complained of difficulty in getting the tithes in, or any work out of the Priory villeins, and on Lammas Eve, Adam Clerk came to Sir Everard in deep distress, having found the trunk of a certain ancient thorn tree on the Manor smeared with blood.

The next day Sir Everard had some business with de Savage, over at Broadwater, and riding home with the two boys behind him as usual, just where the Bramble Hill dropped into the woods, they came upon Ancret gathering simples. They would not have seen her, but that she heard the soft thud of the hoofbeats on the track, and straightened and came down to meet them, trailing her dusty-coloured kirtle like a queen's mantle through the dusty-coloured flowers of late summer, the wild marjoram and the swaying yarrow among the dusty hazel bushes. Randal thought, looking at her, that he had never seen anything human that took on the colour of her surrounds as

131

perfectly as Ancret did. Only those deer's eyes of hers, darker even than Sir Everard's, were bright.

Sir Everard reined up and greeted her courteously as he always did. And she returned the greeting, 'God's joy to you, Sir Everard,' and stood waiting, her eyes on his face, as though she knew he had something to say to her.

'Ancret,' said Sir Everard after a moment, fidgeting with his sword belt, 'if I had not met with you this evening, I should have come to your cottage. Adam came to see me yesterday with a tale of having found the big thorn tree below Long Down smeared with blood.'

Randal, watching her, had a feeling of a curtain being drawn behind her eyes, though they remained as bright as ever.

'Did he so, my Lord?'

'Don't pretend to me that you did not know about it,' Sir Everard said sternly.

'What would d'Aguillon have me do?'

'Put a stop to it; it is dangerous.'

Ancret came a step nearer, and laid her hand on Valiant's neck, looking up into the knight's face with those dark, curtained eyes. 'This year is not like other years. This year the people are afraid. And when they are afraid, men turn back to the gods that they knew before ever they knew Christ. Be glad that it is no more than a cock's blood smeared on a thorn tree.'

There was a pause, Valiant standing stone still under Ancret's hand, though Randal's and Bevis's horses fidgeted behind him, swishing their tails against the flies. Then, leaning down a little from his high saddle, Sir Everard asked quietly, 'What is it, Ancret? Is it the End of the World, as the priests say?'

'I do not think so. But this is a strange year, and strange things moving in it.' She hesitated, as though making up her mind whether or no to say something more. Then she said, 'In the time that it takes for the news to come through Andred's Weald, we shall hear that the King is dead.'

Sir Everard straightened in the saddle with a jerk. 'That kind of talk is folly. How can you know, before the messenger arrives?'

'I dreamed last night that I saw a red-haired man lying under an oak tree, with an arrow in his heart,' Ancret said simply, 'and his blood soaked down into the roots of the tree, and the tree strengthened and put out new leaves, so that he and the tree were one.'

A few days later they heard that the Red King was dead, shot while hunting in the great New Forest that he had made for his pleasure.

Some people said that his friend Sir Walter Tyrrell, who had been with him that day, and was not to be found afterwards, had shot him, either by accident or sick, like most of England, of his harsh rule. Some believed that Brother Henry, who had lately joined him in England, had loosed the arrow. Certainly he had been quick and purposeful in action after his brother's death, securing the fealty of as many of the leading Barons as he could gather in two days, and crowned at Westminster on the third, before the Archbishop of York could get to him, so that the thing must be done by the Bishop of London. But still, deep under these surface reasons for the King's death, ran a dark whisper that no man spoke aloud. Red William had belonged to the Old Faith, scarcely paying even lip service to the faith of Christ, all men knew that; and he had red hair, even as the man under the oak tree of Ancret's dream. Red, the colour of fire, of blood, of sacrifice. Was it not always a red-haired man who died for the life of the people?

The new King issued promises of just government to his Kingdom; he flung the hated Ranulf Flambard (no longer Bishop of Durham) into the Tower gaol; he brought back the gentle old Archbishop of Canterbury, whom William had hounded into exile. Late that autumn he took for his Queen Eadgyth, the orphan daughter of Malcolm of Scotland, who was descended through her mother from the great King Alfred whose White Horse of Wessex still had power to set men's hearts aflame. Most of his Norman subjects mocked at the marriage, but when the news reached Dean, Sir Everard, standing at the head of the South Field to see the great ox-plough turn at the autumn ploughing, said to Bevis and Randal beside him, 'Our Henry may be his brother's murderer, but he is a wise man as well as a strong one. Did I not once say to you that the time will come when there will be no more Norman or Saxon, but only English? This marriage, for all that the fools among us laugh at it, will help to make one England.' He paused, watching the wheeling cloud of gulls behind the plough. 'Already we begin, a little, a very little, to be one people. And I think that before so very long, maybe even before another harvest time comes round, we shall need all the unity we have if we are not to fall under the Norman's heel again.'

'How odd,' Randal thought, watching him. 'He has forgotten that he is Norman himself.' But both boys knew what he meant. William was dead, and Robert home from his crusade and sitting in his Duchy again without even having to pay back the ten thousand marks for which he had pawned it. But assuredly he would not be content to sit there long, while for the second time a younger brother wore the crown of England.

'It is between the two brothers, now that William is gone to his account,' Sir Everard said after a while, 'and neither will rest until one is the death or the master of the other.'

But all that seemed very far away from the ordinary men in the fields, more concerned with the winter wheat than the affairs of their lords. The year that had seemed so strangely fated was passing; they felt that the shadow which had lain so dark across the land was slipping away behind them. They were no longer afraid, and so they left the old gods, and went to church again; and because the clergy preached hell fire and their consciences were tender, they grew afraid as they had not been before, of those among them who still danced for the Horned One in the woods or smeared honey on an oak tree. So there were a few witch hunts, and folk looked askance at any old woman they passed gathering simples in the lanes, and made the Horns with their fingers to avert evil. Even Ancret, going into Steyning to sell her spare honey, found that the folk were careful not to meet her gaze or step in her shadow, though on the Manor they had too many memories of warts charmed away and fevers cooled by her for any such folly.

Summer came again, a still summer evening with sheep shearing over and the hay making almost done. And the time of which

Sir Everard had spoken, when Saxon and Norman English must stand together or fall again under the spurred heel of Normandy was almost come.

Through the spring, news had come on every south wind of supporters flocking to Duke Robert's standard. As early as February, Ranulf Flambard had escaped from the Tower and fled to him (though there was a whisper that his escape had been arranged, and he was gone overseas as a spy for King Henry). Now, in these last weeks, the news was of a war fleet gathering on the Normandy coast. The English fleet was at sea already, the feudal levies and the Fyrd had not yet been called out, but the more alert of the knights up and down the coast were making ready their men and stores against the call-out that they knew must come.

That day Sir Everard had been going through the Manor's war gear, with the two boys to help him and gain experience; making sure that the leather jacks were well oiled and stout, and that no dagger had a sprung rivet, testing the war-bows and seeing to the supplies of arrows and spare bowstrings. (Every man kept a hunting bow hidden in the thatch of his hut, though it was against the law; but the stout, four foot war-bows that could send a shaft through ringmail were kept locked away and only issued for practice or the real thing.) Now, after supper, he had strolled out to sit on the edge of the cider press at the high end of the garth, with the two boys and the hounds sprawled at his feet.

The sun was westering behind Long Down, the shadows creeping towards them across the turf, but the tops of the apple trees were still touched with sunlight that seemed all the more golden because there had been rain earlier. The rain had brought out the good smells of the summer earth, and Randal, sitting on his heels and playing with a half-grown puppy of Joyeuse's, caught, through the tang of woodsmoke and stable droppings, the scent of the hay in the long pasture, and a whisper of something else that might be honeysuckle but was more likely elder. The thrush who had had his nest in the pear tree by the gate was singing as he sang at this hour every evening; and there would be a new moon presently.

Reynfrey had gone into Steyning to take their tithe of strawberries to the Priory. The Dean strawberry bed, begun by
Bevis's mother with wild strawberry plants gathered from all
over the Manor, as well as plants that Sir Everard had had
specially brought for her from Normandy, and later tended by
Sybilla and Ancret for her sake, was the only one in that part of
Sussex, and every year the Prior of Steyning made a great point
of receiving his tithe of the little sweet, scarlet fruit. What an
odd world it was, Randal thought, in which you saw to the
rivets of your helmet and sent your tithe of strawberries to the
Priory on the same day. The Prior would have kept Reynfrey
for supper, but he should be back soon.

'Everything looks so peaceful,' Bevis said suddenly, glancing
about him. 'It seems almost too strange to believe, that in a few
days we shall be facing Duke Robert's army.' His eyes were wide
and bright, and he sat with his new sword across his knees,
fondling it. As d'Aguillon's body squire, he would be going with
him as a right; but Randal was going too. He did not think he
could have borne to be left behind, and the stronger the hay
smelled and the sweeter the thrush sang, the more he thought
he could not have borne it. Well, there had been no question
of that; he was sixteen, and Sir Everard had said to him days
ago, 'When the call-out comes we shall need every man we
can raise. There's an old leather gambeson in the armoury
kist, Randal. Go and see if it fits you.' It did not fit him
very well, being somewhat large, but it had horn scales on
the breast and shoulders. Only Reynfrey was to be left behind, and Randal did not see how the old man-at-arms could
bear that. Maybe one did not care so much when one grew
old?

Matilda, sitting against d'Aguillon's knee, raised her head to
listen. She was very old now and quite blind, so that her eyes in
the evening light were milky, but she could still hear as keenly
as any of the other hounds. Luffra pricked his ears and sat up,
and Joyeuse swung her tawny head towards the gate. A few
moments later they all heard it; the beat of horse's hooves
drumming up the track from the ford.

'That will be Reynfrey now,' Randal said.

Sir Everard was listening with a little frown. 'If it is, he's riding as though the Wild Hunt were behind him!'

'Maybe it is the call-out.'

'We shall know soon enough.'

The hoof-beats swept nearer, nearer, came to a trampling halt before the Hall. Urgent voices sounded, and a few moments later—they were all on their feet by now—Reynfrey appeared round the end of the Hall and came half-running up the garth towards them.

'Good God, man, what's amiss?' Sir Everard said, for the old steward was panting so much when he reached them that for the moment he did not seem able to speak.

'All Hell broken loose in Steyning, that's what's amiss!' Reynfrey rubbed the back of a hand across his sweating forehead. 'There's some wandering friar been stirring them up for days, Brother Thomas at the Priory told me—and there's the market crowd, o'course, today, and they'd been drinking— and then the shout went up——' He drew a deep breath and seemed as though he were trying to straighten out the urgent tumble of words. 'There's a witch hunt started and they're heading this way over the downs. They'll be here by dusk!'

'This way? Why this way?' Sir Everard snapped.

The two men looked at each other for one sharply silent moment, and then Reynfrey said, 'Ancret.'

Randal felt everything go still and unreal about him. 'Witch hunt! Witch hunt!' The words, hideous as leprosy, seemed mouthing, gibbering, screaming themselves over and over in his head. If there had been wind and storm and the tree tops bending double he could have taken it in more easily; it might even have seemed less horrible; but on this still, hay-scented summer evening . . .

Sir Everard had swung round to his grandson. 'Bevis, go and fetch Ancret up to the Hall.'

'I'll go too,' Randal said, as his fellow squire swung on his heel to obey, but Sir Everard stopped him.

'She will come for Bevis alone, if she will come for anyone; and I have other work for you. We must get in all the men near at hand, and for safety's sake the women and children also had best come up to the Hall.'

Afterwards, Randal's memory of what came next was always blurred, as though he were remembering it through running water or drifting smoke. He was pelting down the village street, scattering dogs and cats, pigs and chickens, thrusting into one after another of the villeins' hovels, shouting his warning of the witch hunt, shouting to the men, 'D'Aguillon wants you!' To the women, 'Best get the bairns up to the Hall out of harm's way.' Pelting on again with the women squarking behind him as loudly as the scattered poultry. Bevis joined him before the end with a couple of the house churls with him and the news that Ancret was safely up at the Hall; and they finished the round-up between them. When they got back to the Hall at last, Randal was carrying a sick child for its mother, and Bevis and another man were dragging a wildly bleating goat between them, because the miller's wife, whose darling it was, refused to come without it.

In the Hall, Sir Everard stood by the hearth, with Reynfrey and the men of the Manor gathered about him, and the women huddled in the farther shadows against the gable wall.

'Na, na, there is naught to huddle like sheep for,' he was saying with a touch of exasperation. ''Tis not Duke Robert coming down on us, but a mere market crowd from Steyning with too much cider in their bellies.'

But the fore-shadow of the witch hunt was on them, and Randal could not help seeing how even some of their own Manor women had drawn aside from Ancret, looking at her a little askance, as though in some way the fact that the witch hunt was for her made her something to fear, a kind of danger point like an oak to draw the lightning.

She stood, tall-seeming as always, and looked round at them, then turned her dark gaze to Sir Everard. 'You should have left me to take to the woods.'

'I'll have no one of my Manor hunted across country like a deer,' Sir Everard said briefly.

She walked out from among the women, her dusty-coloured kirtle drawn contemptuously close about her, and came to the

138

fire. None of the men drew away from her, but Alfwine the ploughman made the sign of the Horns, carefully hidden behind his back. But not carefully enough. Ancret flicked him with her eyes. 'At the least I should have had the deer's kinship with the woods, and the woods would not have been afraid of me.' Suddenly she turned from them all, to the young squire loosening his new sword in its sheath, the only one of them all who mattered to her. And her narrow face broke up a little. 'Young Master, are you afraid of me, too?'

Bevis left his sword to itself, and put his arms round her as though he was comforting a child. 'You are all the mother I ever knew. How should I be afraid of you, Ancret, dear?'

It was growing dusk by now, though outside the thrush was still singing. The sick child whimpered, and was hushed by its mother. All colour and substance was draining out of the Hall, save where, close about the hearth, the light of the low fire woke the warm, earthy colours of the villeins' homespun, and showed the look on their waiting faces.

There was not much longer to wait. Suddenly head after head turned, eyes widening; one man licked his lower lip, another half-pulled the knife from his clumsy leather sheath, as the first distant sounds of shouting splurged up into the evening quiet beyond the thrush's song.

'Here they come, then,' Cerdic the oxherd said.

Nobody answered him.

The sounds were drawing nearer; a ragged surf of shouting, with something of the same note of menace that sounds from a disturbed nest of wild bees; the ugly, inhuman voice of a mob. Randal, waiting with his hand on the dagger in his belt, his eyes on d'Aguillon's face like a hound that waits for orders, realized that they were coming straight over the shoulder of the downs towards the Hall, and even in that moment it struck him as odd that they should not seek Ancret in her own cottage; for there must be some among this Steyning crowd who knew where she lived.

Sir Everard, his sword still in its sheath, strode towards the door, Bevis and Randal at his shoulders. They could see the witch hunt coming now, over the shoulder of the turf below

Long Down; a ragged, loping skein of figures strung out like
hounds on the scent. Some of them had torches, and the flames
streamed out behind them in rags of smoky brightness on the
dusk. They swarmed down into the village kale plots, their mass
growing denser as the stragglers in the rear caught up with those
in front; they were pouring through the gateway under the pear
tree from which the thrush had flown in terror, breaking down
the hedge on either side, bursting and jostling their way through
into the garth. The sparks from their ill-made torches whirled
up into the quiet branches where the fruit was setting, and their
faces in the tattered flare of flamelight were both afraid and
vicious. Randal saw the brightness of their eyes, the dark gape of
their yelling mouths, and the torch-glare on cudgels and quar-
terstaffs and the sharper weapons, the scythe blades or but-
chers' knives that some among them carried; saw also the friar,
face hidden in the forward-drawn folds of his cowl, who strode
in their midst.

'Why doesn't d'Aguillon draw his sword?' he thought, as the
mob, catching sight of them in the doorway, set up a fiercer
yowling and closed in at the run. 'Why doesn't d'Aguillon
draw his sword? The sight of it might stop them. *Why
doesn't——*'

D'Aguillon had flung up his arm, shouting above the tumult.
'What is this garboil that you raise on my Manor? What do
you here on Dean land?'

They were right before the door now, milling round it, but
something in the three purposeful figures standing there and the
glimpse of others beyond, something in the tall old knight confronting them on his own threshold, for a moment pulled them up.

'Send out the witch that you have in your house!' someone
shouted.

'What wicked folly is this?' d'Aguillon's deep voice cut
through the ugly surf of sound. 'You have drunk too much perry
in the Market Place, and dreamed dreams.'

'Do not listen to him!' It was the friar now, crying out in a
high, cracked voice. 'He has the woman in his house and the
woman is a witch! Remember the cow of yours that fell sick the
day after she looked at you, Rafe One-Eye! The Wrath of God

is on this house for the witch's sake. Go you in and fetch her for the burning!'

The surge forward began again, weapons were brandished aloft, torches up-tossed above distorted, howling faces. Sir Everard had left his sword in its sheath as long as might be. Now he seemed to make scarcely any movement, but suddenly it was naked in his hand, a streak of glittering steel barring the doorway. In the same instant Bevis's sword was out, and Randal whipped his dagger from his belt.

'Get back!' Sir Everard cried. 'Get back, you fools! Go home and cool your hot heads and be wiser in the morning! There is no witch here, and I give up to you no woman of my Manor, though you choose to name her ten times a witch!'

They drew back a little, snarling as an animal snarls that is baulked of its prey, but the friar, with arm outstretched in accusation, was screaming them on, lashing up their fear and frenzy.

'Will you give ear to this shielder of Satan's women? Woe, woe to those who suffer a witch to live among them! She will put the murrain on your cattle and the mildew on your fields! She will cast her spells about you to suck out your souls while you sleep, and God will not save you because you have turned your face from Him to leave the witch alive!'

Suddenly there was a rush, and the thing had gone beyond shouting and became fighting: fighting that reeled to and fro in the doorway where Sir Everard still struggled to use the flat of his blade and not the edge. Someone had tried to fire the thatch, yelling that they would smoke the witch out that way if they could get her no other; but the thatch was damp after the rain, and the flames guttered out in a black reek of charring that Randal smelled thick and acrid at the back of his nose as he tramped to and fro with the press of struggling men in the doorway.

Then a man with a broad face made stupid by fear, and a butcher's knife in his upflung fist, leapt in at Sir Everard. Randal caught the flash of the descending blade, heard a sharp cry that seemed torn off before it was well begun, and saw out of the tail of his eye the old knight stagger and go down.

A howl went up from the mob, and they seemed to waver, some to half-surge back in horror at what they had done, while others yet thrust forward. Bevis had sprung across his grand-father's body, the house churls behind him; there could be no more fighting with the flat of the blade. And all the while in the midst of the turmoil the friar was still urging them on, mouthing and shrieking curses and wild accusations.

'Na na, never mind the old one! Kill the young one—the yellow-haired one—I see the witch-light shining round his head! Kill! Kill! *Kill!*'

His hand was outstretched, pointing at Randal, his whole figure seemed contorted by a wild spasm of malevolence, and in the same instant, in the milling press about him, the black folds of the cowl slipped back from his face, and Randal saw it in the leaping red glare of the nearest torch, distorted with hate and rage, but unmistakable.

He gathered himself together and sprang as a wild animal springs; but quick as he was, Sir Thiebaut de Coucy had flashed a dagger from the loose sleeve of his habit to meet him, and the two blades rang together. Some instinct, something in the way the man moved, told Randal that de Coucy wore mail of some kind under his black habit, and a body blow would be well nigh useless; and something in him knew, though there was no time for thought, that failing a kill, the thing was to mark him—a mark that could be recognized afterwards . . . For a few heart-beats of time they reeled to and fro together, unaware of what went on about them, aware only of each other. Randal broke his blade free and struck again, and again felt the blow parried with a shock, as steel met steel, that jarred all up his arm. De Coucy's dagger leapt once more, and Randal felt a fiery flick of pain in his left forearm, and sprang back an instant out of touch, then in again, striving to close with the man—the great black cat, he seemed in that habit, whose claws were one bright dagger-point of death—and beat down his defence. Then de Coucy's weapon darted past his shoulder as he side slipped, with such force in the blow that for one split instant of time the man was off balance; and in that split instant Randal had him by the dagger-wrist and closed with him. He saw the rage and hate in

142

de Coucy's eyes, the man's whole face, close to his own, a blazing mask of hate, and slashed it across the cheek once, twice, the second gash crossing the first.

Sir Thiebaut dropped his dagger and staggered back with a strange, high cry like a woman's, clutching at his face. Randal sprang after him and caught him by the breast of his habit, twisting his hands in the black folds, dagger raised for another blow; but the thick stuff tore in his grasp, dragging away at the shoulder, and the torchlight fell full on the quilted gambeson he wore beneath it. And next instant the man had whirled about with the swiftness of desperation and kicked Randal in the groin.

The boy doubled up, as his world darkened and swam in agony, and when it cleared again, de Coucy was gone. He was on his knees, winded and retching. He glared up at the aghast faces that wavered round him in the torchlight, and used the first shuddering breath that he could draw to rave at them. 'You fools! You duped fools! Don't—you know the difference between a friar and one of Ranulf Flambard's gore-crows?'

Vaguely, as he staggered to his feet, he heard Reynfrey's bull voice calling to the Manor men as a huntsman calls to his hounds. The witch hunt was over and the rabble was in full retreat, blundering away and breaking down the garth hedges as they went. It was partly the stunned realization that they had wounded, perhaps killed, a knight whom all men knew was dear to the old Lord of Bramber who held all their lives in the hollow of his gouty hands, partly the sight of a knight's gambeson under a friar's habit, and the hated name of Ranulf Flambard flung into their midst, that had acted on them like a bucket of water flung over fighting dogs. They wanted nothing now but to get away, to reach their own homes and leave the harm that they had done behind them in the hope that in the morning it would all be a dream.

Reynfrey and half the men of the Manor were away in pursuit of de Coucy, but Randal had just sense enough to know that he could not at the moment join in any chase. If he could be any use anywhere, it would be back in the Hall. He dragged himself back to the doorway, his dagger still naked and red in his hand, heaving aside with his foot the body of a respectable Steyning wool merchant that blocked his way. Then he turned on the threshold, without knowing why, and looking up, saw the pale sliver of the new moon that he had known would be here later, caught like a white feather in the branches of the tallest cider tree at the head of the garth.

# 12

# DE BRAOSE'S BANNER

D'AGUILLON lay just within the doorway, with the hounds crouching about his feet, his head on Bevis's knee, and Ancret kneeling beside him, busy by the light of a brand pulled from the fire that one of the remaining men was holding for her. And Randal, pushing through the throng to his Lord's side, felt a shock of sudden hope. He had thought that d'Aguillon was surely dead, but if he were dead, they would not be cutting away the sodden cloth over the wound and hurrying to staunch the blood like that. Still sweating and sick, he dropped to one knee at the old knight's other side, thrusting away Matilda's anxious white muzzle, and fixed his eyes on Ancret.

She had uncovered the wound now, a stab wound just under the collar bone, not wide, but deep, with the bright heart-blood welling up from it. A hoarse, inarticulate murmur that was like a groan ran through the Manor folk pressing about them, and Ancret looked up.

'Back! Get back now and give him air to breathe.'

Bevis, with very straight lips, said, 'Is it mortal?'

She shook her head. 'How can I tell? Even I? Sometimes the pictures come, the pictures of what will be, but never for any looking of mine. If anyone can save him, then I can, and if I can, then I will . . . Bring me clean linen for the wound, and rugs to carry him up to his own chamber.'

Two or three of the men hurried to bring her the rugs she wanted; and Sylbilla came lumbering with the linen and knelt down beside her, her face all puddled with tears. The fear that had stirred between them and the Wise Woman so short a time ago seemed quite forgotten now, as though maybe Sir Everard's blood had washed it away.

So in a little, Sir Everard was carried up to the chamber over the storeroom, his hounds padding alongside him all the way, and laid on the low sleeping bench. Randal remained beside him, partly to help Ancret, partly for the simple sake of being with his Lord, as the hounds were with him. Bevis, who had the better right, was needed elsewhere, with the search for de Coucy to be sped, and the safety and welfare of the Manor folk to be seen to.

Randal never forgot that scene; Sir Everard lying so still on the bed, his face set and quiet as the face of a knight carved in stone, his great nose pointing to the raftered ceiling, and his shield with its painted device hanging in its usual place on the wall above his head, like the harness of a dead knight above his tomb; the dark woman kneeling beside him, her hands laid with a curious, light purposefulness over the newly dressed wound, rising and falling a little—a very little—with his shallow breathing, as though she sought to drive some life or strength through them into his spent body (and watching her, Randal thought suddenly of the way she had held her hands over his bruises on the day he stole the red amber); the hounds crouching whimpering by the fire that had been made on the hearth; the big Norway goshawk hooded on her perch, with her hooded shadow on the wall behind her.

Presently Bevis came back. He came silently up the outer stair and through the doorway which had been left open to the summer night, and stood with his eyes on the still figure on the bed.

Ancret looked up, never moving her hands. 'I think he will wake soon,' she said.

Bevis let go a little breath like a sigh, and came to the hearth, thrusting back the wild, dark hair wearily from his eyes. 'We're keeping some of the outlying folk and the ones who got hurt in the Hall for tonight. Not that there'll be any more trouble now. De Coucy will be away for the sea coast, if he can see his way for blood. I suppose he was making for his Master overseas, anyway—and the rest are damp timber without him.'

'They have not caught him, then?' Randal said, stupidly, still kneeling beside Sir Everard.

Bevis raised his eyes slowly from the unconscious man, to look at him. 'Oh no. They're still searching the woods, but I haven't much hope now.' There was a puzzled frown between

his brows. 'I suppose because Ancret was here when he came
before, and I told him she was my foster-mother, he thought she
lived under this roof.'

'Ancret was only the excuse.'

'Oh, I know . . . How he must hate you, Randal!'

'Almost as much,' Randal said softly, through shut teeth,
'as I hate him.'

He had risen to his feet as he spoke, and they stood looking at
each other in the firelight. Then he took a step towards the
door.

'Where are you away to?' Bevis said.

'To Bramber, to de Braose."

There was a little silence, and then Bevis demanded, 'And
what will you tell him?'

'The whole truth,' Randal said. The bargain was dead now,
and surely de Braose, with all the resources of Bramber at his
sword hand, might succeed with the hunt where they, it
seemed, had failed.

The older boy nodded. 'I wish you joy of getting de Braose
out of bed at this hour of the night, but any chance of getting
de Coucy will be gone by morning. Off with you, Randal.'

Some while after midnight, when the faint light shining from
the window of St Nicholas' Church showed where the Canons
were at Matins, Randal was hammering with his dagger hilt on
the great gate of Bramber Castle, crying out in answer to the
gruff inquiry from within, 'Sir Everard d'Aguillon's squire,
with an urgent message for the Lord of Bramber!'

Probably if he had been another man's squire they would
not have let him in at that hour of the night, but though
d'Aguillon was only the holder of one knight's fee, and therefore not of much importance, the whole castle knew him for a
friend of the old Lord's. There were grumbles and protests, but
the gate swung open, squealing in the still summer night, and
Randal on Swallow clattered through. There were more protests, more grumblings, but somehow his blazing urgency got
things done. Someone took Swallow, and he was following a
man-at-arms across the courtyard and up the Keep stair. The

smokiness of the guardroom gave place to the smokiness of the Great Hall and the sleepy stirring of human and hound shadows on the rush-deep floor. In the Hall they bade him wait (who 'they' were he did not know, he was too dazed by the things that had happened since sunset). He heard a mutter of voices somewhere, and de Braose's squire came down the snail-curled stair, rubbing the sleep out of his eyes and yawning, as though he were mere mortal instead of body squire to the Lord of Bramber.

'What is it?' he demanded. 'Oh, it's you; you're d'Aguillon's squire, aren't you? What do you want at this hour of the night?'

'Word with de Braose,' Randal said hoarsely.

'De Braose is in his bed.'

'Beg him to see me, all the same. Tell him d'Aguillon lies wounded, maybe to the death, and there is that which he must know——'

'Wait here,' the squire said, and turned again to the stair.

Randal waited for what seemed a long, long time, fretting with his feet among the rushes, the centre of curious stares from all directions. And then the squire came back and bade him follow.

A few moments later he stood on the threshold of the Great Chamber, above the Hall. The huge box bed with its hangings of embroidered stuffs showed tumbled and empty in the light of the newly kindled and smoky torch, and de Braose himself, who had never yet received a messenger in his bed, and clearly did not mean to begin now, half sat, half lay in his great chair before the empty hearth, a cloak of some dark, glimmering eastern stuff powdered with silver flowers flung round him over his nakedness, and his great sword laid across his knees.

Two great boarhounds crouched at his feet, and he had been fondling the savage, rough head of one of them; but his eyes, like the eyes of a sick hound themselves, were already fixed on the doorway when Randal appeared in it.

'What is this that you have come to tell me?' he demanded harshly.

Randal crossed to him, limping still from de Coucy's kick,

and dropped on one knee between the hounds. 'It is true, sir—
a witch hunt——'

'Ah!' de Braose leaned forward. 'I heard there was a garboil
in the Market yesterday, and half Steyning out after a witch.
There are many witches and I took no heed. Was it a Dean
woman, then?'

'Yes. Bevis's foster-mother, Ancret—At least, it was meant to
look like that, but in truth it was stirred up by Sir Thiebaut de
Coucy, in revenge for being worsted over Dean.' Randal
covered his face with his hands, and groaned. 'It's all my
doing.'

'Never mind whose doing it is, beyond de Coucy's.' The old
Lord's voice cut like a north wind. 'So it was de Coucy, was it?
I wondered why he forgot his designs on the Manor so suddenly.
Stop talking in rags and ravellings, boy, and get up and tell me
the whole of this thing, from the beginning, whatever that may
be.'

Randal drew a deep breath, uncovered his face and straightened his shoulders and got drearily to his feet. And standing
before the empty hearth, he told to the fat, sick old man
slumped in his chair, the whole story from the beginning, from
the soft voice and the scent of musk in the darkness of the
Arundel water stair, as he had told it to no one save Bevis.

De Braose's gout-swollen hands tightened on his sword as he
listened, but he spoke no word until the whole ugly story was
told.

'We've beaten the woods for him,' Randal finished desperately. 'They were still searching when I rode away—but it is
in my mind that he has slipped through our hands.'

'And so you come to me to raise the countryside against him.
But can you swear that this friar-leader of the witch hunt *was*
de Coucy? In torchlight it is easy to be mistaken.'

'Even though he wore a gambeson under his habit?' Randal
said quickly. 'At least the leader of the witch hunt did not go
unmarked. Bid your men to look for a man with two fresh dagger cuts in the face, crossing each other—here,' he touched his
own left cheek, 'and see if it be not indeed de Coucy.'

'Your dagger, I take it,' de Braose said.

'My dagger, de Braose.'

The Lord of Bramber seemed to ponder for a moment. Then with a suddenness that made the hounds leap up in bewilderment, he burst into action, hammering on the hearth stone with the chape of his sword and bellowing for his squires in a voice to rouse the whole of Bramber Castle. His body squire, from his place just outside the door, was there on the instant; others came running. He shouted orders at them, sent them hurrying for this man and that, for his chief huntsman and the captain of his men-at-arms. And through it all, Randal stood by the empty hearth, dazed by this sudden, wild explosion of activity in the midst of the sleeping castle, the hardly roused and half-dressed men hurrying in and out, while their sick old Lord sat in his great chair and issued his orders as crisply and clearly as ever he could have done at Senlac.

Presently Randal found that the Great Chamber was quiet again, and empty save for the squire who had returned to his place across the doorway. He could hear a voice somewhere below in the bailey, and the dogs lay down again with protesting grunts. And he saw that the old Lord was looking at him out of the little sick eyes sunk in his pouchy face.

'So? That is all; there is no more that we can do. The hunt is up, and within a few hours there will be a search of every ship or fishing smack that sails from this part of the coast; but—like you, I've a feeling we shall not net him. He must have decided to slip overseas and cast in his lot with Duke Robert, or I think he would not have risked it. He's a coward in some things, and he's no gambler; he'll have had his plans laid.' De Braose's voice deepened suddenly to a rumbling growl that seemed to come from somewhere in his chest. 'But if we do not get the ring-leader, we can still hang half Steyning for this night's work.'

Randal said quickly, though it was quite against his will, for he would have liked to do the hanging himself, 'The man who stabbed Sir Everard is dead, and one or two others. They were all no more than tools of de Coucy's; and I—do not think Sir Everard would want any hanging.'

De Braose was silent a moment, one hand still clenched on

his sword, the other plucking at the silver threads of a flower on his cloak.

'Maybe you're right,' he said at last, broodingly. 'A gentle soul, d'Aguillon, overly gentle, maybe, but it has brought him the love of his stubborn Saxons . . . And if he dies, though I hang all Steyning high as the Keep of Bramber, it will not bring him back to fight old battles with me again.' He seemed to be talking to himself rather than to Randal, and suddenly he noticed it, and glared at the boy as though daring him to notice it too. 'Get back to your Lord, boy; there's nought to keep you longer here, and the Lord of Bramber is away back to his bed.'

It was the first silky greyness of the summer dawn when Randal rode into the Manor garth of Dean again, abandoned Swallow to old Wulf who came hobbling with the spent lantern pale as primroses in the growing daylight; and without waiting to ask news of Sir Everard—he could not ask, the words stuck in his throat, and he must see for himself—stumbled up the outside stair.

The door at the head of it stood open as he had left it, and the solar was awash with torchlight and dawn light that mingled without mixing; the fire had sunk to frilled grey ash on the hearth, the hounds still crouching before it, the Norway goshawk on her perch, with her hooded shadow that had been so black grown thin and tenuous on the wall behind her. Ancret still knelt beside the bed, and Bevis stood beyond it; it was as though nothing, no one, had moved since he left the room. But there was a sound of harsh, quick breathing in the solar that had not been there before, and as he halted in the doorway, suddenly d'Aguillon's voice, hoarse and rattling, said, 'Is that you, Randal?'

Randal was across the room in two limping strides, and dropped on his knees beside the narrow bed. 'Yes, sir, I am here.'

Sir Everard's eyes, seeming darker than ever and sunk into his drained face, looked up at him, frowning a little. 'Bevis has told me—the whole story. And—you have told de Braose?'

Randal nodded. 'I wish—God knows how I wish I had told it before,' he groaned.

'Nay, you judged—that the threat might serve—better than the deed; and you were right, for—has not the threat served—all this while?'

'But afterwards—I should have told you.'

'Na na, a bargain is a bargain, even with—such as de Coucy. Did I not—say that to you before? Never be—sorry for faith kept, Randal.'

They did not find de Coucy; and two days later the message came down-river from Bramber that Sir Philip de Braose was carrying his father's banner to join the King's army at Pevensey, and Bevis in his grandfather's stead was summoned to bring in the Dean men to follow him.

The summons came in the evening to march next day, and before the messenger was a bowshot on his way to the next Manor, Dean was leaping into activity very different from the slow, circling rhythm of the farm that had held it before. The ten men were called in from the last of the haymaking, and Randal, coming into the Great Hall with his own leather gambeson, found the women making ready food for the march, and Reynfrey issuing arrows and spare bowstrings. He said to Bevis, who was there also, 'It must be hard for Reynfrey.'

Bevis looked at him quickly, with some trouble in his face, then gave a tiny backward jerk of the head into the shadows behind him; and when they had drawn aside from the rest, turned to look at him again. Bevis, very tall, very dark, very grave, suddenly not a boy any more, but a man. 'Randal, I—don't know how to ask this of you.'

'What is it?' Randal asked, but even as he asked there was a shock of misery in him, and he knew.

'Randal, it isn't only Reynfrey it will be hard for. You too.'

'You mean—I'm not to go with you to join the King's army?'

Bevis shook his head. 'It is for me to go. While grandfather is sick of his wound, I am d'Aguillon, and it is for me to take his levies into battle. But it is for you, who are also his squire, to stay with him.'

Randal said, mutinous for the moment, 'What would you do if you were all the squire he had? You would have been if

Herluin hadn't won me in a game of chess and given me to d'Aguillon as though I were a hound puppy.' That was unjust to everybody, and he knew it, but he was too miserable to care.

'Then le Savage would have taken the Dean levies with his own, and I should have stayed here. That is the way it must be when a knight has only one squire, this is the way it must be when he has two.' He flung an arm across Randal's shoulder. 'Don't you think I'm heart-sore enough about it?—Oh, curse you, Randal, we've done everything together so many years, I never thought one of us would have to go into his first battle without the other!'

Randal was silent a long moment. He had set so much store by this marching out to join the King's army; he had had impossible dreams of doing great things, the kind of dreams, connected with honour and other shining matters, that you do not talk about even to a stranger, let alone to your nearest friend.

'Very well,' he said at last, hoarsely. 'I'll stay with Sir Everard.'

'Good old Randal,' Bevis said. '*Good* old Randal,' and gave his shoulder the little shake that he used sometimes instead of words. 'Try to send me news at Pevensey, if—when there's any news to send.'

And Randal nodded, and turned away to carry the old leather gambeson with the scales on the shoulders back into the storeroom again.

Next morning Sir Robert le Savage came by, leading his Broadwater levies, and would have gone tramping up to see Sir Everard, who was in a high fever and quite unfit to see anybody, while his men waited below, but that Ancret refused to allow him up the solar stair. He fussed and fumed a little, his big nose reddening as it always did in times of stress, but had to accept her ruling; and Bevis, himself white with worry, soothed him with a cup of the Manor's best cider, before they went on together. Randal, standing in the Hall doorway, watched them ride away, Bevis beside their stout neighbour, his hand on his long new sword, and Dean men and Broadwater men loping

155

behind them, their bow-staves across their backs. Cerdic looked round once, at the turn of the track, as though wondering if he would ever see the village under the downs again. Then they disappeared, heading for the ford.

Randal turned to the steward who stood beside him, thumbs in belt, staring after them too, and said, 'Does it get to matter less, when you're old?'

Reynfrey laughed and cursed on the same breath, and clipped him on the shoulder and bade him get back to d'Aguillon; but he didn't answer the question.

Randal had little time for brooding in the weeks that followed. There was work and to spare for everybody, with the Manor running ten men short and barley harvest drawing on; and when he was not helping Ancret to tend the Lord of Dean, he was working like a villein in the fields. Joyeuse followed him wherever he went, seeming to think that where he was, Bevis could not be far off; and even, as the weeks went by, brought him a flint or a piece of firewood once or twice, though always in a bothered way as though her mind was not quite on what she did. News trickled over the downs from time to time; de Bellême had come out for Duke Robert, bought by the promise of more lands in Normandy, and on the other side of them, de Warrenne, Lord of the Honour of Lewis, was out too. They heard of the King's army mustered at Pevensey, waiting for the invasion, and then that the King's fleet had gone over to the enemy; and they slept at nights half listening for the hoof drum of Norman cavalry sweeping across the downs. They heard that Duke Robert had landed, not at Pevensey as his father had done, as any right-minded conqueror would do, but at Portsmouth; and the King's army was hurrying westward to give him battle. On the day that d'Aguillon, looking like his own grey ghost, first came out leaning on Randal's shoulder to sit in the sun before the Hall doorway and listen to the voices of the reapers in Muther-Wutt Field, they heard that there was to be no fighting after all. The two armies had come together at Alton, and the two royal brothers had met between their armies and come to terms. Henry was to keep England but pay Robert two thousand pounds a year. Robert was to keep all

Normandy save for Henry's own Castle of Domfront, and each
was to be heir to the other if he died without a son.

The English army was disbanded again, and soon after the
last sheaves were carted, Bevis and the Dean men came marching home, Bevis bright-eyed and mocking, saying to Randal,
'Well, you didn't miss much, save for seeing the King's camp
like a city of tents. All we did was to sit on our rumps and
scowl at each other, while Brother Henry and Brother Robert
haggled.'

Somehow it all seemed a little flat.

For a while, Sir Everard continued to mend. The wound
under his collar-bone was healed, thanks to Ancret's salves and
the spells she crooned over them. They had a golden autumn
running late into the winter, and towards the end of it, when
the perry making and winter slaughtering were over and the
pigs had been driven down into the Weald to fatten on acorns,
he was out and about the Manor again. But then the winter
came, with its whistling winds through the Great Hall, its cold
and dark and shortage. Sir Everard developed a dry cough, and
when at last spring came again and the fires of May Eve flared
on the Bramble Hill, it seemed to Randal that his Lord was
thinner and grew tired more easily than he had done last
autumn.

That summer Dean was left in peace to harvest its barley
with its full tally of men, for the King did not call out de Braose,
though he himself spent the campaigning season driving de
Bellême from one to another of his castles; from Arundel to
Bridgenorth, from Bridgenorth to Shrewsbury, and at last back
to Normandy where he would inevitably make common cause
with Duke Robert. Randal thought of Herluin when that news
came, thought of him with a small aching sense of loss. Whenever he heard that de Bellême was at Arundel, he had always
had the feeling that at any hour, at any moment, he might look
down the track to the ford, and see the long, fantastic figure in
monkish black with the golden sleeves come riding up it. And
they would wave to each other in the distance, and when they
came together, Herluin would sit his horse looking down at him,
with that twisted smile of his, and say, 'Well, Imp, was I

right?' and he would say, 'Herluin, you were right.' But now, that would never happen.

There was another sense of loss on Randal, too, that autumn, or rather, the shadow of a loss that was yet to come.

Sir Everard's cough had seemed to improve through the summer, but with the autumn it returned. And on a wild evening of early December, just as he was making ready to go down into the Hall for supper, he suffered a bout of coughing deeper and more racking than any that had gone before. He pressed his hand to his mouth, half leaning over the back of his big chair for support, and when at last the attack spent itself and he took his hand away, it was stained with bright spots of blood.

The eyes of his two squires met for one shocked and sickening moment; and then Bevis, his arm round his grandfather's shoulders, said, 'Go and get Ancret.'

Ancret had lived up at the Hall since Sir Everard was wounded, just as she had done when Bevis was a baby. Randal found her without trouble, and she dropped her work in the strawberry plot and came hurrying, but not, it seemed to him, surprised, rather as though it were a summons that she had been waiting for. When they reached the solar, Sir Everard, looking much as usual, though somewhat spent and grey, was lying back in his great chair beside the hearth, his head turned to watch through the narrow window, the windy sunset beyond the downs that was echoing the colour of the burning apple logs. Bevis stood beside him, and old blind Matilda, who spent all her life now dreaming in the sun when there was any, or by the fire when there was not, lay at his feet. There was a great deal of silence in the room; more silence, Randal thought, than he had heard in a room before.

Ancret went to the old knight, and stooped to look into his eyes. She seemed no more shocked or upset by what had happened than he did himself, and something passed between them that was almost a smile, as though they shared some secret that nobody else knew. Then she brought water with certain herbs broken into it, and bathed his face and hands.

Bevis, watching her, said more harshly than he had ever

spoken to her in his life before, 'Can you not do more than that? More than just wipe off the stains? Something to stop it happening again?'

Ancret looked up. 'Nay,' she said, 'neither man nor woman of this world can do that. The blade pierced my Lord's lung. It is finished.'

And Randal knew what the secret was; the secret that she and d'Aguillon had shared between them this year and more.

Sir Everard looked at his two squires, and his straight mouth curled up at the corners. 'Na na, never wear such down-daunted faces for me. I am an old man, children; I have had a good life, and now the time draws near to lay it down; there is nothing for beating the breast in that.'

His gaze, the dark, straight gaze that Randal had disliked so much in the early days, had gone back to the flaming colours of the sunset that seemed spreading into the room itself. 'I should like to see the spring come running into this valley of ours, once more . . .'

Bevis, with his hand on his grandfather's shoulder, stood also staring into the sunset. His face was suddenly thin and taut, and nothing about him moved except the muscles in his throat as he swallowed.

Randal broke down and cried like a child, with his head on d'Aguillon's knees, the great hounds whimpering against him.

D'Aguillon looked down at his tangle of pale hair with a kind of half-amused wonder, and said, 'Randal—do you love me, then?'

'If you take a half-starved dung-hill whelp and bring it up to be your hunting dog and hearth companion, you're likely to find in the end that the silly brute loves you!' Randal wept, almost defiantly.

D'Aguillon was to see the one more spring that he longed for. Christmas passed, and Candlemas, and the valley was full of the babble of lambs again, and the plovers at their mating up on Long Down; and before the night frosts were over, they made him a little wattle hut like a hunting bower among the apple trees behind the Hall, for he found it easier to breathe there than between walls.

Once or twice that winter, messages had passed to and fro between Dean and Bramber where the old Lord too was dying. The last came on an evening early in April, clerk-written on a scrap of parchment as the others had been.

*I am away; see that you follow my banner as close as you did at Senlac.*

Adam Clerk read it to Sir Everard, and the old knight smiled at the grim jest, and bade them send back word that he rode in the very shadow of de Braose's banner. But de Braose never got that message. A few hours after, they heard that he was dead.

Two days later, Sir Everard, always a quiet man, died on the quietest of spring evenings, with the first white pear blossom unfurling on the old tree by the garth gate, and the first nightingale of the year singing in the river woods.

Matilda, who had lain beside him all that long while, died in the same night. Privately, Randal thought that was Ancret's doing. The old hound could not have been left to grieve, and it saved Bevis, who would have had to give her the mercy-stroke, just so much more of sorrow.

So the dark Norman knight who had held his English Manor for more than half a lifetime, was laid beside his wife in the little flint church in the land that had become home to him; and his Saxon villeins grieved for him as deeply as they could have done for a Saxon Thegn. Bevis took his great sword with the damascened blade and the seal cut in the pommel, and swathed it in oiled linen and laid it away in the armour kist.

'When I am a knight, I shall take it out again,' he said, 'if ever I come to my knighthood now . . .'

If. That was always the question for a squire whose knight died, for he must find another knight with whom to finish out his squirehood; and since a knight was seldom made before his twenty-first birthday, Bevis had still two years to go. No good worrying about that at the moment, though. The thing that mattered now was to see that the spring ploughing got finished and the bank of the stream properly made up again where the winter rains had torn it down.

They had been helping with the torn bank, and were returning, thigh-wet, a few days later, when the hounds pricked up their ears, and Bevis said, 'Hallo, someone's coming.'

Looking down-stream through the hazels by the ford, Randal caught a glimpse of russet and blue cloth and the black arch of a horse's neck, followed by a flicker of chestnut colour where a second rider came after the first, up the steep slope of the bank. A knight, and maybe his squire behind him.

'I believe it's Sir Philip himself,' Bevis said. 'Come on.'

It was Sir Philip de Braose. A few moments later he reined in his big Percheron and stood looking down at the two muddy figures that had broken out of the hazel thicket to meet him. He held his left arm at the stiff falconer's angle, a hooded goshawk on his fist, and Randal saw the little wind ruffle her breast feathers that were barred and splashed brown on creamy amber, like that of an enormous missel thrush. Young de Braose looked at Bevis with the cold, grey eyes that were so exactly the colour of a sword blade. 'Ah, we are well met, Bevis d'Aguillon. I was coming up to the Hall in search of you, but now I need not ride so far.'

'Will you not come up to the Hall in any case, de Braose, and drink a cup of wine?' Bevis said, dripping chalky mud where he stood, but mindful of his duties.

De Braose shook his head. 'When you are a knight, then I shall come and claim a stirrup cup at the door of Dean . . . It was on the matter of your knighthood that I came to speak with you. You have—what—two years of your squirehood left to serve?'

'Yes, if I can find some knight to take me.'

De Braose quieted his fidgeting horse. 'I'll take you. Aylwin here'—with a beck of chin over shoulder towards the young man on the chestnut behind him—'will be made a knight at Whitsun, and after that I shall be in need of another squire. Come up to the Castle tomorrow.'

There was a silence, broken only by the tiny silver ringing of the goshawk's bell as she raised one foot. Then Bevis said, 'You are most kind, my Lord——'

'Nay, you will find that I do not do things for kindness. I

161

remember the friendship that was between my father and your grandfather, that is all.'

'—but there are two of us. Unless you can do with two new squires . . .'

De Braose turned his gaze from Bevis to Randal, and raked him with a long, cool stare. 'Both or neither, eh?'

'Don't be a fool!' Randal babbled under his breath, his eyes on de Braose's face, but his urgent muttering for his foster brother beside him. 'Bevis, don't be a fool—I'll do well enough. I can fend for myself. Maybe I'll do a voyage with Laef Thorkelson. I'll come back to you when you're a knight.'

But Bevis simply was not listening. 'Both or neither,' he said to de Braose with a curious gentleness.

De Braose looked from one to the other, frowning. Then abruptly the frown vanished and he flung up his head and laughed. 'God forbid that I should part Roland and Oliver! Come up to the Castle tomorrow, both of you.'

# 13

# THE RED-HAIRED GIRL

SUNSHINE through the hinder door of the kennels splashed on the brindled and tawny coats of the hounds newly in from exercise. A fly with a dark blue, iridescent body danced and hovered above their heads, just out of reach of their snapping jaws, then zoomed out through the door into the kennel court where more of the great Talbots and Alaunts lay sprawled on the little plot of summer-dry grass. Randal watched it go, his hand still fondling the great rough head against his knee. He had come down from the Keep with word for Guthlac the chief huntsman that de Braose wished to see him about the choice of young hounds for the hart hunting. And when the huntsman had stridden off to answer the summons, he had lingered behind to make much of old Rollo, who was a favourite of his. The afternoon was his to do as he liked with, but he never knew quite what to do with off-duty time when Bevis was not off duty also. Thuna oozed towards him, jealous of the attention he was spending on Rollo, and nosed at his hand, gazing up at him with eyes of liquid amber and bee-brown. Her soft coat in the sunlight was tawny gold, like Joyeuse's at home at Dean.

Dean. His thoughts, lazy in the afternoon heat, went off to the Manor under the downs. It would be good out at Dean now. Probably they would just have finished getting in the hay. It was more than a year since he and Bevis had come to Bramber as de Braose's squires, and the Manor had passed into de Braose's keeping until Bevis reached his knighthood. But Reynfrey was still the steward, and when they got the chance of a few hours at home, everything was just as it always had been, save that Sir Everard was not there. Not that the chance came very often. As far as work went, life was easier as well as gayer than it had been at Dean; there were plenty of amusements, hunting and hawking, minstrelsy in the Great Hall at nights; but the squires were always with their Lord, or at least on call, and it was seldom enough that they could count themselves free for a day or a half-day, to have out Swallow and Durandal and ride home. Maybe it was because these visits were so few and so brief, that they seemed always to shine a little in the remembering, as though they were woven of something richer than the fabric of every day.

Rollo had fallen asleep. He was wise and strong with the garnered wisdom and strength of his many years' hunting; but he was old. Probably this would be his last season. He was hunting now in his sleep, paws and muzzle fluttering, and tiny, oddly pathetic whimpers breaking from his throat as he picked up the scent of the dream hart and belled and bayed the proud and eager message to the dream pack behind him.

'Ho moy, ho moy, hole, hole, hole!' Randal encouraged him softly, his hand on Thuna's head. 'Oyez, a'Rollo, hark to Rollo! Hark to Rollo the valiant.'

Suddenly he became aware of other voices in the kennels, voices away up at the far end, from the direction of the stall where Linnet, de Braose's favourite bitch, lay with her new litter of puppies. The stubborn growl of a boy's voice, and a girl's clear tones raised and angry.

'Let me pass! Let me pass this instant!'

Better go and see what was happening. Randal gave a parting pull to Thuna's left ear, and got up. He went through the next bay of the kennels into the far one—the long range of the building was divided into three so that they could shift the hounds about to clean and air the compartments—and found himself in the midst of a fine battle scene.

In the entrance to the stall where Linnet and her puppies were, Perrin the dog-boy was confronting a tall girl with hair as red as Hugh Goch's, as red as winter bracken with the sun shining on it, that seemed just now to be all but flying out of its two thick braids with fury.

The youngest of the Lady Aanor's maidens had only been at Bramber for a few weeks and Randal had scarcely spoken to her, but he knew vaguely that her name was Gisella, that she was fourteen, and that she came from a manor away northward into the Weald where there were too many daughters even though two of them had been given to a nunnery. Fine, warlike nuns, if they were anything like Gisella, he thought, checking just inside the doorway, and wondering what, if anything, he was to do.

'My Lord gave orders her wasn't to be disturbed by strangers,' Perrin was saying doggedly, with the air of one repeating what he has said before.

'Disturb her? Who talks of disturbing her? Do you think this is the first time I have ever been near a bitch with young puppies?'

'I don't know aught about that, young Mistress. De Braose gave orders——'

'I will explain to de Braose afterwards,' said the red-haired girl with her nose in the air.

'It will be me that'll have to do the explaining afterwards, if I let you in,' Perrin said simply. And then, as she showed no sign of giving way, his voice rising into something that was almost a howl of injury and exasperation. 'Oh *why* don't you go back to your stitch-craft and leave what doesn't concern you to them as it *does* concern?'

The girl's eyes widened. 'Why, you—you impertinent oaf!' she spat, her face bright with fury. 'How *dare* you speak to me like that!' Her hand shot out, and she dealt him a sharp blow, not open-palmed as Randal would have expected a girl to hit, but with her clenched fist on the side of his face.

The sound of the blow fell, duller than a slap, into the close, dog-smelling quiet of the kennels, and for a long moment afterwards nothing and nobody moved. The boy had clenched his own fist, but gave no other sign, and stood staring straight before him with sullen blue eyes, while the mark of the blow flushed slowly crimson on his cheek and jaw.

All the careless blows and casual cruelties of his own early days surged up in Randal in that one moment as he watched, and he longed to catch hold of the girl and shake her until her teeth rattled in her cruel, stupid head. But the feeling was mingled with an exasperated helplessness, because he knew the ways of men and hounds but not girls, and certainly, save for giving her the shaking, which he supposed regretfully was out of the question, he had not the faintest idea how to deal with a girl as angry as this one seemed to be.

'Gervase is trying out a new horse in the river field,' he heard his own voice saying with careful courtesy, as he stepped forward. 'Maybe you would like to come and watch him, Mistress Gisella.'

She swung round and stood looking at him as he reached her side, her eyes flickering with scorn. 'You sound just as though I was four years old and you were trying to coax me out of here with a sweetmeat.'

That, Randal realized with fresh exasperation, was perfectly true.

'If you'd not be treated as though you were four years old, maybe you'd best not behave as though you were,' he snapped. 'Now you come out of here and leave Perrin in peace.'

For a long moment they stared at each other, the girl's eyes stormy and challenging, Randal's grimly determined. Then, with a small, furious shrug, she turned to the outer door. Randal followed behind her as she stalked out with her nose disdainfully in the air.

Outside in the bailey where the heat danced a little on the cobbles, she rounded on him in a fine, singing passion. 'And you a squire—going to be a knight some day, I suppose—and you take that wretched dog-boy's part against *me*, after you heard how he spoke to me!'

'He was in the right,' Randal said levelly. 'He had de Braose's orders. And de Braose was right, too. Bitches are easily upset in the first few days.'

'Do you suppose I don't know that? Always I went among my father's hounds whenever I would; I helped tend the bitches and their puppies. I've been with them when they whelped before now.'

'They knew you; Linnet doesn't,' Randal told her flatly. Then, as he saw her mouth open for a furious retort, he added, 'And maybe you did not hit whoever was in charge of them. It was a coward's trick to hit Perrin.'

She flushed, but said defiantly, 'Why?'

'For the obvious reason that he couldn't hit you back.'

Gisella swallowed, and said in a slightly smaller voice, 'Because I'm a girl, you mean?'

'Oh no. If you had been one of the kitchen wenches I don't doubt he'd have clouted you back as you deserve. Because you are one of the Ladies from the Great Chamber.'

There was a little silence, while they stood in the midst of the crowded bailey and glared at each other, and he saw that she was in some sort driven into a corner. Then she gathered herself together again and lashed out, jibingly. 'It seems you have a vast deal of fellow-feeling for a dog-boy—almost as much as though you had been one yourself.'

Randal's temper went with a twang like a snapped bowstring. 'I was a dog-boy at Arundel, until de Bellême's minstrel won me from Hugh Goch with a game of chess, and gave me to Bevis d'Aguillon's grandfather to be bred up with Bevis,' he told her through clenched teeth. 'I've had a good many cuffs and kicks in my time, more than Perrin, maybe, but none from such a stupid, cruel, heartless little creature as you are!'

'Not until now!' Gisella said, also through clenched teeth, and flashed up her hand and dealt him a stinging, open-palmed slap—a girl's blow this time—on the cheek. 'There! I'm not a bit sorry I hit Perrin, and I'm *glad* I've hit you! That's what I think of dog-boys!' And she whirled about and ran from him back towards the Keep.

Randal stood for a moment watching her, the marks of her fingers burning on his cheek. Then he carefully unclenched his own fists, shook his shoulders as though to shake off the whole stupid incident, and strode off by himself to watch Gervase and the new horse.

Bevis was to be made a knight at Easter time. There would be many new knights made that Easter, five of them from Bramber, for the King was gathering his forces to invade Normandy, and a good supply of new knights was always made on the eve of a campaign.

Duke Robert's popularity when he returned from the Crusade had been shortlived; now his Duchy was in a state of chaos, and his harrassed lesser folk begging Henry to come and

take them. It was the younger brother's chance, and Henry
seized it as he had seized his chance before. The days of the
Lenten Fast were full of the steadily mounting din from stable
and store and armourer's shop. Harness was being readied up,
war gear forged and mended, great bundles of arrows brought
from the fletchers, horseshoes, spare mail and weapons sealed
in barrels against the salt of the sea crossing, sheaves of spears,
bales of bandage-linen and wound salves that the Lady Aanor
and her women had provided, wine and salt meat and coarse
barley meal in sewn skins, all made ready for taking down to
the merchant ships that lay waiting at the wharf below the
Castle mound. And all day and all night the great Castle rang
with the clash of the armourer's hammers, the voices of men,
the neighing of horses and the tramping of feet.

Now Easter was one day past, and the ring and throb of last-
minute preparations that had been silent since Good Friday, had
sprung up again more urgent than ever. Tomorrow the can-
didates for knighthood would keep their vigil in the Castle
chapel, kneeling with the new swords that they were so soon to
use laid before them on the altar steps; Randal, hurrying up
with Bevis and Gervase de Machault to the Keep at supper
time, thought that the ring of hammer on anvil, where the
Master Armourer was renewing a link in a hauberk, sounded
like the note of a struck bell; a fiercely insistent note that seemed
to get inside your head and go on beating there, bright as the
sparks that flew up from the anvil in the hurrying grey and
silver of the windy day.

De Braose's senior squire, a strong and very ugly young man
with a disarming grin and a trick of making friends, flung an
arm across Bevis's shoulder as they hurried. 'I wish you were
going to keep your vigil with the rest of us tomorrow. What do
you want to go skulking off to that Manor of yours on your own
for?'

'Not on my own. Randal is going with me,' Bevis said
quickly. And then, 'Being knighted is one of the things that can
only happen once—like being born or dying. I want it to happen to me in my own place, with my own folk around me.'

'De Braose wasn't best pleased, was he?'

'No.' The seriousness that had touched Bevis's voice the moment before, splintered into laughter. 'He said I was a pest, and the Lord of Bramber had other things to do just now than ride half over to Shoreham for the very doubtful pleasure of dubbing me knight.'

'What did you say to that?'

'I told him I was very sure that le Savage would ride over from Broadwater to give me the accolade, for my grandfather's sake.'

Gervase whistled dolefully. 'And you would really take your knighthood from that old cider barrel instead of de Braose, just for the sake of being at home?'

'He was my grandfather's friend,' Bevis said, carefully avoiding the question, as they swung into the alleyway behind the long row of workshops.

But it had not come to that, thought Randal who had been present at the interview. De Braose was not the man to have it said that one of his own squires had had to turn elsewhere for his knighthood. He remembered the Lord of Bramber saying with a bark of laughter, 'Have it as you wish, then; go free of your squirehood a day early, and take Randal with you. I ride down to Shoreham after the ceremony here is over, on some business of horse transports; and I'll turn aside to give you the accolade if you will give me the stirrup cup you once promised me.' He had even given Bevis in advance the tall Spanish stallion he would have given him afterwards, for it was his custom, as it had been the old Baron's, whenever he made a knight, to give him his first war-horse.

So tomorrow they would ride home to Dean, the Bramber years behind them, and ahead, only a handful of days away, the time when Sir Bevis d'Aguillon and Randal his squire would be sailing with the King's host for Normandy.

At that moment two things happened in quick succession. Firstly Randal saw that somebody had left the garden door open. Usually the door of the narrow Castle garden where the Lady Aanor and her women brought their sewing in the fine weather was shut to keep out stray dogs, pigs wandering from the butcher's yard, scullions and other such creatures. But now it stood wide, letting out the luminous, grey-green turmoil of wind-tossed, budding branches into the garbage-strewn and rain-puddled alleyway below the Keep. Secondly there broke out behind them a great baying and snarling, followed by a rush of flying paws; and two of de Braose's great wolfhounds came streaking past, the foremost carrying a red bone from the butcher's yard, the other in furious pursuit. Math and Mathonwy were brothers, even as Bran and Gerland of the Arundel days had been, but all the Castle knew how little brotherly love there was between them when either had a bone.

'One day these brutes will kill each other,' Randal said, as they circled a pile of stacked timber and sprang yelling into view again; and even as he spoke, Mathonwy, seeing the open door and the sheen of grass and leaves beyond, swerved in his tracks and shot through, followed by Math with every hair along his spine bristling like a wolf's.

Randal heard the rush and scatter of their paws, and the sudden sing-song snarling as Mathonwy, finding that there was no other way out, turned to rend his brother; heard also one small human cry, cut short and not repeated.

'Someone is frightened in there,' Bevis said. 'Come on.'

'No, I'll go. We're late already and you two are on duty for supper,' Randal said over his shoulder, already doubling in his own tracks towards the garden door.

Inside the narrow garden, a tall girl with red hair stood pressed back against the wall in the far corner where the two great hounds had penned her, half engulfed in their struggle as they rolled over and over, each striving for a throathold. Randal saw the strained stillness in her face above the whirling slavering turmoil of their bodies, and dived into the fight himself, no longer Randal the squire but Randal the dog-boy. How many yelling dog fights he had broken up, and how many scars of old bites he had to show for them! He twisted one hand in Math's throat, hammering between Mathonwy's eyes with a clenched fist, snarling at them, not as a man giving orders, but in something very like their own tongue. This was something they were not used to, and it seemed to puzzle them and come between them and their deadly purpose. Mathonwy snapped at the boy's wrist, but did not hang on. Sullenly, panting and snarling, they allowed themselves to be flung apart. Randal caught up the bone from where it lay at Gisella's feet, and turned back to the door, holding it above his head, the two great brutes with every hackle raised along their spines leaping and slavering about him as they tried to reach it. He kicked them out into the alleyway, and flung the bone over the nearest wall, where he thought it might take them some time to find it, then rattled the little deepset door to, and turned again to Gisella.

She had come out from her corner, and stood beside the turf seat under the still bare quince tree. The blue of her torn and muddied kirtle made a patch of strong colour in the hazy greens and greys of the awakening garden, but not so strong as the angry, sparkling red of her hair.

'All's over,' Randal said. 'They can't get in through the closed door even if they wanted to, and they'll take their quarrel elsewhere now.'

'Good,' said Gisella breathlessly, with the colour coming back in two little crimson patches on her cheek-bones. 'So now you can go away and—and not have to stop here and play the hero any more!'

Randal felt slightly jolted in the stomach. He had not expected to be thanked, but he had not expected quite such a rebuff, either. He stood and glared at her, while she glared back. They had taken great care to ignore each other ever since their first encounter, but if she still wanted an open fight, then she could have one.

'If you feel like that, I am sorry I came at all,' he said at last. 'I don't suppose Math and Mathonwy would actually have killed you, they were too busy trying to kill each other. But I thought you sounded frightened—despite being so used to your father's hounds.'

'I wasn't frightened, I was startled,' she said crossly. 'I wasn't expecting anything, and I've never actually had two brutes the size of war-horses fighting on top of me before.'

Something in her crossness struck Randal as funny, and despite himself, he grinned. 'Well, if you want no more rescuing,

173

I'm away. You had best come too, or you will be late for supper.'

'Go and get your supper. I've still to find the Lady Aanor's scissors. She thinks she dropped them here——' And then, glancing down as though she thought he might be hiding them somewhere about himself, she saw his wrist, where the close-fitting linen of his shirt sleeve was torn and stained with crimson, and her face and voice changed on the instant, as though she turned before his eyes into another and very much gentler person. 'Oh! You're bitten! Show me.'

Randal had been bitten so often before he was seven years old that it no longer seemed to him a thing to make a fuss about. 'Not much,' he said. 'Mathonwy was not really giving his mind to it.' He pulled up the tight sleeve and sucked his wrist and spat blood into the roots of a rosemary bush.

'Show me,' she persisted, and when, with a shrug, he held his arm out to her because it was less trouble than refusing, she touched the torn skin with one finger. 'Oh, it *is* a bite! It must hurt—and I didn't even thank you.' She swallowed, and looked up. 'But I do thank you. It was splendid, the way you parted those two!'

'It is a thing I've done often enough,' Randal said. 'I'm a dog-boy—remember?' Odd, how that rankled.

There was a long silence in which he heard the insistent bell note of the armourer's hammer ringing to war, but small and shut out beyond the high wall; and the soft hushing of the wind through the budding twig-tangle of the Lady Aanor's beloved briar roses. Then Gisella said in a small, steady voice, 'I am sorry about that. And I'm sorry I hit you, and I'm sorry I hit Perrin.'

Randal was so surprised that he simply stood and stared at her. And after a few moments she said in the same small, steady voice, 'Now it is for you to say you are sorry that you called me a stupid, cruel, heartless little creature.'

At first he was not sure whether she was laughing at him; then he realized that she was completely in earnest. But he still hesitated. He was not going to say he was sorry for the things he had said if it was not true; oddly, he felt he owed the red-haired girl that, not an empty apology for courtesy's sake, but the truth. But even as he hesitated, he knew that if she was sorry, so was he.

'I am sorry I called you a stupid, cruel, heartless little creature,' he said at last, without a shadow of a smile.

Her eyes were fixed on his face, very wide and grave. Grey-green eyes with a feathering of tawny gold. 'I'm not really,' she said. 'Not stupid and heartless, I mean. But I was so miserable and—and homesick, and I *did* have a lot to do with my father's hounds, and when they said Linnet had got puppies, I thought —I thought I would go and see them, and it would be just a little bit like being at home. And then Perrin wouldn't let me in, and I got angry because I was so m-miserable, and then you came, and I was ashamed as well as miserable.'

'And that was why you smacked my face and flung "dog-boy" at me—because you were ashamed?'

'Yes,' said Gisella simply.

They were sitting, turned to face each other, on the turf seat now, without any recollection of having sat down there, without at all noticing that there was anything odd in their doing so, when they had been enemies so short a time ago.

'Are you still homesick?' Randal said after a little while.

'Often. But I'm more used to it now.'

Another silence, and then she added hesitantly, 'I suppose that is a thing that cannot happen to you, anyway—feeling homesick?'

Randal was gazing into the wind-ruffled grey-green depth of the rosemary bush, as if he were looking through it, and seeing a track leading from a ford, and a thin old knight on a great war-horse riding up it, with a small boy with a whip-scarred back and strange feelings waking in his small, sore heart, mounted on his saddle bow. 'You don't know Dean,' he said, 'or you'd not say that.'

'Dean?'

'Bevis's home—and mine since I was ten years old—over the downs that way, towards the sea.' He turned again to her, with a deep contentment. 'And I'm going back there tomorrow.'

'You? Are you going tomorrow?' she said quickly. 'I knew

Bevis was going, because he wants to be knighted among his own folk. But you're de Braose's squire—you're not going to be knighted yet.'

'I'm only de Braose's squire until Bevis is knighted. When we sail for Normandy, I shall be d'Aguillon's squire, not de Braose's.' Randal hesitated a moment, and then added, 'I shan't ever be knighted, you know.'

She sat and looked at him out of a sudden stillness, frowning a little. 'Why not, Randal?' It was the first time she had used his name.

'It is no good being a knight, when you have not the where-withal to furnish your helm. And it's none so bad a life, being a squire.'

'But that's not fair! You'd make a better knight than some that hold a dozen manors!' Gisella said in swift championship. 'Look at the way you got rid of those hounds—and after I had been so horrible to you!' She looked down at her hands folded in her blue lap, with the shadows of the bare quince branches dancing over them; then up again. 'I am glad it was you that came, Randal.'

'I am glad it was I that came, too, Gisella.'

A gust of wind stronger than any that had gone before swooped into the narrow garden, booming like a breaking sea in the branches of the quince tree, and setting the briars streaming like green spray. The rosemary bush flung up its arms in a sil-very turmoil, and as it did so, something bright among the twisted roots flicked at the corner of Randal's eye. He stooped quickly, and picked the thing from its hiding place. 'Here are the Lady Aanor's scissors that you were looking for.'

With the finding of the scissors, remembrance of the time and the rest of the world rushed back to them. Gisella snatched them from him and sprang up. 'Oh we're so late—so dread-fully late for supper. We must go!'

Randal also had come to his feet, and they stood for one moment looking at each other with a queer, unexpected wretchedness for something that they were losing before it could even be said to have begun. Then Gisella swooped down, and with the Lady Aanor's scissors clipped a sprig from the heart of the rosemary bush—the only sprig that was yet come into flower—and held it out to him.

'There, take it,' she said incoherently. 'You'll be going into battle—it's good to have something that somebody gave you, to take into battle with you.'

Randal took it from her, and stood looking at it, seeing as clearly as though he had never seen a sprig of rosemary before, the shape and the faint, washed-out blue of the fragile petals, and the silvery green of the narrow leaves; catching the dry, aromatic scent that came up to him from between his fingers.

When he looked up, Gisella was already gone, running as she had run that other time.

Randal fished inside the embroidered neck of his tunic and brought out the little washleather bag in which he carried his precious lump of raw red amber, opened it, and slipped the sprig of rosemary inside. He drew up the string of the little bag again, and returned it to the breast of his tunic. Then he too ran, but remembering to close the door in the wall behind him.

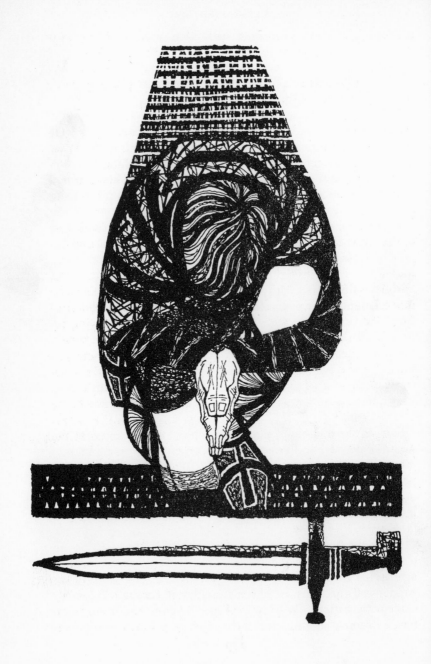

# SIR BEVIS D'AGUILLON

ABOUT an hour before noon next day, Randal and Bevis rode into the Hall garth at Dean, Bevis on the tall bay stallion that de Braose had given him, and Randal leading Durandal beside his own Swallow; the hounds as usual leapt all about them, and the squire years at Bramber were left behind. They were expected, and Reynfrey, who had been watching the track from the ford all morning in the intervals of the other things he had to do, came striding to hold Bevis's stirrup as he dismounted.

'Home again, then, d'Aguillon.'

It was the first time he had ever called Bevis by that name, and Bevis flushed a little as he heard it. 'Aye, home again to be made knight among my own folk, before the ships sail, Reynfrey.' He turned to greet Adam who had come scurrying up from his little cell behind the church when he heard the horses' hooves. 'Come to keep my vigil in our own church, where you made Randal and me keep so many vigils with our Latin when we wanted to go fishing.' And he took the little man's thin, brown hands and stood smiling down at him, then turned to the silently waiting Ancret, and hugged her without a word. Others of the household and Manor had come running at the sound of hooves, and Bevis in the midst of the growing knot of them was greeting and being greeted. But the smell of mutton pottage that had been stealing out to them from the big pot over the cooking fire in the Hall turned suddenly to the smell of burning, and Sybilla fled with a squawk, followed by their laughter.

Presently they ate in the Great Hall, Bevis sitting in d'Aguillon's place at the High Table, with Joyeuse crouched against his knee, and when dinner was over, Adam brought the Manor roll that must be checked and gone through. Reynfrey came with matters of his stewardship to be gone into in readiness for de Braose's coming, and Bevis must go over the equipment and stores of the ten men that he would be leading in a few days to join the King's army. For Dean in its small way was humming the same deep war-song of preparations that they had left behind them in Bramber; all just as it had been nearly four years ago, when the witch hunt came. The witch hunt! There had been no more word of de Coucy from that day; he must have got safely out of the country to join the Duke. Randal, helping Bevis and Reynfrey to check bowstrings, wondered if perhaps he might meet de Coucy in Normandy this summer, and cherished the thought as though it were a smoothly rounded pebble in his hand, everything in him reaching forward to the coming campaign, and Gisella already forgotten altogether.

But towards the day's end, when all things were seen to and set in order, Bevis and Randal went up the valley to find Lewin the Shepherd, and lay on their stomachs as they had done when they were boys, watching the shadows lengthen across the downs.

'If I were going to be made a knight tomorrow,' thought Randal, his nose in the sheep-nibbled grass, 'this is just how I should choose to spend the last few hours: up here with Lewin and the sheep. Nothing moving but the cloud shadows, and all Dean spread out below me from the Bramble Hill to the ford.'

When they got back to the Hall, le Savage had just ridden in from Broadwater. He had sent word that he would come, and here he was, clattering into the garth, his great round face shining in the April sunlight that dappled through the branches of the old pear tree.

Bevis ran to hold his stirrup as he dismounted, exclaiming, 'God's greeting to you, Sir Robert. This is kind of you, when you must have so little time to spare just now from Broadwater's affairs!'

Le Savage clapped a hand like a mottled ham on Bevis's shoulder, his big nose red with emotion. 'All things are in train at Broadwater and I've left Hugo in charge. Couldn't leave you without a made knight beside you at a time like this. Na na!'

Again they ate in the Great Hall; le Savage a good deal—especially of the wheatear pie—and Randal and Bevis rather less than usual. Randal was suffering from an odd breathlessness, a feeling of unbearable solemnity in his stomach that left little room for food. He jibed at himself for a fool; it was not he who was to spend all the long hours of this night's darkness alone in the little church beyond the garth, kneeling before his naked sword laid on the high altar, not he who would kneel down here in the Hall still a squire, and rise up a knight, sheathing his new sword—d'Aguillon's great sword with the seal cut in the hilt . . .

Supper was over and the daylight fading, and Bevis had left the table and turned in the doorway at the foot of the solar steps, looking back for him. They left the Hall and climbed the outside stair together, Joyeuse at their heels. Le Savage looked after them as though wondering whether he should come too, then shook his head and settled down with his cup of home-brewed perry, beckoning with his head for Reynfrey to come and talk to him by the fire, while the churls cleared up the Hall.

Randal set the torch he had brought in the socket beside the empty hearth, and the smoky yellow flare of it sent the grey daylight scurrying into corners where it hung like cobwebs under the rafters. The room felt extraordinarily empty; there had been no life in it for two years. But the sleeping-bench against the wall was made up, with hard, straw-filled pillows and the best sheepskin rug ready for the new Lord of Dean.

Bevis went to the carved kist where d'Aguillon's war gear had always lain, and flung back the lid. The smell of oiled linen and long-stored leather came up to them as he lifted out the great sword in its linen wrappings. Randal took it from him and laid it on the bed; the worn crimson belt with its powdering of tiny golden roses swung free as he did so, a bright slash of colour across the greyish fleece of the rug.

'I'll give it a rub up before you belt it on,' he said.

Bevis was already arm-deep in the chest again. 'I'm no knight that you should be my squire yet, Randal.'

'I shall be your squire tomorrow,' Randal said. 'It is but a few hours. Let me clean your sword for you, Bevis.'

They brought out the nut-shaped helmet in its oiled wrappings, the stained and weather-worn gambeson that Sir Everard had worn so often, the studded leather legstraps; finally, together, they lifted out the great ring-mail hauberk that chimed and rang faintly even inside its linen cloth as they moved it. Sir Everard's shield, the bright bird-snake on it freshly painted and the straps renewed (Reynfrey had seen to all that) hung where it had always hung, on the wall over the bed.

Everything was in perfect readiness, evidently Reynfrey had been busy; and Randal knew that it was really only for a whim that he was rubbing up d'Aguillon's great sword, even as he unsheathed the long streak of wavering, sheeny brightness that was the blade, and began his burnishing, while Bevis, his outer tunic pulled off over his head, stood watching him.

After a few moments he sheathed the blade again, and rose to help Bevis with his arming, and as he did so, their eyes met in the flaring torchlight, with a brightness shared between them. They had shared so many things in their time, but this was something greater even than their red amber had been. Then Randal took up the old gambeson and held it for Bevis to push his arms into the short sleeves, and when that was laced on, set to work on the legstraps. Bevis, being something of a dandy, wore close-fitting hose in the new fashion, instead of the old loose breeks, and the heavy, studded cross-gartering struck Randal suddenly as looking quite ludicrous over them. The laughter rose in his throat, as it will do sometimes when one is not in the least in the mood for it. He gave a kind of whimpering snort, and Bevis, still fiddling with the lacing of his gambeson, looked down to see the jest, saw his own legs, and caught the quick, strained laughter from him so that they rocked together like the veriest pair of urchins. And le Savage, in the Great Hall by the fire, heard them and grumbled to Reynfrey, 'Ah, we did not laugh so, on the eve of knighthood, when I was a boy. But it is different in these days; nothing is sacred to the wild lads now.'

In the cold solar, by the light of the flaring torch, Bevis and Randal had sobered from their laughter, and Randal was helping Bevis on with his hauberk. The thing weighed more than half as much as a man, and hung heavy with the dead, cold heaviness of its interlinking iron mesh as he heaved it up and Bevis, stooping, plunged his head and arms into it. Randal slipped round behind him and heaved it further on over his shoulders. The mail jarred and chimed as Bevis threshed with his arms, heaving also; then he stood upright, his usually pale face scarlet, and the hauberk slid down over his body, a darkly glimmering gown of mail to the knee, the torchlight jinking on his shoulders in flecks and fish-scales of light.

, 'Phew! Somebody ought to invent a better way of getting into a hauberk!'

Randal brought him the great sword and belted it on; lastly the war-mittens. The helmet would be left standing ready on the armour kist until tomorrow, since he must go bareheaded to his vigil; and the mail coif hung loose on Bevis's neck. He hitched at his sword belt, making sure that all was secure, then crossed the solar to take down the gaudy shield, moving less swiftly than usual. He was well used to wearing mail, as was Randal, for it was part of the training of a squire, but however well one was used to it, there was always that slowing up, that faint ponderousness in the movements of a man in full war harness.

He slipped the guige of the shield over his head, and stood a moment as though getting the feel of the harness, with Joyeuse snuffing in bewilderment at his feet and legs. 'It's a good thing grandfather and I were much of a size.' He looked about him. 'Is that everything?'

'Everything save the helmet. You're a credit to your squire.' Randal cast a quick look at the window, where the spring dusk hung blue and opaque beyond the torchlight. 'Time we were away. It is almost dark.'

Bevis glanced once more about the room, as though wondering what strange things would have happened inside himself before he came back to it in the morning with his vigil behind him. Then he whistled to Joyeuse, and turned to the head of the short stair.

Randal lingered just long enough to take the torch down and quench it on the hearth, then he followed.

In the Great Hall the men round the hearth heard the

weighted footsteps on the stair, and looked up, and as Bevis came into sight and checked in the stair-foot doorway, Randal, following close behind, saw their eyes widen in the firelight.

'Splendour of God!' le Savage growled. 'It is d'Aguillon.'

Reynfrey chuckled exultantly. 'Aye, 'tis d'Aguillon. Did you never see before that the boy was somewhat like his grandsire?'

'It is uncanny!' le Savage said. 'He even frets with his sword belt as Everard used to do. I mind him doing it while we waited by the horses on the morning of Senlac Fight.' He tramped to meet Bevis, and clapped him on the mailed shoulder. 'Well, boy, are you ready?'

'Quite ready, Sir Robert.' Bevis looked about him at the familiar faces. 'Where is Adam?'

'Gone to light the candles,' Reynfrey said.

Ancret came through the rest, like a dark shadow cast by the firelight, and set her hands on his shoulders. 'Ah, you have grown into such a tall man that I cannot reach you. Stoop down, little nursling,' and kissed him as his mother might have done.

They were all at the foreporch door now, spilling out into the deepening dusk, Bevis in front with le Savage, Randal following close behind, and the rest coming after him. Candle-light shone dimly gold from the high window of the church as they made their way across the garth; but it was not full dark yet, and Randal could see the familiar outline of the downs high above them, and the pale blur of blossom on the branches of the old pear tree that arched against the humpbacked dark-ness of the thatch.

Adam was waiting for them in the lime-washed church, still fiddling with the wicks of the two altar candles, and the scent of the bees' summer gathering stole out from the warm, golden wax. He came down to them by the door; a thin old man in a rusty brown habit, suddenly near to tears.

'Ah, Bevis, Bevis, my old heart is very full. It is a brave day for Dean that d'Aguillon comes home to keep his vigil in our own little church and be made knight among his own people.'

'For d'Aguillon also,' Bevis said, very quietly.

They stood in a little huddle in the doorway, watching him as he walked forward alone. He was standing at the east end now, dark and narrow against the candles. He drew the great sword from its sheath, and laid it on the Lord's Table, and knelt down, his head bent over his joined hands. The candlelight made a rim of brightness round his dark head; above him in the shadowy saffron of the gable wall the small east window was deeply and luminously blue, and behind him his shadow lay pooled across the long flagstone that marked Sir Everard's grave.

When Randal turned away, he found that the others had gone already. He followed them on feet that dragged a little, like the feet of someone very weary, or very sad; and there was a feeling on him of having just parted from something, a feeling that nothing would ever be quite the same again.

Back in the Hall, they gathered round the fire against the chill of the spring night, and flung on more logs so that the sparks flew upward. Randal, sitting with Joyeuse hunched disconsolately against his knee, heard the others talking, but not what they said; saw their faces in the firelight with a piercing clearness: old, brown Adam growing to look more and more like an autumn leaf these days; Reynfrey who looked, as always, to have been made of harness leather; le Savage with his big red face and bald yellow head—he was the only person Randal had ever seen who had face and head of two completely different colours, and the peculiarity had always fascinated him. But all the while he wasn't thinking of what he was seeing, at all; he was thinking of the little church just outside the garth, and Bevis kneeling with his drawn sword before him at the altar where the tall candles smelled of Ancret's bees.

When the time came, Randal helped as usual to make the Hall ready for sleeping. He brought rugs and straw-filled pillows and made le Savage's bed on one of the broad benches in the warmest and most secluded corner, serving him as Hugo his own squire might have done if he had not been left at Broadwater. But he did not lie down himself in his old place among the hounds by the hearth. Instead, he slipped out through the door at the stair foot, and made his way down to the foreporch end of the Hall, from which he could see the light shining—

more brightly now in the full darkness—from that small, high window under the pear branches.

He could not sleep tonight, warm among his fellow men, while Bevis . . .

A cold muzzle was thrust into the palm of his hand, and as he looked down, a furry shadow pressed itself against his leg, whimpering. Joyeuse too. He stooped and patted her.

'Come too, then, Joyeuse; faithful old Joyeuse—come, girl.'

He crossed the garth, the hound padding beside him, and slipping out through the gate gap, turned aside into the narrow green, tangled alleyway between the church and the hawthorn hedge. It was very quiet as he knelt down—something rustled among the grass and brambles, and then was still again; so quiet that he could make out the faint voice of the winter bourn, that he had always thought you could only hear from the Hall when it was in spate. He wondered if Bevis was hearing it too, inside the church. Joyeuse settled herself against him with a sigh, her great rough head under his hand, and their own quietness became part of the quietness of the night. Bevis need never know that his squire and his hound had kept his vigil with him.

At first light, when the green plover were crying over the downs, Randal got to his feet, cramped, cold and weary; and with Joyeuse still at heel, crept back to the Great Hall. The rest of the household were beginning to stir and must have noticed his absence, but they asked no questions. And now it was almost time to go and fetch Bevis from his vigil.

Randal and le Savage went together, the squire walking a little behind the knight.

The candles had guttered down to their prickets, and Bevis was kneeling exactly as they had last seen him. He did not move when they entered the church, indeed Randal did not think he even heard them. When le Savage stooped and touched his shoulder, he started, and looked up, blinking; then got slowly to his feet and stared about him, as though for the moment he was too dazed to be sure where he was. Then he saw Randal, and smiled ruefully and stooped and rubbed his knees.

They brought him up to the solar, with the first sunlight of a fine spring morning splashing through the tiny eastward-facing window, and stripped him naked, naked as the day he was born; they laid him on the sleeping bench, and piled the sheep-skin rugs over him, carrying out the long, complicated ritual that went to the making of a knight; and all with scarcely a word between them, for it seemed one of those times when there is no use for words. A knight in the making was supposed to sleep before the next stage. Randal wondered if anyone ever managed it, unless from sheer exhaustion. Bevis lay still with his eyes closed, his breath just stirring the curly hairs of the fleece drawn to his chin. But Randal knew that he was only making the pretence of sleeping that custom demanded. Well, he would rest for a while, anyhow, after those long, cramped hours. Le Savage went down to the Great Hall where the morning meal of bread and perry would soon be on the tables; but Randal had no more wish for food than he had had last night. He set Bevis's clothes and harness all in order to be put on again, then went and sat in the sunshine across the threshold of the open doorway, his back against the doorpost, his arms round his updrawn knees.

He heard a blackbird singing in the pear tree, and the deep, full-throated murmur of bees already busy in the fruit blossom, and little by little his head went down until his forehead was resting on his knees.

The next thing he knew was le Savage shaking his shoulder in kindly exasperation, and trumpeting into his ear. 'Splendour of God! Is this the time to be sleeping and snoozing? How if de Braose comes, and our young knight not ready for him?'

Randal glanced at the sun and shook his head. 'He'll not be here yet. But it is time we started, all the same.' He got up and crossed to the bed. Bevis's eyes were open, looking up at him with a little smile. He flung off the heavy sheepskin and stretched his arms wide above his head in the way that he used to do on fine summer mornings when the two of them had slept out on the downs. His arms above the elbows were very white; all his body where the clothes covered it from sun and wind was white as the flesh of a just-ripe hazelnut. He brought his hands down on Randal's shoulders, laughing, and sprang up.

It took a good deal longer to arm him this time than it had done before, because of le Savage's determined efforts to play his part, blundering about them like a good-natured bumble bee, mingling advice on the aims and behaviour proper to a knight, with hearty tugs on the wrong straps and laces at the wrong moment. They bore with him patiently, as though he were a well-meaning, very small child, but it was not easy. Presently Randal looked up from the sword belt. 'Look, I've only slipped it through the buckle and under the loop, and not put the tang through. One pull, and it's off.'

Le Savage snorted in approval. 'Aye, aye, can't spend half the day wrestling to get your sword belt off while the priest waits with his hands out, as I had to, I remember.'

While Bevis was being armed, they had heard the continual tramping of footsteps and the growing splurge of broad Sussex voices from below.

'The whole Manor must be packed into the Hall by the sound of it,' Randal said, standing up from his task. 'And 'tisn't only for free drink. I wonder if any of the old men among them are remembering that Sir Everard was an enemy overlord when they were young.'

Bevis looked at him as though it was a new idea. 'I expect so,' he said slowly, after a moment. 'But maybe it's only with their minds, not with their hearts. I hope it's like that.' He had begun to pace to and fro with that firm, slightly cumbered tread. He could not go down until de Braose came. He went and stared out of the window, leaning his mailed elbows on the sill. 'If blossom is anything to go by, we should have a good crop of pears this year, and enough perry to make the whole Manor drunk at Christmas. I wish de Braose would come; my belly is full of foam.'

De Braose came at last, with a nearing tramp of hooves that swung into the garth and clattered to a halt before the door. They heard the trampling and snorting of horses, the ring of a sword chape on stone. Reynfrey's voice sounded in greeting, and then de Braose's level, rather harsh tones and the jingling tramp of mailed feet. In the solar the old knight and the young, unmade knight and the squire looked at each other. Time to go down.

The Hall was as full of Manor folk as it was at Christmas, when they entered it a few moments later, the ten men of the levy standing together in a knot as though they felt themselves already a little apart from the rest. Even Lewin Longshanks stood just within the doorway, leaning on his crook, huge and quiet as always, and seeming to dwarf the whole place. The Lord of Bramber stood on the slightly raised dais, three other grey-mailed Bramber knights with him, and Adam beside them in the old brown habit that even *looked* as though it smelled of mice.

There was a stir as they crossed the threshold and every face from de Braose's to the boy who scared the crows turned towards them. Le Savage gave Bevis a small friendly push, and he walked forward alone as he had walked last night towards the Lord's Table and the glimmering candles. It came to Randal, watching, that the business of being made a knight was one of the lonely things of life, like being born, or dying.

Bevis mounted the low steps of the dais; Randal saw him give a quick tug to his sword belt, and drew a breath of relief as it fell open in his hand. Bevis laid d'Aguillon's great sword in little brown Adam's hands, and knelt down to take his vows. Adam fumbled with the sword, blessing it, then set his free hand on Bevis's bowed, dark head and bent over him a little. Bevis took his vows very quietly, so quietly that Randal could scarcely catch the words; it seemed as though he were making them to something deep within himself, and there was no need for anyone else to hear.

His vows taken, he rose, and knelt again, this time to de Braose, and set his joined hands between those of the Lord of Bramber. And this time the whole Hall heard him clearly enough, as he took the vassal's oath to his feudal Lord.

'Here, my Lord, I become liege man of yours for life and limb and earthly regard, and I will keep faith and loyalty to you for life and death; God helping me.'

He remained a moment kneeling at his Lord's feet, then rose and turned to take his sword again from Adam. Le Savage stepped forward to belt it on him, and Randal, standing in the doorway, suffered a stab of jealousy. The old fool was fumbling and bumbling with the buckle. He felt Bevis's exasperation as though it were his own and it was all he could do not to start forward and take the strap from the man's fat fingers. But the thing must be done by a knight, and not a mere squire. It was done at last, and Bevis turned to kneel once again, with bowed head, before the Lord of Bramber; and while the whole Hall held its breath, de Braose leaned forward and gave him a blow with his mailed hand, between neck and shoulder.

'Rise, Sir Bevis d'Aguillon.'

Bevis blundered to his feet a little blindly.

There was a long silence, while it seemed to Randal that the almost painful solemnity drained out of the air; and they heard, as he realized they must have been hearing it all along, the horses being walked up and down outside.

Bevis was looking round him as though in search of something or somebody. His eyes lit on Randal by the door, and clearly he had found what he was looking for, and for the moment nobody else in the Great Hall, including de Braose, mattered in the least to either of them.

The Manor folk, his own folk, were thronging round d'Aguillon now, even up on to the dais with de Braose still standing there fiddling with his riding gloves. And as Randal with a sudden joyful sense of having found again something that he thought was lost thrust his way through at last to Bevis's side, the Lord of Bramber brought his hand down once more on the shoulder of his newest knight, laughing. 'Now what about the stirrup cup that you promised me two years since, Sir Bevis? One cup of wine to drink damnation to Robert of Normandy, and I must be away. The ships are ready and we sail on the fourth morning from now if the wind holds. Get your fellows down to Shoreham by the morn's morning.'

# 15

# THE WEALDEN BLACKBIRD

It was strange, but in after years that summer of his first campaign which should have been vivid in his mind with the sharp-edged vividness that belongs to all First Times, never stood out much in Randal's memory. It was as though all the time something within him knew that next summer, not this, was to be the one that mattered.

The day after Bevis was made knight, they marched out with their ten archers down the marshy river valley through the downs to Shoreham, where the horse transports were waiting. They embarked with the rest of de Braose's following, and sailed on an oyster-pale morning tide. They joined a great and ever-growing fleet at sea, and glimpsed among them a vessel flying a pennant like a licking gold flame, which someone said was the King's. Most of them, Randal included, and all the horses, were miserably seasick. And then there was Normandy, dusty already in a dry spring. Henry landed at Barfleur in the Cotentin, his old Lordship, called in his vassals, and the allies—Flanders, Main, Anjou and Brittany—that he had been making for a year and more past, and marched on Bayeux. So Bevis and Randal went into their first battle together, after all. And through that early summer, with the last apple blossom falling and the fruit setting in the Normandy orchards, at Bayeux and Caen and on the rough march to Falaise, Randal gained the experience of a shield-squire, riding into action behind his knight; always a line of squires behind the knights, each to second his own lord in every way, help him if he were thrown, carry his spare lance, receive his prisoners, and in between whiles, maybe strike a blow or two on his own account. Randal came to know the sights and sounds and smells of battle, the dust kicked up by the horses, the rank smell of sweat and the sharp smell of blood, the flying thunder of hooves and the tempest-roar of shouting and the weapon-ring; the vicious sound that an arrow makes, passing within a hand's span of your ear.

When the English army returned home soon after harvest, he had seen his full share of fighting, and had the fading scar of a sword-cut on his forearm to compare with Reynfrey's; but still, none of it seemed very important. They came home with nine of the ten men they had marched out with, leaving Alfwine the ploughman dead before Caen, and the wailing of Alfwine's widow remained ever after the thing that Randal remembered most sharply about that summer's campaigning.

The whole campaign had left nothing settled either way. And next summer it would be all to do again. Henry would not leave matters as they stood; he could not. It must be a fight to the finish between Brother Henry and Brother Robert, now. And according to whichever of them went down, so would Normandy be master of England, or England master of Normandy.

The Manor grumbled when the preparations for war began again, as every Manor in the Kingdom was grumbling, and always had grumbled at such times. 'Ten men short, we were, last harvest and seemingly we'll be getting this one in ten short again—na, eleven, counting Alfwine . . . If our Norman overlords want fighting, let 'em have it to themselves, wi'out troubling the poor folk . . .'

Bevis, hearing two of them in this strain, told them with a flash of angry impatience, 'If you had not all talked like that when your Harold, that you sing so much about, called you to arms forty years ago, maybe you'd not have had us Normans with our wars to trouble you now!'

The villeins withdrew into silence. More than anything else, they were shaken by Bevis having spoken of 'us Normans' when it had been 'us English' with him all his life, as with their old Lord, and on one Manor at least, the grumbling ended.

The swallows were late that year, but they came at last to nest again in the great barn. The May Fire blazed on the crest of the Bramble Hill, and in the midst of making ready for war, it was time for sheep shearing. And then there came a day in early June that was the last day before they marched again to join the King's army. Bevis and Randal were both of them far more sharply aware of tomorrow's march than they had been the year before, maybe because then there had been Bevis's knighthood to think about as well. But they did not speak of it much to each other until darkness came, and they went out together as they always did, escorted by Joyeuse who had long since made it clear to the other hounds that it was her place and her's alone to go with her Lord on his evening round, for a last look at the horses before they slept. It had been raining off and on all day, a soft growing-rain that whispered through the river woods and dripped from the Hall thatch, but it had passed now, and the deep, still darkness was breathing with the scents of wet, refreshed earth; and as they came out from the stables, Bevis checked a moment, sniffing, his head up like a hound's, and said, as he had done so often when they were boys, 'Come away, Randal; there'll be a moon later, and we can't waste tonight snoring in the rushes.'

They did not. Part of that night they spent with Lewin Longshanks up at the summer sheep fold. Later, moving on again, they made a wide cast over the downs that brought them at last valleyward again by the bluff, out-thrust shoulder of the Bramble Hill. The smell of the summer dawn was already in the air, but the moon that had risen now swung high over the downs in a glimmering harebell sky, and the world was bathed in a light that seemed tangible as silver water, so that Randal felt suddenly that if he held out his cupped hands he would feel it trickling between his fingers. Joyeuse, loping ahead of the two young men, and looking round from time to time to see that they were following, was silver too, with no hint of her daytime gold; a silver hound running through a silver night, like some great feather-heeled hunting dog of the Fairy People.

As they came down to the Bramble Hill, the valley began to open to them, and they checked, looking out and down over marsh and woodland and strip-patterned field, to where the Hall trailed its straggle of village down the side coomb, all lying asleep in the remoteness of the moonlight. No, not all asleep, for as they looked, from somewhere at the foot of the village, a flicker of warm yellow light blinked out, telling of a kindled lantern.

'Someone is early astir,' Bevis said.

'Looks like Gudram's cottage; he'll be making ready to do you credit on the march—never one for a last moment flurry, our Gudram.'

'They're good lads to lead, even if they do grumble,' Bevis said, his pride in them lit with laughter.

'We English always grumble,' Randal said, still looking down through the elder scrub towards the tiny blink of gorse-yellow light. 'We always have grumbled and we always will.'

They moved on again, the old companionable silence falling between them once more. But after a while Bevis said, as though he had been following a train of thought, 'We English . . . Randal, do you remember grandfather saying that one day there would be no more Norman or Saxon, but only English? If this summer brings us victory in Normandy—one great victory gained by Norman and Saxon English fighting side by side—I think it will do more than all else could do to hammer us into one folk.' Another long silence, and then, thoughtfully. 'That would be an odd kind of revenge for Senlac!'

The scar of the May Day Fire still showed black on the turf, and at their right hand the great barrow rose, still under the rustling of the night wind through its elder bushes, with the strange potent quality of stillness that it always had—as though it shared in the stillness of the name-forgotten king who slept in the dark heart of it with his wrought gold and his weapons about him.

As Bevis and Randal, touched by its stillness as though it were a great wing that brushed over them, walked slower, and stopped, out of the darkness of the river woods below them rose one clear, perfect note of birdsong, long drawn and insistent, repeated again and again, then breaking into a shining spray of notes, a cascade of runs and phrases that seemed to shimmer on the ear. It was a song that the two young men standing up there among the bramble domes had heard often enough before; but surely it had never sounded quite like this, so that it was one with the white flood of moonlight and the smell of the elder flowers.

'Oh, listen!' Randal whispered, stupidly, for the whole night was already holding its breath to listen. 'Listen, Bevis, it's the nightingale.'

Bevis stood as though he were rooted, like the brambles and the elder scrub, into the hill beneath his feet. His head was up, his gaze not turned down to the dark woods below from which came the song but going out up the curving length of the dearly familiar valley to the long, low huddle of the Hall that he had been born in, under the steep stride of Long Down, and the Manor Mill by the ford. His thin face was remote and far off, as Randal glanced aside at him, as though he were hearing something else, something that was beyond the singing. In a little, he shook his head. 'It's a song spun from the moonlight. But if it were me up here in the hollow hill, and I were to wake tonight, it would not be the nightingale but the speckle-breasted thrush or our Wealden blackbird I'd be listening for, to tell me I was home again.'

Joyeuse, who had been rooting under an elder bush, came padding back to lay a rolled-up hedgehog at his feet. She was the only dog Randal had ever known who would carry a hedgehog without tearing her soft mouth to shreds. And Bevis stooped to fondle her head as she thrust against him. 'Nay, now, leave poor Tiggy be; what harm has he ever done you? But thanks for the parting gift, all the same.' He straightened up with a little shake of his shoulders and looked about him. 'It's been a good night, this one; the kind of night that is good to remember. But we must be getting back now, or we'll be all unready when the time comes for the march.'

The first blue mist of the September evening was beginning to rise, though the swallows still swooped and darted in the last of the sunlight about the battlements of Tenchebrai and over the heads of the two opposing armies encamped below. Randal, on his way back from seeing to Durandal, who like most of the spare horses was picketed at an outlying village, paused where the woods fell back a little, to glance out over the wide valley of the Orne. He could see the great castle still flushed fiercely tawny by the westering sunlight, though the huddled roofs of the little town at its foot were already dimming into blue and violet shadows, and the faint blue twilight and the autumn mists were creeping out from the oakwoods to mingle with the smoke of countless cooking fires that made a drifting haze of their own all across the great camp. Knowing where to look for them among all the other tents, the awnings and flying banners, the crowded fires and horse-lines, he could just make out the big, checkered tents of the Counts of Maine and Brittany, each pitched among their own men, and closer at hand, on a knoll of rising ground in the midst of the English camp, that had been an orchard before they cut most of the trees down to make room for it, the great weather-worn, crimson pavilion of Henry himself.

It was more than a fortnight since the English army with its Cenommanian and Breton allies had come out of the oakwoods by the wild road north from Domfront, and settled down to besiege this great Castle of William de Mortain—de Mortain, Lord of Pevensey in his day, until, like de Bellême, he had forfeited his English lands for rebellion against the King, and, also like de Bellême, had made common cause with Duke Robert in revenge. More than a fortnight—the smell must be getting somewhat thick in Tenchebrai by now, Randal reckoned. Well, one way or the other, it looked as though the siege could not last much longer, not now that Duke Robert had brought up his own forces to relieve his henchman's stronghold. Couldn't see the Norman camp from here, it was hidden by the oakwoods, but awareness of it seemed to quiver like thunder in the air over the whole valley; and every soul in the English camp knew that somewhere—not in the great crimson pavilion, but out between their two armies, maybe in the lea of a beanstack or under a poplar tree by the track side—Brother Robert and Brother Henry were met this evening as they had met between their armies before, to talk of terms.

Would anything come of it this time? Randal wondered. Fiercely he hoped not, as most of the camp were hoping not. Nothing save fighting could settle the thing in the long run, but one great battle now might do it, the one great victory that Bevis had spoken of, that would bind Norman and Saxon together in the common bond of Englishry. Was that what was coming tomorrow?

The chatter of a magpie from the woods behind him called him back from tomorrow, and he remembered that it was no part of a squire's duties to be standing thinking his own thoughts on the fringe of the war-camp. He strode on again, whistling tunelessly as he went, casting wide through the edge of the woods so as to come down from above on the derelict tanning shed where Bevis and a handful of other young knights had taken up their quarters; it was quicker so, than trying to make one's way through the teeming thickness of the camp.

But without knowing it, he must have made a cast wider than usual, and so he came on a place in the woods that he had not found before, a small clearing among the denseness of the moss-floored oakwoods, and in it a hovel of wattle and daub under a ragged thatch that gave somehow the effect of a filthy old straw hat pulled over its eyes, squatting amid seven gnarled and ancient apple trees, two bee skeps and a tethered goat. On one of the trees, and only one, the apples were already ripe; small, greyish apples with a scent of fennel about them that reached his quick nose even as he checked and stood looking up into the lichened branches. It was one of the tasks of a squire to forage for his lord, but in any case the idea of apples, the crisp juiciness of apples, at the end of that dusty day—Normandy seemed to him dustier than England—would have pulled Randal up in his tracks. While he stood there, a woman came out through the smoky darkness that hung like a curtain at the doorway of the hovel, with a wooden milking pail in her hand.

She was a very old woman, scrawny and twisted as one of her own ancient apple trees, with her head tied up in a folded cloth and little bright black eyes in a face all fallen together and made up of earth-coloured wrinkles. She checked at sight of Randal, and fixed him with a bright, beady stare, blowing her crumpled and toothless mouth in and out, but she did not seem surprised at his appearance; probably he was not the first of his kind to pass that way, and he rather wondered that she had managed so long to keep the goat.

'Well then, Englishman or Breton or whatever you be, and what is it that you're wanting?'

'Apples,' Randal said. 'A handful of apples for my knight.'

She let out a squawk of laughter and set down the pail. 'Sa, sa, it is only a boy after all! How old is your knight?'

'Two years older than I am,' Randal told her with dignity.

She flung up her hands. 'Does Henry of Coutances fight his wars with children, then?'

Randal would have protested hotly at this, but he had a feeling that to leave well alone, though bad for the dignity, was the way to get the apples he wanted. So he grinned cheerfully at the little old woman, standing with his feet planted wide apart, and towering over her, with his helmet, which he had unbuckled and pulled off, swinging in his hand.

'Maybe—but give me the apples, old mother.'

She looked up at him slantwise like a bird. 'Aye then, take as many as you can carry in that iron cap of yours, and give me a kiss for them. 'Tis a long and a weary long while since a fine young man kissed me.'

It seemed fair enough. Randal stooped, and put his free arm round her for good measure, the helmet still in his other hand. She smelled sour, but it was not the kind of sourness that a hound would have objected to, and nor did Randal. He kissed her, laughingly and kindly and clumsily, and stood back, grinning still.

The old woman cackled like a hen. 'None so bad, my bold young squire! None so bad for the first time.'

Meeting the snapping, cackling amusement in her little black eyes, Randal felt himself flushing. 'How do you know it was the first time?'

'Easily enough!—Any woman could tell you as much,' she said scornfully. Then, voice and manner abruptly changing, 'Aye, but there's another thing I'll tell you that's none so easy, about yourself,' and before he knew what she was about, she had put up her old, clawed hands and taken his face between them, and drawn it down to look into his eyes. 'When to-morrow's sun goes down, you'll be no man's squire, but your own knight.'

Randal felt a little prickling chill in the back of his neck; but he laughed, and shook his head between her hands. 'I shall never be my own knight. I'm the kind that stays a squire always. It costs money and acres to be a knight, and I have not anything of my own, save my sword and helmet.'

'None the less,' said the old woman very softly, 'knight you will be, before another sun goes down, and as to the acres——' Her voice trailed away; her hands were still on either side of his face, and he felt that he could not break from their hold on him, or maybe from the hold of her eyes. They were small, hard, bright eyes, their darkness very different from the shadowy darkness of Ancret's eyes, and he saw the reflection of himself in them, and the leafy reflection of the apple branches behind his head. Yet suddenly he had again the feeling he had had once when Ancret held him so, of sinking down into their darkness as into dark water, only this time it was a darkness of rustling leaves. In another moment they would part and let him through and close again behind him, and he would see—he would know—something that he could not bear to know. Already he could see it dimly, moving to meet him through the leaves . . . And then a bird flashed across from branch to branch of the apple tree above him, so close that the beat of its wings was in his ears; the sudden movement broke the spell, or else, as Ancret had done, at the last instant she let him go. 'Ah, but leave that for now—leave that until the hour brings it,' and she dropped her hands and stooped for the milking pail.

Randal stepped back, oddly shaken, and not sure why. For the memory of the uncanny moment was passing almost as soon as the moment itself.

'If you can foretell the future, tell me if we shall join battle tomorrow,' he said, jeeringly.

'Oh, aye, there'll be fighting tomorrow,' she told him, almost without interest. And something in her tone made him think again of Ancret, and Ancret's people, watching the later folk come and go, conqueror following conqueror, like a little wind through the bramble bushes. But if tomorrow did not matter to her, it mattered to him . . .

'Shall we win? Old mother, shall we win?' The question stuck in his throat.

She shot her lips in and out at him. 'Maybe you will, and maybe you will not. Have I not told you enough? Whoever has victory, I must milk the goat.' The last words were tossed to him over his shoulder as she hobbled towards the tethered animal. 'Away with you now. Fill your helmet and go.'

Randal stood for a moment looking after her, frowning a little as he tried to remember—something that he felt he had only just forgotten. Then he turned his attention to the apple tree, and picked his helmet full of little grey, fennel-scented apples. He hesitated when he had done, looking again towards the old woman, but as she still kept her back to him and had seemingly no more thought for him nor for anything save her milking, he finally shrugged, called out to her, 'God keep you, old mother. Thank you for the apples,' and set off once more on his interrupted way back to the tan shed.

He walked with the apple-filled helmet in the hollow of his arm, not whistling any more; thinking. Had she spoken truth? Was he really to win his knighthood tomorrow? Oh, but how could he ever be a knight? He shook his shoulders and determined to think no more about it, and of course went on thinking, dreaming a little, as one does dream of the shining and impossible things happening . . .

When he got back to the tan shed the day had faded almost to dusk, and the fire of brushwood and heathersnarls that burned in the wide, nettle-choked entrance had begun to cast a fluttering, tawny light over the faces of the men gathered about it and up into the lower branches of the giant old hornbeam that grew before the door. Martin, Gervase de Machault's squire, was roasting a rabbit over the fire on the point of his sword, and Gervase was there, and several of the young knights who had been squires with Randal and Bevis at Bramber. But of Bevis himself there was no sign at all.

'He's gone off to settle some trouble between his fellows and de Salynges',' Gervase told him, without much interest. Quarrels were common between the different Manors.

Randal hesitated, wondering whether he should go after him,

and if so what he should do with the apples, and in that moment a square and freckled youth said, 'Hé! I smell apples!' and reached out to grab. Others followed the action, and Randal stepped back, laughing but determined. 'Hands off, sirs! I forage for my own knight, not for you!'

'How many have you eaten yourself?' the freckled one demanded cheerfully. Wilfred was a Saxon. There were beginning to be a few Saxons and half Saxons among the young knights, these days; and, surrounded by Normans, he and Randal had always bickered together in friendly fashion when they were both squires. But it was not quite the same now that one of them was a knight.

'Does my helmet look half-empty?' Randal demanded, suddenly a little stiff.

One of the others sat forward, grinning in the firelight, his arms round his updrawn knees. 'Squire Virtue! Don't you like apples, then?'

And a third joined in the good-natured baiting. 'Splendour of God, you shock me, Roger! Do you suggest that Randal would pleasure himself on apples meant for Bevis's belly? Don't you know that Randal would give Bevis his head if Bevis had a use for it?—Randal, wouldn't you give Bevis your head if he asked you?'

Randal laughed, but felt himself flushing, and before he could answer the sally, Gervase struck in, saying as Randal had done a few moments before, 'Hands off, sirs!' Then with a grin towards his own squire, carefully turning the rabbit on his sword point, 'I'd like to think Martin would do as much for me.'

It was full dusk by now, and growing misty. Below them the cooking fires of the main camp were a little blurred, and shadows of bowmen and men-at-arms came and went between them and the brightness. A shadow loomed up through the twilight, and took substance, and Bevis emerged into the firelight that jinked on his ringed hauberk and the nasal of his nut-shaped helmet. The others greeted him with a cheerful clamour.

'Ohé Bevis! You've been a long time! Have your fellows slit the de Salynges throats to a man?'

'Not quite,' Bevis said, folding up beside the fire, and tipping his head for Randal to unlace his helmet, 'though there were knives out when I got there.'

'Were there so?' Gervase said. 'And what did you do about that?'

'Called them every name I could lay my tongue to in Saxon *or* Norman, and banged a couple of their silly heads together. All's well now . . . That rabbit smells good.'

'Never mind that rabbit,' Wilfred sniffed. ''Twill do no more among this lot of us than to flavour the black bread. Here's Randal come by a whole helmet full of apples and will not let us so much as smell one until you have eaten your lordly fill.'

But the one they called Roger, sobering all at once, said, 'Never mind the rabbit *or* the apples. Is there any news?'

'Yes.' Bevis ducked his head out from under the helmet as Randal lifted it off, and pulled back the mail coif from his flattened dark hair. 'Henry's back in camp. No terms.'

'So——'

'So we fight tomorrow.' He cocked up his head as he spoke, his eyes full of little dancing lights from the fire. 'Listen—you can hear it running through the camp, now.'

They listened, all of them sober for the moment. Randal, leaning back on his knees to lay Bevis's helmet beside his shield against the fire-dappled bole of the hornbeam, heard the voice of the little stream that had once fed the tan pits, and beyond it the evening voice of the great camp that seemed, even as he listened, to rise and quicken and take on a new urgency. So the old woman had been right in that at least . . . Oh, but it was an easy guess, anybody's guess. When he had asked her who would have the victory, which was a harder thing, she had turned sour and gone to milk the goat. And as for the other things she had said—there was a sudden flutter of wings among the branches of the hornbeam, as of a bird disturbed in its roosting by the firelight and the voices, and he half remembered something—something that had to do with the old woman . . . then lost it again as Gervase said quietly, 'It's Michaelmas Eve tomorrow. I'd forgotten; but one of our old

men-at-arms was saying that it was forty years ago on Michaelmas Eve that the Conqueror landed at Pevensey.'

'Forty years to turn the tables,' someone else said, and all
round the fire the young men looked at each other.

Then Bevis stretched his arms above his head, his thin face
splintering into laughter. 'That's for tomorrow. Meanwhile—
apples! Where are those apples of yours, Randal?'

The moment passed, and a little puff of laughter caught from
Bevis blew in behind it, for it seemed to them good to take life
none too seriously on the eve of battle. And in a little they were
all munching the small, grey, fennel-scented apples from
Randal's helmet that stood propped beside the fire, while they
waited for the rabbit to finish scorching.

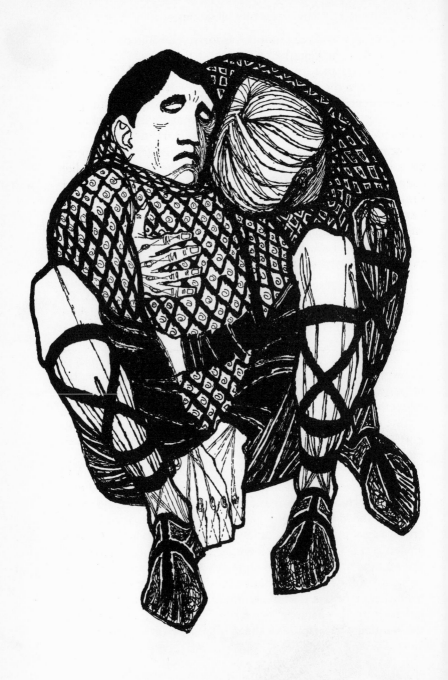

# 16

# MICHAELMAS EVE

It seemed odd to be waiting on foot to meet the shock of the Norman charge. Always, until now, the time of waiting for battle had meant to Randal the smell of horses, the uptossed mane and ceaseless, restless trampling; Swallow fidgeting under him, the nervously flicking tail of Bevis's war-horse just ahead. But the Saxon in him found it familiar, all the same. 'This is the way my mother's folk waited for war. This is the way we waited at Hastings, forty years ago.' And he was glad of it because it meant going into battle with one's own men, instead of being cut off from them in another part of the battle line, as had to happen if one's own men were foot soldiers. He was as proudly and harshly aware of the Dean men somewhere among the archers of the ranks behind him, as he was of Bevis standing spear in hand just in front.

Henry had dismounted his whole vanguard, indeed most of his army save for the Breton and Cenommanian cavalry on the left, and formed them into a solid phalanx to confront the Norman cavalry. It was only partly the old Saxon battle formation, for the men who had waited dismounted with Harold at Hastings had formed a single line of wedges; and this solid phalanx, built up of three such lines close behind each other, was of the Byzantine school. The combination was a new thing that had not confronted Duke Robert's cavalry before, and whether it was a good thing or a bad only that day's fighting would show.

Away ahead of him through the spears, through the blue and green, russet and crimson of lesser banners, Randal caught the golden gleam of the King's banner, lifting and spreading sideways on the dry, gusty wind, and only a little behind it the blue and gold of the lion battle badge that de Braose had taken after his father. It was a day of changing lights and eddying, dust-laden wind, this Michaelmas Eve; a day of pale, dry colours, the weather-worn stones of the great Castle itself that frowned out over the two armies, the sombre, gold-flecked darkness of the oakwoods, the fading tangle of wild marjoram along the river banks, and the stubble of the spent corn-land, all a little paler than usual. And even among the two great armies, no depth of colour nor spark of light on hauberk ring or shield boss; only the constant dry, dusty movement of banners and pennoncels in that little fretting wind, and the darting to and fro of swallows overhead.

Duke Robert, Randal knew, was in command of the Norman centre, William de Mortain of the vanguard and de Bellême of the rear. De Bellême . . . Looking out over the empty strip of corn and beanfields between, to the dun-dark masses of the Norman cavalry with the farther woods behind them, he remembered with sudden, startling vividness the white face under the flame of red hair that was just a little darker than Hugh Goch's, the voice with its hint of mockery that was just a little darker, too. And where de Bellême was, there would de Bellême's minstrel be also. Odd to think of Herluin somewhere among those waiting enemy ranks—or maybe, since he was a singer of songs and no fighting man, with the camp servants and the baggage train. But Taillefer, the Conqueror's minstrel, had ridden with him at Hastings—had led the charge, singing one of the songs of Roland, tossing up his sword and catching it again as he rode. He could imagine Herluin doing that, Herluin with his casual, loose-limbed grace and drawling courage. He could imagine how the sword would flash in the sunlight, bright as the images of the Song of Roland . . .

But there was no sun, nothing bright and flashing save the notes of a Norman trumpet blowing thin on the fitful wind, for the end of the waiting time and the onset of battle.

Randal felt his heart tighten under his breast bone as the trumpet echoed away into silence between the oakwoods, and in its place came the sudden, swelling thunder of horses' hooves rolling towards them. The English ranks braced themselves for the shock, the dismounted knights and squires of the foremost ranks settling each his spear butt under the hollow of his instep as though to take the shock of a charging boar. Randal, crouching to his own spear with the rest, saw with painful acuteness how the pattern of the hauberk rings across Bevis's slim, braced shoulders slid with the tensing of the muscles underneath. Then the whole Norman van led by de Mortain was upon them. The English ranks shuddered as a dyke shudders under the blow of a breaking sea, but stood firm, and a roar burst up from both sides as defiance and counter-defiance and the blood-rousing battle-shout was flung to and fro above their heads.

How long that phase of the battle lasted Randal never knew; it was a thing without form and without time; a blind, slow reeling back and forth of two great armies locked together like two wild beasts that have found a hold but cannot shift it to a death grip. It might have been a few heart-beats of time or a whole day before he became dimly aware of a fresh outburst of cries and shouting, a fresh sweep of drumming hooves away to the right, and supposed that the Bretons and Cenommanians were charging in on the flank. But he saw nothing of all that, and after the one moment, thought nothing of it either. For him, Tenchebrai Fight was the trampling struggle of the mere hand-ful of men and horses nearest about him, and the sudden fierce exultation as he realized that they were no longer reeling to and fro over the same ground, but the English were moving for-ward, slowly but remorselessly forward, after the golden flame that was the King's banner.

It was no longer the time for spears, but out swords and drive home the slow, deadly charge that was gathering momentum as a wave; drive forward, plough forward into the Norman foot, following the King's banner, and the gold and azure of de Braose's lion; and above them, no swallows now, but the dark deadly flights of arrows lacing the pale September sky.

'Bramber!' They were shouting all about him.

'Bramber!' Randal roared at the full pitch of his lungs, his chin driven down behind his shield, and his sword busy in his hand.

And then, seemingly out of nowhere, a flying squadron of Norman cavalry crashed down upon them, and the world ex-ploded into a tangled and swirling welter of pounding hooves and slashing sword-iron and savage, up-flung horses' heads with wild eyes and flaring, blood-filled nostrils. Randal saw a horseman stoop from the saddle at Bevis, and as Bevis sprang to meet him, he heard, even above the vicious uproar of battle, the crash and grind of blade on blade. And in the same instant another Norman swung his horse down on them and assailed the young knight on his unprotected side. As in some horrible dream, Randal, locked in desperate combat on his own account, saw the man lean from the saddle with upswung blade, and the crashing blow that tore away Bevis's shield and bit deep into his shoulder. He saw Bevis stagger and go down, beaten to his knees. And even as, breaking through the guard of his own enemy, he sprang forward to cover him, the second Norman spurred forward his snorting and wild-eyed steed, trampling the crumpled figure under the great, round hooves.

It was all over almost before it was begun, but for one jagged instant of time that had the intensity of a lightning flash, Randal saw the face of the second Norman. In the heat of battle, and part covered as they were by the mail coif and the helmet with its broad nasal, he might not have known the snarling features again, but there could be no mistaking the livid criss-cross scar on the left cheek, that his own dagger had set there.

He gathered himself like an animal to the kill, flung back his hampering shield, and sprang.

De Coucy had just time to recognize his assailant, just time to see death coming at him in the white, blazing face of the young squire, and no more. Randal sprang sideways under his guard and flung himself across the horse's withers, making the great brute plunge and rear. He had hurled the man back half out of the saddle by the impact of his own body against him, his left arm was round him as de Coucy's sword arm flew wide, and for one instant they glared face to face, even as the Norman toppled sideways from the saddle with Randal still clinging to him: down and down among the plunging hooves of battle. They were broken apart by the fall, but Randal, falling uppermost, was on his knees almost before he hit the ground. He flashed up his own sword and brought it hissing down on de Coucy as he struggled to rise. The blade hacked through the rings of the Norman's hauberk, through flesh and bone, and he slumped back, his head all but smitten from his shoulders, while his great horse plunged away riderless into the mêlée.

Randal, struggling up through the trampling press, knew no hot joy of vengeance, the vengeance he had waited for so long, no thought for anything save Bevis. But the fight had closed over between him and the place where Bevis had fallen, and he was being picked up and borne along like a bit of flotsam on the slow, resistless flood of the English advance. There could be no beating back against that flood; nothing to do but go on. He went on. The smell of blood was in the back of his nose and a crimson mist of it swimming before his eyes, and only one thought in his bursting heart,—if Bevis were dead, to avenge him on the whole Norman army. The red, uncaring, berserker fury of his forefathers woke in him and roared up like flame, and he forgot that he was anything but a high wind and an avenging sword. He thrust forward into Bevis's place, into the ranks of the knights storming at the tasselled heels of de Braose's golden lion, into the mass of the Norman infantry that had already begun to crumble and break apart.

English Henry's new formation had proved its worth. They said that de Bellême and the rear squadron had been swept clear off the field, that Duke Robert had been captured by Waldric, Henry's Chancellor, and de Mortain by the Bretons. They said that four hundred knights had been killed or captured besides countless men-at-arms and foot soldiers. But none of it had any meaning for Randal. The sun that had begun to make a brightness in the breaking sky was still high above the low wooded hills, for at the last it had not taken many hours of this Michaelmas Eve to reverse the work of that other Michaelmas Eve, forty years ago; and he was squatting beside Bevis, who had been carried back to the derelict tanning shed where they had made their headquarters last night.

The shed was crowded with wounded; but Bevis had demanded to remain outside, telling the men who carried him that he had liefer do his dying in the open air. So he lay under the great hornbeam, by the scar of last night's fire, with his head and shoulders propped on his high, crimson saddle. He was still in his hauberk; they had unhelmed him and twisted a mass of rags round his shoulder to staunch the bleeding, and that was all. Gervase, nursing a gashed arm of his own, knelt at his other side, and a little knot of Dean men had already gathered, and stood leaning on their bow-staves in silence close by; but Randal was not aware of them at all, only of Bevis.

'But you'll mend,' he was saying, desperately, stupidly, as though by repeating it he could force it to be true. 'You'll do well enough by and by. You'll be all right, Bevis——'

But he knew, all the time, that Bevis would not be all right.

'De Coucy's horse—trampled on me. I'm—about broken in half as well as—bled white. Shan't last till evening, old lad.'

Randal's fists were clenched and driven together in his sense of utter helplessness as he looked down into the grey, sweat-streaked face of his foster-brother.

Bevis turned his head slowly on the high, red saddle, to return the look, frowning with the effort that even that small movement cost him. 'Randal, I—something I want to tell you.'

Randal nodded, his gaze never leaving the other's face.

'You remember once when we—were lads, I asked you what —you would do if ever your chance of knighthood came, and— you said you'd refuse because you—couldn't furnish your helm?'

Randal nodded again, wordlessly. How odd that that had once seemed to matter.

'You'll be—able to furnish your helm—after all. I have spoken with de Braose—oh, long ago, and he—it is in my mind that he will give you Dean to hold in my stead.'

There was a long, long aching silence. They heard the distant sounds of the camp and the spent battlefield, the voice of the little stream, and the soft stirring of wind in the mazy branches of the hornbeam; but all from far off, beyond the borders of their own stillness. Then Randal said dully, 'But I am not a knight.'

'That is a thing that—can be amended.' There was a shadow of laughter in Bevis's face, an echo of it in the painful, breathless whisper that his voice had become. 'You're too—humble-minded, that's—your trouble. You've proved yourself—well enough, all these two summers in Normandy. And today— they've been telling me how you—fought today. Like three men! Go you to de Braose and—ask for knighthood at his hands. He'll—give it to you.'

There was another silence, and then Randal said unsteadily, 'I had sooner ask for it at yours.'

'At mine? Nay now, that's—foolishness fit for a woman. Stand you in better stead in—after years—to have it from the Lord of Bramber.'

Randal shook his head, stubbornly, blindly. 'I'm not very interested in after years, not now. If I am—if you judge me worthy of knighthood, let you give it to me, Bevis. I—don't want it from anyone else.'

Bevis lay looking up at him, his face very still under the shifting shadows of the leaves. Then he said, 'Have it your own wilful way. Gervase, you'll be his sponsor? Raise me up . . .'

Gervase raised him against his shoulder. Randal came slowly to his knees, his head bent, lower, lower. He knew, through all his own body, the effort that it cost Bevis to raise his arm. He felt it fall in a light, fumbling blow between his neck and shoulder. So little ceremony needed, in the end, to make a knight; no ceremonial arming, no vigil—oh, but he had kept his vigil, a year and a half ago—nothing but Bevis's spent hand falling on his shoulder in the accolade. 'Sir Randal of Dean.'

So Randal, who had never thought to be a knight, had his knighthood after all; and would have given all the world to be only Bevis's squire again.

Bevis looked about him at the Dean men, as Gervase laid him down, seeming to notice them for the first time.

'Well, I've done my best for you both,' he said. 'Lord and villeins. Na na, don't all of you look—as though it was end of—the world that we didn't have—six years ago.' And a little later 'Will—somebody bring me some water?'

One of the men—it was Gudram of the apple tree—took up the nut-shaped helmet and turned away to the stream, and came trudging back with it half full of water. This time it was Randal who raised Bevis against his shoulder, and taking the helmet from Gudram's hand, held it to his foster-brother's dry, white lips. Bevis drank a little, but he could not keep it down. It came up again, beaded with dark grains of blood. Randal wiped the stain away, and did not lay him back but continued to hold him.

Gervase had withdrawn a little, and sat nursing his arm, with his back to the hornbeam bole. No one moved among the Dean men, and amid the swarming life of the English camp, and the tramp of men bringing in more wounded, it seemed that Randal and Bevis were alone with each other as they had so often been alone on the high downs at home with only the green plover calling.

'My sword——' Bevis said after a while, his lips scarcely moving. 'Grandfather's sword—yours now, Randal.'

Randal was still holding him when, an hour later, he opened his eyes once more and looked up into his face, with the quiet contented look of so many summer morning wakings.

'Randal,' he said again. Then his gaze drifted past the other's face, into the brightening sky beyond the rustling branches of the hornbeam. 'Look, the clouds are flying like banners above Long Down. We shall have wild weather tomorrow.' He stretched himself all out with a long sigh, and turned his head in the hollow of Randal's shoulder as though to sleep again.

A soft gust of wind swooped at them under the hornbeam branches, setting the shadows flurrying, and when it died into the grass, Randal laid Bevis's body down, with a stunned emptiness inside him as though something of himself had gone too. As he did so, the tramp of spurred feet checked behind him, and a shadow long in the westering light, fell across the grass. He looked up slowly, and saw de Braose standing beside him.

'They told me d'Aguillon was wounded,' he said. 'I came as soon as might be.'

'You're just too late,' Randal said. 'Just—too—late, de Braose.'

De Braose looked down at the body of his youngest knight. 'So I see,' he said in his harsh, clipped voice. The iron-grey gaze shifted deliberately to Randal. 'Come up to me in my tent, in an hour's time.' And with a brusque nod, there being no more that he could do here, and many things that he must do elsewhere, he turned on his spurred heel and tramped jingling away.

When he was gone, Randal turned his attention with a dull, conscious effort to the Dean men, where they stood looking to him now to make the decision and tell them what to do.

'Ulf, go you and find out where they are taking the slain. The rest of you go down to the cooking fires and get something in your bellies, you'll be needing it. Come back after; we shall have to carry him somewhere—wherever it is.' And as they trailed heavily away, and only Gervase was left, sitting against the grey bole of the hornbeam, he bent again over Bevis's body. There was something that he must do before he took the great sword, something that to him mattered even more. He slipped his hand into the breast of the loosened hauberk, and pulled out the little washleather bag which Bevis wore round his neck, and from the bag, bloodstained now, Bevis's nut of red amber. It lay dark in his hand, keeping its secret, until a gleam of the westering light striking through it woke a spark of the old fire even as he watched. He dragged up the little bag that hung round his own neck, opened it with fumbling fingers, and took out his own piece that was twin to the other: precious, half magic Gold of the Sea that Laef Thorkelson had brought from half the world away. As he did so, something else spilled out with it; a sprig of rosemary, dried and crushed, its flowers shrivelled to brown wisps that crumbled at a touch. He picked it up, and the aromatic ghost of a fragrance came up to him from between his fingers, bringing for an instant other ghosts with it; the narrow, waking garden at Bramber, a girl with red hair . . . With a sudden confused feeling that the thing was in some way precious, he dropped it with his own half of the red amber into the bag round Bevis's neck and slipped it back inside the loosened hauberk, over Bevis's quiet heart.

Bevis's half of the red amber he stowed in his own breast. Then he set to unbuckling the great sword with the d'Aguillon seal cut in the hilt.

# 17

# KNIGHT'S FEE

It was sunset, and the clouds which Bevis had seen as flying like banners from Long Down, were banners indeed: vast, tattered, gold and purple, fire-fringed banners of victory streaming all across the sky, as Randal made his way through the camp towards de Braose's tent. The wind had begun to rise, and smoke from the cooking fires billowed all across the camp, and he heard snatches of talk around him that had the same ragged, shining, torn-off quality. An old knight, leaning on his sword, cocked an eye upward and said to another beside him. 'Splendour of God! Will you look at that sky! Just such a sky we had on the evening after Senlac fight, as though Harold's golden banners had been caught up in the sunset.' And an archer, squatting with his bow-stave across his knees beside one of the great cooking fires, spat contentedly into the flames, and announced to the world at large, 'Eh, lads, if ever Norman cries Senlac after us in the roadway, I reckon we just turn and cry 'Tenchebrai' in his teeth, from now on.'

Randal heard them as he strode by, but as though they came from a long way off, outside some black barrier that walled him in. He had left Bevis lying with the dead in the Abbey Church below the Castle, and the stunned emptiness that had been all he felt at first was beginning to wake into intolerable pain. He wanted to crawl away into the woods, away from all men, like an animal that has its death hurt. But de Braose had bidden him come in an hour, and the habit of obedience had been drilled into him.

De Braose's pavilion was pitched not far from the greater one of the King, which stood dark and empty now, for Henry supped in Tenchebrai tonight. The entrance flaps were looped back, and the flames of the dead apple branches burning on a field hearth just inside seemed in the shadows to echo the streaming banners of that fiery and victorious sky. The aromatic scent of the woodsmoke reached Randal before ever he came to the threshold, stealing out to swirl and eddy with the autumn wind through what were left of the apple trees. Squires were setting out the trestle table for de Braose's own supper, while two or three camp curs who had wandered in in the hope of bones and gristle later, were sniffing expectantly among the rushes. Several knights were gathered there already; among them Randal saw vaguely the round, red face and kindly, rueful eyes of le Savage of Broadwater. And de Braose himself, his helmet off and his coif hanging loose about his neck, stood by the fire, face to face with a tall man in black, sombre as a monk, save that no monk would wear garments of that outlandish sort—a slender, loose-limbed creature with pale, mocking eyes, and a lock of mouse-coloured hair hanging limply across a high, sallow forehead: nothing changed in twelve years, save that the bitter, laughing, twisted lines of his long, mobile face were bitten a little deeper than when Randal saw them last, and he carried no little gilded harp, but wore a sword belt and an empty sheath of fine, embossed leather, the sword that had evidently been in it standing propped against the bench behind de Braose.

And so, checking in the opening of the tent, after twelve years Randal saw Herluin the Minstrel again.

'We must see that you are well bestowed. Robert de Bellême's own minstrel should fetch a good ransom,' de Braose was saying bluntly.

Herluin shook his head a little. 'I doubt it, do you know. They tell me that de Bellême has come in to make his submission, and will of a surety be stripped even of his Norman possessions, now that Henry is Lord of Normandy. Not, I fear me, the moment to be indulging in luxuries such as the ransom of a mere minstrel.'

'A pity,' de Braose said, meaningly.

'Yes, is it not? It seems that you will have to trade me cheap —hy my! Almost for nothing!—or have me on your hands for life.'

'Not on *my* hands,' de Braose returned with a glimmer of a smile, stripping his great war-mittens between his fingers. 'I dare say Henry may well find it amusing to possess a minstrel captured from one of his brother's barons—especially since Rahere shows signs of exchanging his motley for a monk's habit and his harp for a rosary.'

'It was once said of me by de Bellême, my Lord,' Herluin said in a tone of gentle reverie, 'that so far as he knew there was no way of—persuading me to wake the harp against my will.'

'I wonder. Henry has ways of—persuasion . . .' de Braose's hard eyes flicked towards the tent opening, and he saw Randal standing there with the fires of the windy sunset behind him. But Randal was not looking at him, he was still gazing at Herluin; and in the same moment, as though feeling the intensity of the gaze upon him, the minstrel turned and saw the haggard young man in the opening.

'Herluin!' Randal said, as their eyes met.

Herluin looked in silence for a moment, and the wicked, winged lines of his eyebrows drifted upward. 'Well, Imp! Not maybe the happiest of ways to meet again.'

'Ah, of course.' De Braose's hard voice came between them. 'I had forgotten that you two were of old acquaintance.' He gestured with his war-mittens to Herluin to stand aside, and turned his full attention to Randal. 'Come here!'

Randal came, walking heavily like an old man, and stood before his overlord.

'You know why I sent for you?' How intently the man was looking at him, the hard, grey eyes raking into him as though seeking to uncover what lay behind his outward-seeming and form some judgement.

'Yes,' Randal said. 'Bevis told me—before he died,' and was aware of a sudden movement from Herluin, who never made sudden movements.

'I will give you Dean to hold for a year,' de Braose said abruptly. 'At the end of that time—we shall see. Meanwhile, the end of a campaign, when the shield squires have proved their mettle, is as good a time to be making new knights as the beginning of a campaign, when one makes them for the sake of fresh fighting blood. Kneel down.'

Randal remained standing. No longer like an old man, but

very young, very straight, very proud for all the haggard misery in his face.

'I have my knighthood already, de Braose.'

He saw de Braose's brows snap together, and added, his hand on the engraved pommel of the great sword at his side, 'At Bevis's hand. Sir Gervase de Machault stood sponsor for me.'

De Braose's iron-grey gaze flickered a little in the silence that followed. 'So-o. It seems that I am too late for all things today— Sir Randal.'

Sir Randal. How strange it sounded. Sir Dog-boy, Randal thought, with the harsh mockery of it tearing at his chest. All that way he had come, and he would have been so proud to be a fellow knight of Bevis's—and it was only by Bevis's death that he could furnish his helm. Life was very bitter, very cruel, and he wished rather desperately in that moment that he too was dead. He was saved from his moment of black despair by the sudden ripple of reflected firelight as a log fell, on the blade of Herluin's captured sword where it leaned against the bench behind de Braose. Herluin's sword—Herluin a captive, and in need of help . . . Herluin had said once that Randal had lived with hounds so long that, together with most of their faults, he had learned their chief virtue of faithfulness. Randal could not know that, but it was true.

'De Braose, it is the custom, I know, to make some gift to the Church or to the poor, for the first act of one's knighthood. May I, instead, pay the ransom for a friend?'

'Meaning de Bellême's minstrel,' de Braose snapped.

'Yes, sir.' Randal caught at the tail of his eye another movement from Herluin, startled and quickly suppressed. His eyes were on his overlord's square, uncompromising face, begging him to understand and show mercy. He knew that he was taking on a crushing burden for Dean. 'Oh, I know that I could only pay it off a little at a time; Dean is not a rich Manor, but if you will set Herluin free now, I will clear the debt though it takes me twenty years.'

'And I have promised you Dean for only one,' de Braose said. 'If at the end of that time I do not choose to renew the fief—what then?'

Randal was silent. He simply did not know what then. He felt how ridiculous his offer had been; there must be something he could do—some other way—but he could not think of it.

'I am not a man given to easy kindness, as you will know by now,' said the Lord of Bramber. 'I give nothing for nothing. For your good service these two summers past, and for the old friendship between d'Aguillon and de Braose, I have given you Dean to hold by knight's fee. I take that back now, and make another offer. I will give you the minstrel to do with as you choose, *or I will give you Dean.* The choice is yours.'

There was a long, dragging silence. Randal's fists clenched slowly at his sides, and he no longer looked into de Braose's face, but into the red heart of the fire brightening as the windy daylight faded. Le Savage, on the edge of the firelight, protested explosively down his nose. 'That's too cruel a choice to set the boy! You can't do it, de Braose!'

'I can, and I will,' de Braose said, simply; and something of the cold iron that showed in his eyes sounded also in his voice.

Every face in the dim, fire-reddened pavilion was turned to the two standing beside the field-hearth. Herluin's expression, as he looked on, was a strange one under the circumstances; a look of interest that seemed to be quite detached from himself, and something that was almost amusement in his pale, bright eyes. A dog began to scratch in the silence, and scratched on, and on . . . Randal was still staring into the fire, while slowly but without any kind of wavering, his mind made itself up. A few moments ago, he had thought that he had nothing more to lose; now he knew that he had, and he must give it. He knew that it had been Bevis's last wish that he should hold Dean, but Bevis would understand. There were certain things that a man could not do, certain debts that he could not leave unpaid. In an odd way that he could not have put into words, he felt that Bevis, whose body would sleep in Normandy, was part of Dean, part of the marshes and the downs and the river woods in springtime, woven into them by his love. Nothing could ever take Dean from Bevis now; the Wealden blackbird would always sing for him . . . For himself, it meant that he must go all his life in exile, but there was no other way. He raised his head

221

slowly, and looked at de Braose through the faint waft of wood-smoke fronding across his face, and ran the tip of his tongue over his lower lip because it was uncomfortably dry.

'I beg you give the Manor to someone like Gervase, who will be good to it—to the land and the villeins,' he said.

There was a soft rustle of movement among the watching knights. Herluin made a small gesture of applause that was only half fantastic. The dog finished scratching and wandered out. De Braose stood for a long moment more, looking at the young knight, and still stripping his great war-mittens between his hands. Then he turned and tossed them on to the bench behind him with an air of *finish*, and swung back to Randal.

'So.' He nodded. 'The colt is worthy of his breakers. I was none so sure, before, though you should have had the Manor at least for the year to prove your worth; but it is in my mind that he who keeps faith in one thing, even to the breaking of his heart, is like to keep it in all. You're a fool, Randal, but such a fool as I would have among my fief knights. Take Dean, and this minstrel of yours also. Pay me for the one with a stirrup cup each year over and above your knight's fee, and for the other—do with him as you will.'

In the first instant Randal was not quite sure that he had really heard it. Then, very slowly, the words sank in and became part of himself. His eyes were on de Braose's face all the while. If the Lord of Bramber knew that in that instant he had gained for life a liege man who would follow him into Hell fire to bring him a cup of water if he were damned and thirsting, he showed no sign of doing so; but every other man there saw it plainly enough.

Randal did not attempt to thank him; he had no words—no words of his own, only the words of the vassal's oath, that Bevis had spoken at his own knighting in the Great Hall of Dean, a year and a half ago.

In the smoke-filled and fire-flushed pavilion, with a few battle-weary knights and a captive minstrel looking on, while outside the triumphal cloud banners faded over the battlefield of Tenchebrai, he knelt in a passion of gratitude, and set his hands between de Braose's.

'Here, my Lord, I become liege man of yours for life and limb and earthly regard, and I will keep faith and loyalty to you for life and death, God helping me.'

Two dawns later, Randal took his leave of Herluin the Minstrel, in the lea of an apple orchard on the edge of the English camp. The camp was smaller than it had been, for the King and his Bishops and certain of his English Barons had by now made their quarters within the walls of Tenchebrai. De Bellême had been dismissed, humiliated and raging, with his freedom but little else, to almost the last of his Norman estates left to him. The dead were buried, and the swallows, gathering for their flight south, swooped and darted once more about the Castle walls.

It was raining, soft swathes of rain that were scarcely more than mist, and the moisture spattered cold from the branches of the apple trees. Somewhere in the rain a trumpet sounded thinly for watch-setting, and a horse whinnied, and someone went by whistling a snatch of a Breton tune. The blue waft of woodsmoke from the cooking fires drifted to them, mingling with the chill, grey freshness of the dawn. Beside one of those fires they had sat together late into the night before, silent for the most part, talking by fits and starts, of all that had happened in twelve years; of Dean and Arundel, of Sir Everard and de Coucy—of Bevis . . . But it seemed to Randal now that he had left unsaid so many of the things that really mattered. At the last moment, he said one of them.

'Herluin, come with me back to Dean.'

Herluin's brows drifted upward under the lank forelock, and his winged mouth curved in mockery. 'Hy my! Are you, then, one of the Barons of the land, to keep a minstrel in your Hall?'

'I did not mean as a minstrel,' Randal said. 'I just meant—come.'

'Nay then, what should I do, save grow moss, on a downland Manor?'

Randal was silent a moment, rebelling against the implication, yet knowing the truth of it. Herluin and Dean were of two different worlds.

'You'll go to de Bellême, then?'

'At least life will never be dull, where de Bellême is.'

'And you think it would be, with me?'

Herluin's face cracked into its slow, twisted smile. 'I think it more than likely.'

And then he set both hands on Randal's scale-clad shoulders, and stood looking at him, almost as searchingly as de Braose had done, two evenings ago. 'You are not yet bearded to compare with Sir Steward Gilbert at Arundel; but tell me now, was it a good thing that I did, when I gave you to Sir Everard, twelve long years ago?' He was not asking in a spirit of 'did I not tell you so?' He was asking the question because he wanted, wanted badly, to know the answer.

Randal gave him back his look, levelly—even in that moment it seemed to him odd that Herluin's eyes were on a level with his own instead of glinting and glancing down at him from somewhere tree-tall above him.

'Two days since, when I was yet Bevis's squire, I would have told you yes, a thousand times,' he said at last. 'Now, I am a knight, and Lord of my own Manor, and Bevis is dead; and I should maybe have a less sore heart if you had never even played the game of chess that won me from Hugh Goch.' His voice, which had been hoarse and steady, cracked desperately in the middle. 'I don't know, Herluin, I don't know.'

But even as he said it, he knew that it *had* been good; for the sake of all that Dean had given him and made of him, for the sake of the friendship he had shared with Bevis, that could not be lost, even though Bevis was dead. He brought up his own hands and set them over the minstrel's and bowed his head for an instant on to the other's neck.

'It was a good thing, Herluin,' he said, 'a good thing that you did, all those years ago,' and dropped his hands and stood back.

Herluin kept his hands on the young knight's shoulders a moment longer. 'So; and truly I think that for Dean also, for the folk and the fields of the Manor, which must otherwise have passed to a stranger's hand, the matter will prove to be none so ill. God keep you, Imp.'

He slipped his long musician's hands from Randal's shoulders so lightly that Randal never felt them go, and turned away, leaving the boy standing there under the apple trees in the rain, with the waking sounds of the English camp behind him.

# 18

# THE LORD OF DEAN COMES HOME

TOWARDS evening of a wild day in late October, Randal dropped from Swallow's saddle in the courtyard of Bramber Castle. He was quite alone, the Dean men, and Bevis's horses which were his now, left behind him in Normandy with le Savage, for the King and the main part of his army were not yet coming home. Henry had held a Council at Lisieux and soon there would be another at Falaise, for the reforming and future handling of the Duchy that was once again one with England. But there was so much to do, and already the year grew late for embarking an army; so it could not be before spring, now, that the King would be home. Meanwhile de Braose had sent Randal back with letters for his Seneschal at Bramber, and for the Lady Aanor, before the winter storms shut the seaways.

The rain that had come with him all the two days' ride from Pevensey had fled away for the moment, and the streaming cobbles washed clear of their accustomed filth shone silver-gilt, the puddles reflecting the ragged lake of clear sky over the battlements, and in the old days Randal's heart would have lifted to the sudden blue and silver flashing out of the grey like a sword from its sheath; but not now: all that seemed dead in him now, and left behind him with Bevis at Tenchebrai.

An ancient stable-hand had come hobbling out to take Swallow from him, and a small, impudent varlet not much older than he had been when Herluin won him from Hugh Goch came darting down the Keep stair, grinning as he recognized the mired and weary knight who had just ridden into the courtyard, and shrilling like a curlew to know whether de Braose and the rest were near at hand. Already a little crowd was gathering, of women and boys and old men. There were few of fighting age in Bramber now.

'Na na. De Braose and the rest will not be home before spring,' Randal told him, standing with his hand on Swallow's wet and drooping neck. 'I am come back with letters from my Lord to the Lady Aanor. Where may I find her?'

'In the Great Chamber. Have you seen much fighting?'

'Enough . . . Run then, and tell her that I come, and that all is well with the Lord of Bramber.'

The boy darted off again, and behind him, slowly, wet and saddle-stiff and desperately weary, Randal was climbing the familiar Keep stair. He was passing from the wind and the scudding silver-gilt light that was beginning to fade, into the smoky dimness of the guardroom; climbing still, from the guardroom to the Great Hall and then to the Great Chamber above it: the Great Chamber that he had come to know so well since he spoke there with the old Lord of Bramber on the night of the witch hunt. Now a fire leapt on the hearth, and the fluttering light of it warmed the grey stone walls and the hangings of the huge box bed against the chill and the changing lights and glooms of the wild autumn day. The Lady Aanor sat in the carved chair by the hearth, where the old Lord had sat that long-past summer night with his sword across his knees, her year-old son sprawling with the wolfhounds among the strewn rushes at her feet, while scattered about the room two or three of her women were busy at their spinning.

She had been busy, too, on the embroidery of a wall-hanging to keep out the draughts, but she had let the work fall in a drift of soft, dark storm-colours across her lap, and sat looking towards the stairhead arch as Randal appeared in it.

'Why, Randal, God's greeting to you. Garin says that you bring me a letter from my Lord.'

Randal shook the beading rain from the horn-scaled shoulders of his hauberk, and crossed the floor to kneel among the hounds and sprawling baby, holding out the packet that he had brought from his wallet.

'De Braose greets you, and sends you this, my Lady.'

She leaned quickly forward and took the packet from him,

her plump face alight with eagerness—for the marriage, made
by Red William for his own ends, had grown to be a happy one,
and the Lady Aanor, who had first come to Bramber riding her
big white mare as lightly as a boy, was running to soft, sweet fat,
like a full-blown rose in the sunshine.

'You are welcome twice over, then, once for yourself, and
once for what you bring!' she said, and made a little gesture to
him to rise, before she took her scissors to break the yellowish
wax with its impress of de Braose's seal, and opened the crackling sheet of parchment.

Randal got to his feet again, and stood looking down at the
embroidered stuff that flowed from her lap to the floor. He saw
an oak tree with three acorns and seven leaves, a hare and a
fallow doe beneath it, a bird in its branches, all worked in those
sombre greys and russets and dim violet colours, and one unexpected note of brilliant blue in the bird's wing that was like
the sudden flashing out of blue and silver from the grey tumble
of storm-clouds that had greeted him for a brief moment in the
courtyard.

But the brightness had fled onward, and the Great Chamber
was already darkening with the next storm of rain. The shutters
of the weather windows were closed against the wind and wet,
and the rain rattled on them and drove hissing down the slanting smoke vent into the fire, making the ash logs spit and steam;
but under the steam and the smoke that billowed into the room,
the hollow heart of the fire seemed to glow all the brighter, red
gold, the colour of Randal's red amber—Bevis's red amber—
with the sun behind it.

There was another note of fire colour in the Great Chamber,
flaming out of the greyness by one of the open windows. It
teased at the corner of Randal's eye until he raised his head
and glanced towards it, and saw Gisella sitting in the deep
embrasure, watching him, with the grey storm-rain driving behind her head, and the back-wash of the wind fretting the wisps
of bracken-red hair about her face.

He had not seen her since the evening in the Castle garden, a
year and a half ago. Bevis and he had not come up to Bramber
at all last winter, there had been so much to do at Dean. And

when they had come up to the Castle in the spring, with preparations in full spate for Henry's second invasion of Normandy, she had not been there. He remembered vaguely having heard that she had gone home on a long visit to help with an elder sister's wedding; he remembered still more vaguely that at the time he had been sorry. But with so much else happening, he had scarcely thought of her since. He remembered that evening in the Castle garden now, sharply and painfully, even to the way the shadows of the budding quince tree had danced, and the dry aromatic scent of the sprig of rosemary that she had given him. And because Bevis was dead, the memory hurt him unbearably, as the sudden dazzle of blue and silver in the courtyard had hurt him, so that he swerved away from it in his mind and would not remember at all, and stared back at Gisella with almost hostile eyes.

Gisella in the window met his look, puzzled. She seemed to be waiting for something, and then he saw her give up waiting. She cocked up her chin with a sudden resolve, and laying aside her spindle and distaff with its load of saffron wool, got to her feet and came to stand before him.

'I will take your helmet for you,' she said, and put up her hands to the strap that held it to his mail coif.

But Randal's own hands were before her, and he stepped back a pace until his head struck against the raised stone of the hearth. 'Na, I can do well enough for myself.' He freed the buckles with a savage tug, and pulled off the heavy, nut-shaped headpiece.

Two bright patches flamed up on Gisella's cheek-bones, and he saw the war-light that he remembered of old flickering in her eyes. 'Are you afraid that I shall dint your precious helmet? You are not the first knight that I have unharnessed, Sir Randal!'

Randal looked at her again, quickly, startled by her words. 'How did you know that?'

'Well, of course I know who I have unharnessed and who not! Does it seem that I am quite a fool?' she retorted, wilfully misunderstanding him.

'No, I meant—about my being a knight.'

'You are, are you not, in spite of telling me that you never would be?'

'Yes.'

Gisella hesitated, her eyes moving over him with a kind of ruthless, detached interest, and returning to his face. 'I do not know. You don't look like a squire any more—and that sword; it's no squire's blade.'

'It was Bevis's sword,' he told her after a moment.

Her face changed in the swift way it had, all the sparkle of temper draining out of it. 'Oh no!' she said quickly and softly. 'Bevis—is Bevis——?'

He looked at her with dull eyes. She was outside the dark barrier of his misery, and he could not reach her, even if he had wanted to.

'Bevis is dead,' he said, and turned his shoulder on her. He saw the Lady Aanor look up from her letter, and forestalled her kindness as he might have shielded a raw wound from someone's too searching touch, saying roughly, 'My Lady, I have letters also for Sir Herbrand the Seneschal. Give me leave now to go and find him.'

The storm blew and drenched itself out in the night, and the world had turned gentle when Randal set out next morning for Dean. The tall elms by the Mill stood up, half bare already, but lamp gold against the tawny paleness of the downs beyond, and the dog-rose tangle among the hazel bushes was set with the scarlet flame-points of rose hips as though to light him on his way through the quiet, grey morning as he rode up from the ford. But Randal saw nothing of that. To him it was dusk, under a sunset sky that was like the echo of a brighter sunset somewhere else; and he rode with ghosts, hounds long dead that came running to meet him, and old Sir Everard's voice calling to them, 'You will let them know through half Sussex that the Lord of Dean comes home!' A long-legged boy in russet hose dropping out of the pear tree by the gate . . .

'The Lord of Dean comes home.'

It was the thrusting and barking of real hounds about him now, as he swung down from the saddle in the Hall garth, and

231

he realized that he must have come right through the village without seeing it at all—or rather, seeing it across twelve years. The hounds fawned about him, Joyeuse carrying an old shoe of Bevis's in her mouth. The household was gathering in the wake of the hounds. Randal stood with his arm curved over the warm grey arch of Swallow's neck, and looked back into their eager, questioning faces, and knew that this was the worst moment of all. He heard their voices without knowing what they said. He did not know if he answered them; but if not, they must have read his news in his face, for he felt his own grief reaching out to engulf them too. He saw them standing back from him a little, staring at him, without noisy sorrow, in a silent and almost sullen grieving, after the manner of the Saxon kind. He saw Adam Clerk's face among the rest, white and stricken and suddenly very old. Reynfrey's big hand was on his shoulder, and he felt it shaking; Sybilla, making less outcry than for many smaller griefs, though the tears trickled down her fat cheeks, was bidding him come in, promising him something to eat. Odd how one still had to eat . . .

But the worst thing of all was Joyeuse pattering round him, looking for something—someone—who was not there. She nudged the old red shoe against his legs, whimpering, but would not give it to him when he stooped for it. It was not for him she had brought it. He fondled her head, seeing the greyness of her muzzle, and realized for the first time that Joyeuse was old. They had called her Joyeuse, though it was a sword's name and not a hound's, because she had been such a joyous puppy; but now she was old and grey-muzzled and not joyous any more.

'He is not coming,' Randal told her, choking; and she looked up into his face with a piercing whine, trying to understand. 'No good looking; he will not come again—poor old lass, not any more.'

Suddenly he had had all that he could bear. 'I—am not hungry,' he told Sybilla. 'Give me some supper when I come back—someone look after Swallow . . .' and he turned and strode blindly out from the garth, round the end of the little flint-walled church, and up towards the downs.

Joyeuse followed a little way at his heels, then turned with a distressed whimpering and padded back towards the Hall, and Randal went on alone.

There were goldfinches on the seeding thistles and wild marjoram beyond the garth, jewelling the grey day with their forehead-rubies and the blink of gold on their quivering wings, but Randal did not see them, he did not see the familiar upward sweep of the downs that was tawny as a hound's coat, silvering as long, cool swathes of air went by. He climbed on, blindly, leaving the tilled land and the woods behind him, into the emptiness. He did not know, he did not even question in his own mind whether it was the downs or Lewin Longshanks that he was going to; in a way they were the same thing in his mind. Strength and unchangingness; and he needed them now . . .

He saw Lewin from a long way off, sitting on the crest of Long Down against the drifting sky, with the Dean sheep grazing in a quiet grey crescent in the steep coombhead below him, and in the same instant the shepherd stirred, put up one arm in a slow, wide gesture of greeting, and got to his feet. He did not come loping down over the rolling fall of turf to meet him, but remained quietly leaning on his crook, with the dogs crouched on either side, to wait for his coming. And Randal, returning the greeting gesture, climbed slowly on and up. He climbed straight through the flock, the sheep raising their heads as he passed to stare at the armed man in their midst, then returning peacefully to their grazing.

The two men came together on the broad downland ridge with nothing higher than themselves save a kestrel hanging in the sky above them. The big, fair shepherd in his sheepskin mantle, with the quiet of the high and lonely places about him; the young knight still in hauberk and helm with his shield strap creaking across his shoulders, still mired with yesterday's long, hard riding, haggard and red-eyed. They stood looking at each other for a few moments, without any further greeting. Then Lewin asked in his gentle growl, 'Where's d'Aguillon, then?'

'Dead,' Randal said. It sounded such a little word, in the immensity of the downs.

In the silence that followed, he heard suddenly the faint

*shish-shish-sh* of those long, cool swathes of air moving through the tawny grass, and the thin, shining song of a lark lost somewhere high overhead.

'Aye, I thought it might be that,' Lewin said at last, his quiet gaze still on the younger man's face.

How they came, soon after that, to be sitting side by side on the sloping turf, Randal never knew, save that when one was not going anywhere or doing anything, it always seemed more natural to sit than stand on the slow, quiet swells of the downs. There they sat, with the prick-eared dogs, Lewin with his crook lying beside him, Randal dandling his great sword across his knees. Lewin glanced aside at it, after they had kept silent for a good while. 'D'Aguillon's sword.'

'He gave it to me,' Randal said.

'When was he killed then? Was it at Tence—Tenchebrai? We heard there was a great battle at a place called Tenchebrai.'

'Aye, at Tenchebrai. It was a great fight—broke the power of Normandy.' In a dead, level voice he began to tell the other how it had been. 'Henry dismounted most of his army to take the shock of the Norman charge—so that in a way we fought as Harold's men fought at Hastings. It was queer, that. We held the charge and we pressed on against the Norman foot, and the battle began to break up; but a squadron of their horse came against de Braose's men—de Coucy was one of them.' He turned a little to look at the gravely listening man beside him. 'Always de Coucy, as though even in the chances of war his fate was woven with Dean's. I was close behind Bevis and saw it all happen. Another Norman took him first, and while his sword was busy to the full, de Coucy took him cross-wise and cut him down before I could reach him to cover him with my shield, and the horse——' he bowed his head for a moment on to his sword arm that lay across his updrawn knees. 'The horses trampled on over him. He died before evening.'

Lewin said, 'You killed de Coucy?'

'Oh yes,' Randal said very gently. 'I killed de Coucy.'

A long time passed before either of them spoke again. Presently one of the sheep wandered too far from the rest of her kind. Lewin pointed her out to the dogs beside him, and they streaked away, running silently, belly to ground, to head the straggler back into the flock, and then, their task accomplished, returned to fling themselves down again, panting, beside their master. Then Lewin said, 'Who is the new Lord of Dean?'

The skies had begun to break up, and faint blurs of brightness to drift across the downs. Far below them and a mile away, a ragged wing of sunshine brushed across the thatched roofs of the Manor Hall and its byres and barns, waking the colour of the three great fields, fresh from the autumn ploughing, and the gleam of the tall straw-stacks in the garth.

'I'm afraid I am,' Randal said.

It was so long before Lewin answered that he looked round. The shepherd was watching him with those far-sighted, very blue eyes of his, that met his own haggard gaze and held it in a long, considering scrutiny. At last he nodded. 'That's as it should be. 'Tis a thankless time any stranger would have had of it, I'm thinking, but the Manor will accept you. Aye, and for more than that barley-coloured thatch of yours.'

Yes, Randal thought, the Manor would accept him. In an odd way it had already done so on the night that Lewin showed him the nameless flint weapon, the night that he had seemed, for one instant that was outside time, to see the shadows of the wolves leaping about the lambing fold . . . His thoughts turned, as always when he remembered that night, to Ancret, who belonged to the world that he had glimpsed then. Ancret with her ancient wisdom and her ancient magic, who had been Bevis's foster-mother. And he drew his legs under him to get up. 'I must go to Ancret. I should have gone to her first, before someone else told her about Bevis.'

'No hurry for that, then. You'll not find Ancret on the Manor, no more.'

Randal checked his movement to get up, and looked at the older man with startled eyes. 'Not find her? Not—dead too?'

'Na, na.' Lewin shook his head. 'Cerdic saw her walking up over the shoulder of the Bramble Hill, way back a moon and more gone by—'bout the time of Tenchebrai Fight, I reckon. Her didn't come back, and her won't now.'

Randal said, 'But she's part of Dean!'

'Aye, her's part of Dean; a villein, tied to the land like the rest of us,' Lewin agreed, watching his new Lord. 'Send after her and fetch her back, if you can find her.'

'Don't be a fool,' Randal said wearily, his arm across his up-drawn knees, and his forehead on his wrist. He was remember-ing, against the darkness of his closed eyes, Ancret's face as he had seen it that first time of all, shadowy against the berry-laden branches of the elder tree, hearing her voice as she told Bevis that she would always be there for his finding, so long as he needed her. So long as he needed her. She must have known when she walked up over Bramble Hill and away, that her foster-son's need of her was finished, and he would not come seeking her again. She must have known how it would be, that first time of all. He remembered her hands on either side of his face and her eyes holding his own, so that he seemed to be sinking down into the darkness of them, down and down . . . 'The old blood runs strong, and comes again into its own again; you should know that, you that Sir Everard brought home on his saddle bow.'

Why had she not hated him? Knowing what she knew even then, why had she not hated him? The answer came to him in Ancret's voice, remembered across twelve years, but clear as though the words were murmuring that moment in his ear, sounding in the faint soughing of the air through the long grasses. 'We, who are an older people still, who were an old people when they raised the grave mound on Bramble Hill in the days when the world was young, we see the conquerors come and go again, and marry and mingle, but we know that all things pass, like a little wind through the bramble bushes.'

Only the downs went on, the downs, and life itself, whatever happened to the people who lived it. The wolves leaping about the lambing folds, and the men with their spears; Harold dead at Hastings, and Bevis at Tenchebrai, and all the while, the little wind blowing over the downs, and harvest following seed-sowing, and the new life coming at lambing time. In a few days, he thought suddenly—and the thought woke in him as un-expectedly as the blue of the bird's wing flashing out from among the dun and grey and violet colours of the Lady Aanor's embroidery—he would take time off from the autumn work of the Manor, and go up to Bramber and get word with Gisella again. He did not get as far as thinking that now he was a knight, standing well with de Braose and holding his own Manor, her father would likely enough give her to him if he asked. It was much too soon for that. He simply thought that he would go and get word with Gisella again, and tell her that he had carried her sprig of rosemary through those two long, blood-stained summers in Normandy. But not how he had parted with it; that was between himself and Bevis, for all time.

'It's a good Manor,' he said. 'Looks as though we're ready for the autumn sowing.'

# Historical Note

THE Mowbray revolt of 1095 really did happen, and Hugh Goch was caught up in it, just as I have told in *Knight's Fee*. All the other campaigns and uprisings in the background of the story are historical. In 1094 there was a great rising of the Welsh, and in the next year William Rufus marched into North Wales, but the expedition had little effect; in 1096, having lent his brother, Duke Robert of Normandy, the money he needed to go on the First Crusade, he crossed the Channel to hold the Duchy while the Duke was away. In the spring of 1097 more Welsh troubles called him back, and again he marched into Wales, but when the revolt died down in the autumn, he returned to Normandy and set himself to secure and make strong the Norman borders. That done, he returned triumphantly to be crowned a second time in his new Westminster Hall. But less than a year later, on 2 August 1100, he was shot while hunting in the New Forest; and it was for his younger brother Henry to hold England.

Henry did not have an easy time, for Robert was back from his Crusade now, and wanted England as well as Normandy. He bought the allegiance of several of Henry's greatest Barons with promises of lands in Normandy; and on 20 July 1101 landed at Portsmouth. On this occasion the two brothers came to terms without a battle. Henry was to keep England but pay Robert £2000 a year, and Robert was to keep all Normandy save for Henry's own castle of Domfront. Afterwards, Henry dealt with the Barons who had turned against him; and by spring 1102 it was Robert de Bellême's turn, and the King drove him out of one after another of his English castles, and finally overseas.

Meanwhile, the people of Normandy who had been so glad to see Duke Robert back from his Crusade, were becoming sickened by his weakness and his cruelty; and they appealed to Henry to come and take the Duchy. In April 1105 Henry invaded in force, and though he had to draw off in August, in June of 1106 he invaded again, and in September the great battle of Tenchebrai was fought, which ended all Norman resistance to the English for a long while to come.

So much for the events. For the people—most of them are real too, the greater folk anyway; de Braose and de Bellême and Hugh Goch; but not Herluin the Minstrel nor de Coucy nor Bevis nor Randal. D'Aguillon is not a real person but he comes of a real family; several d'Aguillons followed Duke William from Normandy, and by the time the Domesday Survey was made they were settled here and there throughout Sussex.

You may wonder how the Saxons and Normans in the story talk to each other so easily; but I believe that very soon after the Conquest, certainly as soon as the first Norman children born in England had begun to talk at all, they would have used one tongue as easily as the other, speaking Norman French to their fathers and their fathers' friends, and Saxon with their nurse and the grooms and dog-boys, and sometimes—for there were many mixed marriages—with their mothers too.

The Old Faith was the faith of all Europe, long before Christ. It lasted on, side by side with Christianity, right through the Middle Ages, though by then most people had forgotten what it was, and called it witchcraft. The people who held to it believed that a God-King had to die every so often, and be born again in a new God-King, just as the year dies in the winter and is born again in the spring, and that only so could life go on. William Rufus belonged to the Old Faith, and many people still believe that he was chosen to be the 'Dying God' for that particular time. If so, he may have been on the whole a bad man, but he was certainly a very brave one.

# Glossary

ACCOLADE   The blow on the neck that makes a knight.

ALAUNT   A kind of hound.

CHAPE (OF SWORD)   The metal guard on the end of the sheath.

COIF   A close-fitting hood.

FEALTY   Allegiance.

FIEF   A knight's holding of land.

FURNISH ONE'S HELM   A colloquialism: to provide one's own horse
   and armour and keep up the way of life fitting to a knight.

FYRD   Militia.

GAMBESON   The padded tunic worn under the hauberk.

GARBOIL   Unseemly noise and turmoil.

GUIGE   The strap of a shield that goes round one's neck.

HAUBERK   A chain-mail or scale-mail shirt.

HONOUR   A Baron's holding.

JACK   A leather tunic

KIRTLE   A shirt or tunic.

KIST   A chest.

NASAL   The nose-guard of a helmet.

PRICKET   A kind of candlestick with a little spike on which to stick
   the candle.

SEISIN   A piece of turf or a small object given in token of ownership
   of land etc.

SENESCHAL   Steward and manager.

TALBOT   A hound.

TITHE   The tenth part of the harvest etc. paid as tax to the Church.

WOLF'S HEAD   Outlaw.

[